## "What have

Becks had gambled away her future, and her daughter Pippa's, on a whim of independence and an unfulfilled dream.

"Look at me." Carlos's soft tone captured her attention. "What did you see when you looked at your burned building?"

"At first I saw what it could be, a marvelous soccer complex where everyone would have fun and be competing hard, but then..."

He gently cradled her chin with his hand and she appreciated his touch. Those charming crinkles around his eyes deepened, and he was that much more attractive. That look in his brown eyes reminded her of the summer days while they were dating. "Then what?" he asked.

"I saw what exists right now, a mess of monumental proportion, a shadow of what it was meant to be."

"Sometimes it takes the worst before the best can be realized."

Was their worst behind them? Did it take three thousand miles and nine years for their best as friends, as more than friends, to be realized?

Dear Reader,

It's holiday time in Hollydale! When I first met a happy Becks Harrison Porter in *The Sheriff's Second Chance*, she was a professional soccer player expecting a baby girl. When I uncovered the layers of Becks's life, I discovered her struggles, including her rivalry with her twin sister. A couple of years later, she's suffered through a nasty divorce and moved back to Hollydale, where she's rebuilding her life. With Christmas fast approaching, fire comes close to destroying her new soccer complex.

While fighting that fire, Becks's former fiancé, Carlos Ramirez, sustains what might be a career-ending injury. He's the third generation of Ramirez firefighters, and he doesn't know how he'll break it to his family that the streak might be finished.

During this holiday season, Becks and Carlos have to accept themselves and learn that some of the best things, including love, are worth the wait. Fortunately for them, the residents of Hollydale and the Christmas season provide some happy times for them to rekindle their romance. I especially loved meeting Carlos Claus.

I love hearing from readers. Please check out my website, tanyaagler.com, or follow me on Facebook at authortanyaagler.

Happy reading!

*Tanya*

# HEARTWARMING

## *The Firefighter's Christmas Promise*

---

*Tanya Agler*

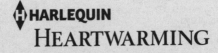

# HARLEQUIN®
## HEARTWARMING™

ISBN-13: 978-1-335-58467-0

The Firefighter's Christmas Promise

Copyright © 2022 by Tanya Agler

Recycling programs
for this product may
not exist in your area.

For questions and comments about the quality of this book,
please contact us at CustomerService@Harlequin.com.

Harlequin Enterprises ULC
22 Adelaide St. West, 41st Floor
Toronto, Ontario M5H 4E3, Canada
www.Harlequin.com

**Printed in U.S.A.**

**Tanya Agler** remembers the first set of Harlequin books her grandmother gifted her, and she's been in love with romance novels ever since. An award-winning author, Tanya makes her home in Georgia with her wonderful husband, their four children and a lovable basset, who really rules the roost. When she's not writing, Tanya loves classic movies and a good cup of tea. Visit her at tanyaagler.com or email her at tanyaagler@gmail.com.

### Books by Tanya Agler

### Harlequin Heartwarming

*A Ranger for the Twins*
*The Sheriff's Second Chance*
*The Soldier's Unexpected Family*
*The Single Dad's Holiday Match*
*The Paramedic's Forever Family*

Visit the Author Profile page
at Harlequin.com for more titles.

This book is dedicated to my youngest child, Matthew, who is analytical and thoughtful. On his first Christmas, he became enthralled with lights and decorations. To this day, he's always the first in the car during the family's annual trip to a local holiday light display. I'm so grateful he's made me appreciate the holiday season that much more. I love you, Matthew!

And to all the firefighters, first responders and frontline workers who give up holidays with their families, thank you for your service and dedication.

# CHAPTER ONE

WITH THE CLOSING happening yesterday on the future Mountain Vista Soccer Complex, the air around Becks Porter seemed that much sweeter. Good thing, too, since she'd sunk every penny of her life savings into the venture. This North Carolina property, perfect for six outdoor fields alongside the prefab building that contained enough room for four indoor ones, was hers and hers alone. The future was now.

Becks dug her ground cleats into the grassy field closest to the majestic view of the Great Smoky Mountains that sold her on the location. From here, the gentle slope, now stark with gray branches of oaks and maples awaiting that first blanket of snow, gave off a peaceful vibe. She inhaled one more breath before exhaling into her metal whistle for the sheer joy of hearing the echo. Then she texted her staff she was on her way to join them for her first official meeting on the actual premises. With Thanksgiving a memory and Christmas on the horizon, parents would be seeking ways for their preteen children to run off steam throughout the long winter months, and grandparents would be searching for presents more unique than the usual colorful sweaters or lava lamps. Becks had the perfect answer for them. A gift certificate for soccer lessons at the new complex run by a former professional player, the only one of its kind in the area.

She contained her excitement at entering the building situated a fair distance away from the indoor soccer facility. While she'd have loved for the buildings to be closer together, the offices of the one-time industrial facility were made separate so the heavy machinery wouldn't disturb employees. Someday she might be able to change that, but not today. With the utilities turned on this morning, the planned facility upgrades would commence in earnest so the first sessions would take place as scheduled in late January. Still, who'd have guessed a steel mill could be converted to an indoor soccer facility with a little money and a lot of imagination?

Becks proceeded to the closest gathering space. Her newly hired staff of four sat in metal folding chairs around a makeshift table. She had already been hard at work on the new website, registration, and coaching strategies with three of her employees throughout the day. The fourth had spent his time on assessing renovations.

"Thank you for going on this journey with me. With hard work and a vision, the Mountain Vista Soccer Complex will be one of the top ten soccer academies in the Southeast, if not the nation, by this time next year." She outlined the agenda for the rest of the meeting and led off with Stan the groundskeeper.

Stan, who was in his late fifties with a baseball cap and a brown flannel shirt and dusty jeans, ran through his extensive list of tasks that needed doing. Becks opened her mouth to ask a question, but he'd only paused for a breath. "I spent all morning inspecting this building. Started the afternoon in the indoor soccer facility. Plenty that needs doing."

She waited another minute, and this time he had finished. She turned to her assistant, Sharlene.

"Any word from Kick, Goal and Score yet?" Becks asked. "The partnership with them is key to getting more signups from the parents of tweens and teens all over the region."

Part of her business plan depended on aligning the complex with an established company with a track record of coaching successful players. Known for their aggressive approach, Kick, Goal and Score promoted themselves and their affiliates extensively. They also helped organize summer soccer camps and travel leagues for the best of the best rising talent. In return for exclusive rights to her complex, they'd pay her more than enough for her business to thrive.

Sharlene pulled out her phone. "Stacy, Wallace Key's assistant, emailed a few minutes ago. She's coming on Friday."

Doing a mental happy dance, Becks turned her attention back to Stan. "It's Tuesday. That gives you three days. Will you have the goals set up and that hole filled in?"

He removed his cap and scratched his bald head. "Thought I had a month to finish everything. Can't guarantee the goals. I have the supplies ready. Fixing that hole is my top priority, but it won't happen if I'm sitting around talking. I'd best get to work if you can do without me."

"Not a problem." Becks thanked him while he replaced his cap and ducked out of the room.

"If it's okay, I have to be going, too. My daughter's arriving with my little grandbaby in an hour. Have I shown you my latest pictures?" Sharlene raised her cell phone for them to see the photos and express polite admiration, although Becks was confident Sharlene's grandson couldn't hold a soccer ball to Becks's daughter, Pippa.

Tonight she'd take Pippa out for tacos to celebrate getting the business officially up and running.

"Anything else, Sharlene?" Becks asked.

The older woman fluffed her gray hair and then lowered her phone. "I'm working hard on an opportunity that'll raise community awareness, but I'll fill you in later."

Sharlene headed for the door and Becks stayed behind with her two other employees, a married duo who served in various roles, including the director of training and registrar respectively. Becks clutched the soccer ball next to her laptop bag and bounced it on her knee. "Up for a quick practice session?"

Dante Jones nodded while his pregnant wife, Amara, shook her head. "I'll watch while you two kick the ball around."

"We won't be long. I have to pick up Pippa from day care in half an hour."

Outside, Becks went through her stretching routine while Dante made sure Amara was bundled up, wrapping her scarf around her neck twice for good measure. Once upon a time, Becks's former fiancé, Carlos, had done the same for Becks, but he'd broken off their engagement rather than support her dream of becoming a professional soccer player, and the less she thought about Pippa's father and her ex-husband, Jack, the better.

She and Dante got started but within seconds, Becks navigated the ball past the former collegiate star and kicked it so it sailed into the goal area. Her knee might be sore tomorrow morning, but it was nice to know she still had it.

Her phone rang, and she stopped. "It's my lawyer, Penelope. I'd best take this." Had she forgotten to sign one of the forms at the closing? "Hi, did I accidentally sign something as Becks instead of Rebecca?"

"You remember that matter you referred to me a couple of months ago? The one regarding Pippa?"

Becks gripped the phone, not liking the tension in Penelope's usual cautious tone. "Hold on a second. This sounds serious." Becks begged off to Dante and Amara, who confirmed they'd be at the complex bright and early tomorrow. "I'm back."

"Do you have a minute to drop by my office today?"

Stan stomped her way, and he didn't look happy. "Can you hold that thought? Sorry." Becks joined Stan, who muttered something under his breath.

He stared at her through slitted eyelids. "Did you inspect the property before you signed those papers?"

"I toured the buildings with the seller, who assured me everything was up to code." But it wouldn't have mattered. This property was the only one in her hometown of Hollydale or the surrounding area that fit her price range with sufficient acreage and square footage. "I bought the property as is."

He removed that too-familiar baseball cap and scratched the top of his head. "Your wiring's shot in parts of the indoor facility, and the sprinkler system needs updating around the second and third fields."

It could be worse. Somehow. "Can you fix that? Or will I have to subcontract the work?" The extra cost might make opening on time difficult, and her business plan didn't have that much wiggle room. "How many changes are we talking about anyway?"

While money was tight, the players, whether five or ninety-five, came first. She wouldn't compromise anyone's safety.

"I'm heading to Farr's Hardware now. I'll give you a ballpark figure tomorrow, but it's not going to be cheap." He stormed off before she could ask any more questions.

Penelope's voice calling Becks's name reminded her of her lawyer's presence on the line. Becks brought the phone back to her ear. "You have my full attention."

"Drop by my office as soon as possible. My paralegal has already left for the day so come on back."

Becks had gone from elation over closing on her dream property to concerns over impending repairs in her immediate future. She'd have to prepare herself for whatever Penelope had to tell her.

Less than a half hour later Becks's mouth dropped. She reread the order from the California judge allowing Jack to have joint custodial rights. "Please tell me this isn't so. He's coming this Saturday to take her for the whole month of December?" Becks felt empty as if someone had sapped her strength. "I live in North Carolina now. Can we appeal to the court system here?"

"No. Your legal state of residence with Jack at the time of the divorce was California. They have jurisdiction." Sympathy shone in her friend's brown eyes.

"Give me some hope, Penelope. She's only two years old. She's never been separated from me before, especially not at Christmas. She doesn't even know Jack."

Becks could say the same thing about herself and this latest stunt of his. After he lied and lied before admitting his infidelity, she'd immediately flown back to Hollydale with Pippa in tow and started divorce proceedings. Since she hadn't forged ahead with a prenup, he'd taken half of her career earnings.

Never again would she fall off the deep end and feel so vulnerable.

"As your friend, I know how badly he hurt you, and starting a custodial battle after two years apart from Pippa doesn't help my low opinion of him." She set the stack of papers on the desk next to her glasses and met Becks's gaze. "As your attorney, however, I have to tell you that the judge's reasoning is airtight. You're going to have to let her go."

That last ember of hope was snuffed out, and Becks wrapped her thick gray sweater around her.

If the best lawyer in Hollydale, if not the entire state of North Carolina, said Becks's case was futile, she'd have to meet Jack at the airport and deliver their daughter to him. Once again, Jack had won.

Somehow Becks would face the holiday season without waking up to Pippa's joy on Christmas morning.

"Thank you for telling me in person."

Moments later, Becks sat in her car, staring at the steering wheel, numb and hurt. Part of the reason she was opening this soccer academy was as a means to provide for her daughter so Pippa wouldn't have to depend on Jack's low amount of child support. Without Pippa at the dedication and first kickoff next month, the joy of bringing her dream to life seeped out of her.

WITHIN SECONDS OF the alarm sounding in the station, Carlos Ramirez tugged on his big black boots, followed by his pants and hood. His firefighter gear went on in less than a minute, but his father, Roberto, the fire chief of Dalesford County, emphasized safety above speed. That was wise advice that Carlos tried to heed every time he suited up.

For now, however, every moment counted, and Carlos grabbed his turnout gear and sat on his pack in his seat on the first engine. Sirens confirmed the second was close behind. He finished closing his coat and let the adrenaline take over. While he hadn't visited the Mountain Vista Soccer Complex yet, several of the firefighters, including the three on his crew, had discussed forming a team for a friendly game against the local police. Just after midnight, less than eight minutes since the call came into the station, they arrived at the scene. Already the dense acrid smell of smoke permeated the air.

Carlos could only make out one window of the commercial building that had smoke billowing from it, with flames licking the air. From his vantage point, the sprinkler system didn't seem to be functioning. That would make the team's evening that much harder, but he'd faced worse before.

Ned Grayson, the battalion chief, barked out orders, and the crew got to work.

Carlos's chest tightened before he let instinct and training kick in. He took up the first connected hose and entered the building. The firefighters from the second engine were searching for anyone or thing in need of rescue. So far, it seemed as though the building was empty. With the crew's combined efforts underway, he focused on fighting the smoke and flames around him and aimed his hose at the base of the fire. He swept the water in an arc from side to side.

In an instant, the smoke changed color from a billowy gray to a fierce black. The heat intensity dialed up a notch, noticeable even through the thick protective layers that covered his body. He adjusted the spray and soon the flames flickered low. Still, the sheer volume of smoke impacted visibility.

"Clear out." A voice came through his headset. "Let the remainder of the fire burn itself out."

"Negative on that. Confinement is near," Carlos said into his mouthpiece, careful to keep the spray of water pointed at the dwindling fire on the AstroTurf covering.

"Copy that, Ramirez. Stay the course." The battalion chief's voice came over the frequency and issued other orders.

His vision blurred. Carlos stayed low on the AstroTurf until he found his path blocked. He considered backing up when something crashed behind him. Pivoting, he found a wedge of ceiling had broken off. He tried going around the obstacle, but more debris lay in front of him and soon he lost his footing. His legs became entangled in a web of rope, the goal, he realized too late, and he landed hard. His body jarred from the impact. In his fourteen years as a firefighter, he'd only suffered minor scrapes yet the instant pain throbbing in his ankle and up his thigh let him know that this was something more serious.

Carlos spoke into the headset. "Grayson, are the EMTs still here?"

"Affirmative." Static cut through Grayson's connection. "Do you require assistance?"

"Negative." At least he hoped that was the case. The last thing he needed was ribbing from being unable to navigate around a simple net and goalposts. Just to be sure, Carlos stood and put weight on this injured leg. To his surprise, he could do so. Whether it wasn't so bad or simply adrenaline keeping him upright remained to be seen. "Concerned about my ankle."

"Get out of there. The rest of the crew can handle what's left." Ned's order came through the headset. "Bukowski, cover Ramirez."

Carlos limped until he reached the door. With the fire out and visibility restored, the rest of this night would be straightforward, except for the cog he'd placed in the wheel.

Ned and a paramedic, Mason Ruddick, met him at the entrance.

They attempted to carry him to the ambulance, but Carlos waved them off. "I can walk."

Despite the activity surrounding the two engines, someone on the sidelines caught Carlos's attention. It was as if the breath had been sucked out of him as he caught sight of Rebecca Harrison for the first time in years. While she preferred the sportier nickname of Becks, she'd always be Becca to him. His first love and the only woman he'd ever asked to marry him.

With her crystal blue gaze focused on the building, he was unsure whether she'd seen him. Her bright red hair was still styled in a short cut that framed her heart-shaped face. Did those fifteen freckles still grace her nose or had time added to that number? A bright blue anorak covered her tall, athletic body, only a few inches shorter than his five-ten frame. When she'd worn heels to their prom, they'd been eye to eye. They'd continued dating while she'd attended college, and he'd proposed right before she graduated. They'd set a wedding date until she decided North Carolina wasn't for her.

"Ramirez? I need to check you out now. You look like you've seen a ghost." Mason tugged at his arm. "Ned and I can get you to the ambulance faster if you wind your arms around us.

Or you can stay here while I bring the stretcher to you."

"I'm good." Carlos freed his arm and removed his headgear. "This is probably nothing. Get the exam over so I can help with the cleanup."

"I have to fill out an incident report so let Ruddick do his job." Ned brooked no argument, and Carlos turned his attention away from Becks toward the ambulance.

Carlos settled on the stretcher and pulled off his boot. As soon as his ankle was free, it swelled and the bruising became apparent. A sprain was going to mess up the firefighter's annual exam he had scheduled only months away. If he couldn't perform his most basic job tasks by then, would his job and any future promotions be in jeopardy?

Mason poked and prodded along the top of Carlos's foot, and Carlos braced his hands on the stretcher. Anything to keep from crying out from the pain shooting through his foot and lower leg. "Already hurt that much, huh?"

Carlos should have known he couldn't fool Mason, who was a straight shooter and a great paramedic. "Nothing I can't handle."

Even so, his mind was already racing. For four generations, at least one Ramirez followed in the family footsteps and chose this profession. With his two sisters choosing other careers, he'd been the one Ramirez to embrace the call. Carlos couldn't see himself doing anything else. He loved everything about being a firefighter, especially helping people when they were most vulnerable.

"Save the strong talk, Carlos." Mason opened his medical bag and then continued his evaluation. "First, I'm checking the arteries in your foot and leg. Good. No damage there."

Carlos sucked in another breath, and Mason's partner, Jordan Bonetti, slipped on an oxygen mask, preventing Carlos from talking. After a minute of more prodding, Mason removed the mask and brought out a chart. "On a scale of one to ten, what's your pain level?"

He considered playing down the injury, but, under Ned's and Mason's watch, Carlos couldn't. "Now that you've touched it, about a six."

Mason removed Carlos's right boot and touched the side of his ankle. "Your left ankle is significantly warmer, and the skin color is already mottled. There's no bone sticking through the surface, but until you have X-rays, I can't tell for certain whether it's a sprain or broken. Can you wiggle your toes?"

Carlos attempted and gave up. "Hurts too much."

Mason turned to Ned. "I'm taking him to Dalesford General. I'll follow up with you for your incident report."

"Appreciate it." Ned patted Carlos's shoulder. "I'll update the fire chief. He'll inform the rest of your family."

Carlos didn't doubt that his father would break the news to his mother and sisters, same as he knew his mother would believe him on death's door until she saw him for herself. "It's just a sprain."

The ambulance doors closed, but not before he glimpsed Becca.

Who was he kidding? He had no right to think of her as Becca. Toward the end, she'd made it clear she was Becks to everyone, including him.

He kept repeating his mantra that this was only a grade-one sprain throughout the ambulance ride and subsequent X-rays. In spite of his words, his ankle appeared more swollen and bruised with every passing minute. In no time, Carlos was back in the ER, unaccustomed to being on this side of the treatment table. He didn't like it one bit.

Dr. Wang strode in, concern written on his brow. "Eventful night, huh?"

"Give it to me straight. Is my sprain a grade one or a grade two?" Carlos feared a grade three sprain, as that would indicate ligament damage, the worst-case scenario. One little trip and fall and bam. His firefighting career could be over in the blink of an eye.

"It's not a sprain, Carlos." Dr. Wang tucked his tablet under his arm and met Carlos's gaze. "Your ankle's broken."

# CHAPTER TWO

THE EXTERIOR FLOODLIGHTS shone brightly on the outdoor soccer fields, illuminating the fine sheen of snow intermingled with gray ash from the fire. Becks finished updating her mother, who assured her that Pippa was asleep and hadn't even noticed Becks was gone. She ended the call, her exhale of breath fading away in a puff of white in the chilly mountain air. Now that the emergency vehicles had left, Becks could at last assess the initial damage.

Everything was far worse than she'd feared. The tire tracks of the engines left deep gouges in the soccer field closest to the indoor complex. The pungent stinging smoke permeated the air, and made her throat ache.

This might spell the end of her dream of bringing a first-rate soccer academy to Hollydale. That, along with the thought of Jack coming for Pippa, made her legs wobbly.

Roberto Ramirez had just arrived on the scene too. Until Carlos broke off their engagement, she had thought this man would become her father-in-law. Little did she know at the time that it would only be the first of several future disappointments. But she'd rebuilt her life after Jack's infidelity. She wouldn't let this fire be the end of the Mountain Vista Soccer Complex.

"Chief Ramirez." She pocketed her cell. "I'm so thankful for what the firefighters did tonight."

"It's our job, Miss Harrison."

"Please, call me Becks." She'd kept her married name Porter for Pippa, although, at times, she thought maybe she should revert to her maiden name. She faced the building, the smoke still dissipating. "Can it be salvaged?"

That wasn't what she wanted to ask. Earlier, she'd seen someone who looked like Carlos leaving in an ambulance. Why was he transported away? Was he okay?

Her old feelings for her former fiancé came back in a rush, which she tried to ignore. He broke it off with her, and she'd sought the arms of a charming soccer coach shortly after arriving in California. It wasn't Carlos's fault she fell for Jack.

"We can make an appointment for tomorrow, once I've inspected the premises during daylight hours." Chief Ramirez started to walk away.

She couldn't hold back any longer. "Did I see Carlos earlier?"

A brief flash of concern highlighted the chief's dark brown eyes, an older version of his son's. "Yes. He was one of the firefighters on the scene."

"Was he hurt?" Of course, he was. Ambulances didn't leave an emergency with a firefighter for no good reason.

"Not seriously. I visited him in the hospital and he's recovering. I wanted to check the scene for myself before I headed home."

That was a relief about Carlos. Becks shifted, the cold beginning to go to her core. "What about the cause of the fire?"

"I'd prefer not to speculate at this point."

"Can I continue to conduct business in my administrative building? It's across the way." She pointed it out, hoping for one victory tonight.

Becks scrutinized the chief's gaze while he gauged the distance between the buildings and their proximity to the soccer fields. "Until I give the all clear, I'd prefer you work at another location. Shall we make it nine thirty tomorrow?"

She nodded, and he took his leave but not before presenting her with a blanket for comfort. It did little to warm her. Numbness began overtaking the adrenaline, and for the second time that night, self-doubt struck at her core, but she swept it away.

Arriving home, she filled her mother in on the fire, a needed hug her mother's instant response. Becks lingered for one more minute, inhaling her mother's sweet floral scent before breaking contact. Her mom left then with her daughter's promise to bring Pippa to her home rather than Tiny Tots later that day. Becks checked in on a sleeping toddler. Her red curls almost covered her teddy bear, Grizzie, tucked securely in the crook of her arm. Becks lingered in the doorway before taking a shower, thankful the smoke smell was gone. If only it were that easy to repair all the damage.

She changed into comfy yoga pants with a sporty pullover and let her dogs, Gomez and Morticia, outside. Soon, they returned. After a series of stretches, she powered up her laptop. Something was still missing. Her phone! She ran out to the garage and grabbed her phone from the console of her SUV. *Drat.* She'd activated the Do Not Disturb feature at the scene of the fire. Scores of texts greeted her, many from Sharlene and her friends and neighbors.

Returning to her dining room, which would serve as her office for now, she made herself comfortable with a blanket and a cup of coffee. The caffeine and adrenaline from the night's events should keep her eyes open and her mind sharp enough to pull an all-nighter. She'd have plenty of time to sleep once Jack collected Pippa.

For a good five minutes, her fingers kept typing and deleting the text before she hit on the right tone to let everyone know she was fine and the complex was mostly fine, too. Then her body started shaking uncontrollably. She couldn't stop trembling. She'd almost lost so much tonight, but thankfully, no one was hurt. That was the main thing.

Except, someone was hurt. *Carlos*. Ever since he'd broken off their engagement, something would often trigger a memory. A sunflower like the one he gave her the first time he asked her out on a date. The song he always hummed when he washed his car. A badly knitted scarf from the one time she'd attempted the hobby convinced she'd be good at it since her twin sister, Natalie, was. She wasn't, but she and Carlos had laughed over that scarf.

She scrolled through the texts but didn't find any new information about Carlos. Maybe her friend Lindsay Ruddick would know something since her husband, Mason, was the paramedic on call tonight. Or maybe her best and most obvious choice was her brother, Mike, who was also the sheriff. Seeing the time, it was late, so she'd seek out answers tomorrow.

Becks picked up her mug and sniffed the aroma of the coffee, prepared with vanilla creamer and three sugars, just the way she liked it. She had to do something about what had happened. *Insurance*. This late at night she logged onto the website of her insurance provider and emailed them.

The words began to blur together. Rubbing her neck, she decided she'd rest her head for five minutes and then visit websites of contractors who were specialists when it came to fire damage. No sooner did she lay her head down than a hen pecked at her leg.

Becks shifted her weight. "Go away, bird."

A giggle penetrated the fog.

Chickens didn't giggle. Wide awake, she looked at Pippa, her daughter's green eyes dewy and large. She thrust Grizzie toward Becks. "We're hungry."

"It's the middle of the night, darlin'. Come on, I'll tuck you into bed." Becks wet her mouth, her tongue feeling dense and thick. She noticed sunlight flooding in through the bay window and grabbed her phone. "It's already nine?"

With Pippa on her heels, Becks ran to the crates in the mudroom between the garage and kitchen. Gomez and Morticia circled their crates like jackals and barked when she and Pippa entered the room. "Some alarm dogs you are. Why didn't you wake me?"

Pippa tugged on her mother's yoga pants while Becks opened the crate doors. "I spilled milk."

"What?" The question slipped out way too loudly, and Pippa's little lip jutted out with a quiver. "It's okay, darlin'. We'll clean it up together."

Gomez and Morticia didn't run to the back door like they usually did. Instead, they sprinted to the refrigerator, where a carton of milk lay on its side on the floor, and began lapping up the creamy liquid. How Becks missed that in her rush to the dogs she didn't know. She grabbed their collars and led them to the back door. "Thanks, but I don't need you two to get stomachaches."

Pippa was too short to unlock the top safety latch, and the second Becks let go of Gomez's collar, he dashed back to the milk. Flipping the latch, she threw open the door, only to find her dad on her stoop. He extended his arms, and she flew into them. "Oh, Dad."

"When you didn't show up with Pippa, we thought something might be wrong."

She sniffled once and pulled away. "I fell asleep." The sight of her tall father with his thatch of white hair and wise blue eyes gave her strength.

He bent down, and it was Pippa's turn to embrace her grandfather, her curly mop of red curls blending in with his red flannel shirt.

"Grandpa Carl!" She stepped back and hung her head. "I not supposed to make cereal."

On that note, Becks ushered the dogs outside and her father inside before closing the door. "I'm running late."

He picked up Pippa and tweaked her cheek. "Your grandma told me to come get you and bring you back to our house. Natalie's on her way over with Danny and Shelby. You'll love playing with your cousins." He met Becks's gaze. "What happened last night is such a shame. If you need us to keep Pippa for a few days, she's always welcome."

Her father didn't know about the court order yet. She'd wait until tonight to tell her parents. "Thanks, I don't know how long I'll be today. The fire was limited to one building, but there'll be a lot to figure out. I need to speak to the insurance company as soon as possible. I'll rebuild better than ever."

With the chief waiting for her, she kissed her dad's cheek and Pippa's. Then she hurried on her way.

AFTER CARLOS WAS discharged from the hospital in the wee hours of the morning, he asked his sister Graciela to bring him home despite Mami's protests she wouldn't hover. They arrived at his ranch-style, one-story home, and he went straight to bed. He tossed and turned, wondering what he could have done differently at the scene. Instead, the four walls of his bedroom crowded in on him, and he came to terms with his new reality. His ankle was broken. Without ligament damage, however, there was a good chance he'd resume his normal activities in about six weeks. Eight, tops.

Would there be complications with his ankle for next year's physical exam? Would this cause him to lose out on a promotion to battalion chief if it came up?

Those questions kept him awake until he smelled coffee. He grabbed his crutches and made his way to the kitchen where his sister was dressed for work. Graciela motioned him to the table and handed him a cup of the steaming brew.

"I'm sorry for all the times I ever teased you about your braces," Carlos said.

"Sure you are." Graciela raised her own cup and downed the contents. "I have to head to work. Mami said she'll drop by as soon as she can."

After his sister left, he made himself comfortable on his couch. He opened the thriller he'd been reading for a month, ever since Halloween, and then closed his eyes. When he woke, sunlight was shining through his living room window. Drips of water fell from his eaves to his front porch, last night's snowfall melting away, same as his morning. With some effort, he assembled a sandwich and downed his anti-inflammatory medication, saving the pain meds for nighttime.

Resting, with his lunch beside him, he wondered what his crew was doing this afternoon. The daily check for inventory of the items on the engine and verifying fluid levels would already have gone down. If he recalled correctly, the second-grade class of Hollydale Elementary was scheduled to visit today. Seeing the innocent round faces, each eager for a plastic hat and a kind word, was the ultimate reward for a firefighter.

This job was like air and water to him. He cherished every aspect of his life, even the poky spring in the mattress where he spent the night shifts when he wasn't called to a medical emergency or a fire.

The heel of his foot itched, and Carlos longed for a good long scratch, rather impossible with the lime-green fiberglass cast covering the ankle, foot and lower leg. For now, he couldn't get it wet or place any weight on his left leg. After he stopped taking the painkillers, he could drive himself around, something that wouldn't have been possible if he'd broken the right ankle.

His doorbell rang, and he reached for his crutches. He welcomed his battalion chief, Ned Grayson, who handed him a get-well card signed by his fellow firefighters, although each of them had sent texts or called already. He kept his composure while Ned cleared his throat and said, "The pain meds must be taking their toll. You look ready to call it a day."

"It's only noon." Carlos made it back to his chair, but one of the crutches fell to the ground.

Ned righted it.

Carlos grunted his thanks. "Have a seat?"

"Thanks. Since you'll be on worker's comp pending the incident investigation…" Ned leaned forward. "Did the doctor say anything about whether you'll be cleared to return to work?"

The truth became clear to Carlos. This visit wasn't so much about the card as it centered on his future with the department, something he wouldn't know until the final prognosis.

"It was a simple fracture. No surgery necessary. So, I'll get an ankle boot in four weeks. That's when they'll know for sure if there was any ligament damage." Carlos looked around and knew he'd be climbing the walls if he were left alone the full month. "But I can drive and use crutches."

"What about desk duty? Did the doctor say anything about clearing you for that?"

*Desk duty.* In some circumstances, it was where injured firefighters figured out what they could do with the rest of their lives. Some of them did make it back to the crew, but a good many went on to other county government positions or found work in the private sector.

Carlos flexed his right ankle. "I can start next week."

"I'll need written authorization…" The doorbell rang, and Ned jumped to his feet. "I'll answer the door for you."

Ned disappeared, and Carlos leaned back in his recliner. Closing his eyes, he considered what he'd be doing. Most likely, county inspections, paperwork, and the like. He'd have to use some of this time to consider all his options, such as what his backup plan was if he could no longer serve as a firefighter.

Voices echoed in the foyer. One of them was his mother's.

"I've come to stay until you're fully recovered." His mother, Fabiana, had paired her festive holiday sweater with black jeans. She rolled in a suitcase, placed the cake carrier on the coffee table and then patted his cheeks, her fingernails painted a pretty red. "I made your favorite tres leches cake."

"Thanks, Mami." He tried to rise, but she pushed him back down.

"Do you see this latest streak of gray? I call it the Carlos Special to go along with the ones from your father and sisters." Fabiana pulled a strand of her hair in a straight line in front of his face. "I'll need my hair dyed for sure this week. You and your father are going to keep Mitzi Mayfield Thompson in business at her beauty parlor until she's a hundred and still keeping all of us enthralled with her stories."

His mother might have been short in stature, but she was big on drama. Her friends, who called themselves the Matchmaking Mimosas, believed themselves responsible for a few of the recent love matches in Hollydale.

Ned shifted his weight and picked up his uniform hat from the corner of the sofa. "I'll be going. We'll talk tomorrow, but I'll need what we talked about in writing."

He disappeared, and Fabiana began bustling around the room, collecting Ned's disposable coffee container from The Busy Bean along with Carlos's half-full cup of water. "I knew I should have moved in last night. Do you want more water with lots of ice? And how about I whip you up something for lunch?"

"Mami, you're a guest."

She froze as if he'd thrown a pie in her face. "I'm not a guest. I'm your mother."

He stilled her arm with his hand. "Sure, you are, but you don't have to wait on me."

She broke free and headed toward the kitchen. "I'll put a lot of ice in your water, just the way you like it."

Actually, that was the way his sister Graciela preferred her drinks, but he didn't have the heart to correct her. When she brought him a fresh cup, he smiled and placed it on the table. "Thanks, Mami."

"Don't mention it. That's what mothers are for. Now about lunch?"

"I made myself a sandwich." It sat untouched on the end table as he wasn't hungry. He hadn't been since the accident. Whether it was the medication or lack of exercise or what, he wasn't sure, but he anticipated a return to his normal appetite eventually.

"Why don't you take a nap? I'll run to the store for the ingredients for my special mojo marinated pork. It tastes better if I let it sit overnight, but it'll still be passable." Fabiana patted his face once more. "I don't know if I told you this last night, but I love you."

Only about twenty-five times, but this had nothing to do with her forgetting if she'd said it and everything to do with the worry she'd been feeling. He smiled and closed his eyes for a minute.

A few minutes later, he woke to the smell of something delicious. He glanced at his watch, shock skittering down his spine. He'd slept for over seven hours. Fabiana bustled into the living room with a table tray in her arms. "Good evening, sleepyhead."

"You shouldn't have let me sleep that long." He reached for his crutches.

"What do you need? I'll get it for you."

"Trust me, Mami, I need to do this by myself."

Her hearty laugh let him know she understood his meaning, and he returned several minutes later to a plate of pork and yellow rice and grilled vegetables on the tray situated by his recliner.

"It smells wonderful. Thank you." He situated the crutches and lowered himself, taking care not to put any weight on his foot. "But you don't need to stay on my account."

She sat on the couch and deposited a cloth napkin on her lap. "How are you going to get around? How are you going to take care of yourself?"

He did likewise with the napkin she'd laid

next to his plate. "I've been on my own for several years and done just fine. I'll manage." His mouth watered at the aroma of his mother's special marinade, the orange, lime and mint combining with other spices for a coating that was out of this world. The first bite melted in his mouth. "It's delicious."

"It's not as good as if I'd taken my sweet time about it. And speaking of taking your own sweet time, it's a shame you don't have a wife here helping you, caring for you." Fabiana finished cutting her meat before spearing a piece with her fork.

"Yes, because you and Dad and Graciela, not to mention several of my crew, weren't enough people crammed into my ER cubicle in the two hours before I was discharged." He took another bite, savoring the flavors.

"Seriously, Carlos. You're my baby boy. I want to see you settled. I want grandchildren."

Carlos laid down his fork. "Now you have Marisol." When his sister Gisele called to tell them she'd eloped with her boyfriend, they'd welcomed her new husband and his twelve-year-old daughter into the family. His mother was a grandmother at last. "Gisele is very happy with Javier."

His mother's dark brown eyes glistened. "Did I tell you the news? They're moving to Hollydale. I'll love having a granddaughter and spoiling Marisol." She waggled her finger in front of him. "Ever since you moved back, you won't let me set you up, and there's no better time to go out on a first date than when you have a broken ankle." Fabiana stopped for a bite of food.

The memory of Becks's bright blue eyes, curious and caring, danced in front of him. She'd seen him at the fire. He was sure of it. Even if she hadn't, he would have noticed her, even with his injured ankle. From his position on the stretcher, she wore her red hair cropped in a style that highlighted her cheekbones. He shook away the image.

"I don't understand your reasoning. There's no worse time. I can't walk, and I don't know what might happen with my job right now."

She swallowed and then sipped her water. "Nope, it's the perfect time. Trust your mother."

The doorbell rang, and he sent a mental note of thanks to whoever it was. He reached for his crutches, but Fabiana jumped to her feet. "I'll see who it is and send them on their way. You need to rest more."

She disappeared into the foyer, and he stood. Using his crutches, he navigated his way and found Becks with his mother.

"Carlos." That deep husky voice of hers made it seem as if no time had passed since the last time he'd seen her. She'd wanted him to reconsider breaking up with her, insisting she'd return home after the season. He refused to hold her back.

In that time, she'd married, had a child and divorced. At least that's what he'd heard since his return to Hollydale.

She held out a pink box with Night Owl Bakery in black looping letters on top. "Can I come in?"

Fabiana shook her head. "I made him my special tres leches cake, and Carlos needs his rest."

He snorted and both women glared at him. "What?" He kept a grip on his crutches. "A minute ago, Mami, you were trying to set me up with every single woman in town, and now a beautiful unattached one appears at my doorstep and you can't wait to get rid of her."

"Carlos Roberto Ramirez, your father and I raised you better than to talk to me like that," Fabiana huffed.

"That's right. You did raise me well, and I'm capable of being here by myself." He nudged her suitcase with his right crutch. "You'll be more comfortable at home. Say hello to Dad and tell him I'll talk to him and Ned tomorrow."

"Well, since you do need the rest, we'll both be going." Fabiana picked up her suitcase and frowned. "Surely Becks parked behind me."

"Actually, I parked on the street."

His mother walked over to him, raised herself on her stiletto boots and brushed his cheek with a kiss. "If you need me, you call me, day or night." She picked up her suitcase and glared at the pink box in Becks's hands. "Store-bought dessert, humph."

Fabiana sailed out in regal fashion. Carlos shifted his weight, and Becks continued gripping the box.

"Hi, Becca." His special name for her slipped out before he could help it. "Um, Becks."

She tapped the box. "I shouldn't be here, and this really doesn't even begin to make a dent in what I owe you. I mean, you hurt yourself saving my complex."

"I was only doing my job." He tried standing

straighter, but a person could only do so much on crutches. "You don't owe me anything."

She flinched and nodded. "It was just a shock seeing you last night and then finding out you were hurt. I just wanted to tell you we don't have to tiptoe around each other. The past is in the past, where it should be."

"It was a long time ago." She'd had the world at her feet with that professional soccer offer. She hadn't needed to be stuck with her small-town fiancé. Considering it hadn't taken her long to replace him, he'd been proven right. He wondered if he should invite her in. Hollydale was a small town with a big heart, so they'd cross paths often. "We should clear the air. Come in for a minute?"

"My parents are expecting me, and I'll only get to tuck in Pippa a couple of more times before she goes to California for the holidays." More emotions flitted across her face until guilt settled there. "You're right, though. We're bound to run into each other. It's best if we can pass each other without ducking behind corners."

Lines of stress creased her forehead. He raised his right crutch and pointed it toward his living room. "Sounds like we both need a moment to relax and talk. Join me?"

She looked longingly at his couch. "I've been on the move all day. One minute won't make that much of a difference."

One minute sometimes made all the difference.

Surprised at her decision to relent and stay, he led her into the living room, where he claimed the recliner.

"By the way, the cupcakes are a guilt offering. I'm sorry about what happened to you."

"It wasn't your fault." He understood guilt. He'd endured it after breaking up with her, enough to book a flight to California to try for another shot with her before her twin sister lowered the boom. Becks had moved on so fast.

She nodded and clutched the box to her chest. "Well, my mother taught me always to bring something when I'm a guest. I thought red velvet cupcakes used to be your favorite, but since your mom made her famous cake, you won't need these."

"Red velvet is awesome. Thanks." He leaned forward and gestured her closer. "Give me the box."

She hesitated and looked at the tray. "Did I interrupt your dinner?"

"I'm an adult. If I want to eat dessert first, I can." She handed him the box, and he pulled out a cupcake, the cream cheese frosting all but calling his name. He unwrapped a cupcake and sank his teeth into pure lusciousness. For the first time since the accident, the pain dulled and his appetite returned. He extended the box to her. "Want one?"

"No, thanks. How do people clear the air after nine years? That's a long time. Too long for grudges." She played with the edge of her coat and stood. "Do you need anything before I leave? Water? Milk?"

"No, I'm good. But I do need one thing from you."

"Name it."

"It shouldn't be this awkward between us. Can we move on?" Talking to Becks had always been the easiest thing in the world, even in those gawky teenage years when nothing seemed to come easy.

She fell back on the couch and looked at him, the years melting away. The carefree Becks whose world revolved around soccer and him showed herself. Then her blue eyes became guarded again. He longed for another glimpse of the Becca he used to know.

"Time's passed, Carlos. We're not the same people anymore."

"You're right, so we should get to know each other."

The wariness in her shoulders took him by surprise, another facet of her personality that was different from the fearless Becks of so long ago. "Sometimes the past is best left alone."

"I disagree. Our past molds us into who we are, but our future is what we make of it. Knowing your options and mapping out a plan help people survive."

"But, you of all people know you can't always rely on just one plan. Sometimes you have to take a chance and go for it."

And that had been their downfall. He'd been so sure she'd take the option that wouldn't include him he didn't take the option of trusting her. And she'd scored by leaving Hollydale and achieving her dreams of playing soccer professionally.

There were so many options now. What if he asked her out? What if this little spark of attraction could turn into something more? Too many routes in front of him, and in his present state he didn't dare choose one.

He finished off the cupcake. "Thanks for deciding to go for it and check up on me."

Becks always had assertiveness to spare. That was one of the reasons he'd fallen for her and proposed.

"Like you said, we have to get past the awkwardness," she said.

"So, where does that leave us?" He balled the wrapper and deposited it on his dinner tray.

"That leaves us with me wishing you a good night." She pointed to the cake carrier. "No matter where I ordered a tres leches cake in California, I've never tasted another as good as your mom's."

"She says love is the special ingredient. What she doesn't know, though, is the cake's my father's favorite, not mine." He'd never corrected his mother about that either. After all, she'd believed it for so many years, why hurt her feelings? He stared at the box of cupcakes. "I'm partial to red myself."

Red velvet cupcakes, red fire trucks, and a certain redheaded soccer player. Great things came in threes.

"That's my favorite color, too. Pippa prefers pink. Speaking of my daughter, I have to leave. I need to have a conversation with my parents about her."

"Is something wrong?" That protectiveness he'd always felt around her kicked up once more.

"Are you sure you want to hear all of this?"

He nodded at her questioning gaze.

"My ex-husband has finally decided he wants to be part of our daughter's life and a judge agreed with him. He's picking up Pippa on Saturday. They're spending Christmas at his beach house in California."

"That's rough, Becks. I'm here the next time you need someone to listen."

"Next time? Thanks, but I don't think that's a possibility. Those cupcakes are a one-time offering." Her underlying meaning was clear. She'd moved on and he should do the same. "It's time for me to go." She eyed his mother's cake carrier with a hint of longing.

"Why don't you take the cake home with you?" He stood and reached for his crutches, a reminder he wouldn't be active for the next several weeks.

"I couldn't possibly."

"It's my way of thanking you for being the first to make a peace offering." The best thing was to let her go. Just as he had to accept his broken ankle and that he was the one who'd ended their relationship, leading them down different paths.

"So you're saying I earned this cake?"

That challenge was so her that he had to laugh. Then he grew somber. He had to know. Had she been telling him the truth when she said she'd come back to Hollydale in the off-season? "You know I didn't believe you."

"About what?" She blinked, confusion written all over her face.

"I thought you'd outgrown Hollydale. Outgrown me."

She met his gaze, and her eyes darkened to navy. "I'm sorry you didn't know the real me. I value loyalty, and I'd never betray a relationship where I pledged my love."

He broke the gaze and made his way to the cake carrier. He handed it to her. "This cake has your name on it."

"I really shouldn't, but my daughter Pippa loves cake. Having this cake might help me face telling her about her trip to California a little easier." He'd missed that smile, the one that brought roses to her cheeks. "Thank you."

He saw her to the front door and noticed her apple scent, making him too aware of her, of too many memories. This new Becks was so different from the girl he remembered from years past. He'd never seen her hesitate while accepting what she'd wanted. He'd never heard that kind of bitterness from her younger self. Though her eyes softened when she talked about her daughter. Still, she was a far cry from the happy go-getter he'd fallen in love with.

He locked the door behind her, hobbled into the living room and sat again in his recliner. As he shoved pieces of pork around his plate, he hoped now he'd stop comparing every potential girlfriend to the illusion of his first love.

# CHAPTER THREE

BECKS AND PIPPA giggled over the last bites of dessert, perfect for a Friday night pick-me-up. Even now, a few days old, Fabiana's tres leches cake was every bit as good as she remembered, and then some.

Only one other conversation in her life was as bittersweet as her dining room talk with her daughter to explain why Pippa would be spending Christmas away from her mother and extended family. A long time ago, she'd accepted her dream job of playing for a professional soccer team in California, following her college graduation. Instead of a give-and-take conversation about making the relationship work, she'd been shocked when Carlos had simply broken off their engagement. Boarding that plane and flying to Los Angeles a week later, without any meaningful follow-up communication between them, was one of the hardest things she'd ever done.

That same bittersweet agony would be felt

again tomorrow, only this time Pippa would be boarding the plane and Becks would be the one left behind at the airport.

"Mommy go up in sky, too?" Pippa looked adorable with white frosting dotting her lips and cheeks. There was even a smidge on her forehead. "You come with me and Grizzie."

Becks's chest squeezed at Pippa's smile, the one that usually got her whatever she wanted, within reason. "Not this time, darling girl."

Her mountain of tasks prevented her from flying to California with Pippa, although she'd stay at the airport until she made sure the exchange with Jack went smoothly. Until she was satisfied that Pippa was emotionally secure, she'd remain at that airport.

Becks had an upcoming meeting with the fire chief and county inspector regarding the follow-up safety of the burned building. That would lead into an afternoon of negotiations with the insurance agent, followed by two appointments with construction crews. Today's meeting with Kick, Goal and Score had once again fallen through the cracks. Their email postponing the interview for the proposed partnership and extra visibility landed in her inbox this morning. She took comfort that Pippa would have a marvelous time with Jack, who'd mentioned the beach, theme parks and zoos on a videoconference call.

Jack was squeezing two and a half years of fatherhood into one month, but who was counting?

Ever since she returned to Hollydale, she'd let Jack and his infidelity rob her of any joy. Like the fun so evident on Pippa's face right now after finishing her small piece of cake. That betrayal just as they were about to celebrate their fourth wedding anniversary had cut her deeper than she'd realized.

Letting go of that type of hurt wasn't easy, but maybe she could while not forgetting it. Maybe the best way to win back her life was turning a new page and choosing happiness. Wasn't that one of the reasons she'd moved back to Hollydale?

For the past two years, she'd supported herself and Pippa by using her college degree in physical therapy and worked at a local rehab facility. That only reinforced what she really wanted to do, coaching soccer and starting this academy. She'd bought the first available property that suited her needs, one that allowed her to be in charge of her destiny. And yet disappointment was seeping into her at how fate seemed to be working against her.

As soon as she led Pippa into the bathroom and wet the washcloth for her daughter's face, her cell phone rang. *Jack.* Probably a last-minute question about Pippa's schedule or updated information about his flight, although a text would have sufficed.

"Hello, Jack." She transferred her phone to her other ear and wedged it with her shoulder. "Hold on a second. I'm washing Pippa's face." Once she'd finished the task, she settled Pippa in her bedroom with a book and Grizzie. "I'm sure your daddy is excited about tomorrow. Get some sleep, pumpkin."

Oddly, she thought she heard an automated voice announcing departures in the background, but Jack wasn't supposed to leave for North Carolina until tomorrow. Was this call letting her know he was arriving early? That was probably for the best, and she regretted not coming up with that solution herself. One morning of adjustment for Pippa with both of them was better than handing her off at the airport.

Becks kept Pippa's door open and moved to the living room. "Are you at the airport already? You'll have to rent a car or use a service to get to my house. Did you reserve a room at the Eight Gables or are you crashing on my couch?" If that was the case, how would Pippa feel about finding her father here in the morning?

"I'm at LAX, but not for the reason you think." He sounded too happy for this to end well for her. "Becks, I've had a once-in-a-lifetime offer."

For Jack, that could only mean one thing. "Did you get the call from one of the European teams?"

"Yes, and Steph and I are about to board for New York now. We're flying to Lisbon tomorrow."

"But Pippa doesn't have a passport. And who's Steph?" Jack had disregarded her feelings in the past, but she wouldn't stand by and let him take Pippa abroad.

"Hold on." His muffled voice came through like he was carrying on two conversations at once. "Still there?"

"How am I supposed to get Pippa to New York, Jack? I'm not putting her on a flight by herself. And who is this Steph?"

"Steph is my girlfriend. We've been dating for six months. She's helped me see I need to be a dad to Pippa. She's the one. My true love." Becks braced herself for some reaction, but there was nothing. Her feelings for Jack as anything other than Pippa's father ended long ago. "This is my chance at a coaching position for a team in Europe. Pippa would be a distraction."

*"A distraction?"* Becks couldn't hold back. "Our daughter is anything but that. She's a wonderful little girl and you won her over with the video chats. She's excited about the ocean and the zoo."

"Don't put words in my mouth, Becks. I have a lot on my plate. Pippa and I will connect next summer."

"You can't promise your daughter something and then back away, Jack."

"I thought you'd have been thrilled to keep Pippa for the holidays."

This type of passive aggressive behavior was something she didn't miss about their marriage. He was half right, though. She was thrilled about this turn of events. "I am. I just don't want her to be disappointed."

"She's only two. She won't even know I'm not there. Look, Steph's waiting for me, and the plane's about to board. You'll love Steph. Everyone does, and so will Pippa. Steph's dad is great, too. He's the one who arranged for this chance with the team. With any luck, by next summer, Steph and I will be engaged. Pippa can be our flower girl. Gotta go."

Silence met her before she could say anything else. She stared down the hallway, wondering how to break the news to her daughter that she wouldn't be going up in the sky after all.

## CHAPTER FOUR

CARLOS FLEXED HIS left leg out of the open door of the SUV his father used for official county business. He waited until Roberto brought him his crutches. At work, he always referred to his father by his first name or as chief, careful to keep their professional and personal relationships separate. Thankfully the ride out to the Mountain Vista Soccer Complex hadn't been long. Since they'd be walking over gravel, Carlos preferred using the crutches rather than the knee scooter his orthopedist Dr. Patel had suggested.

Roberto handed him his crutches, and Carlos thanked him. To his trained nose, a faint whiff of smoke still hung in the air. The chill of late fall hadn't dissipated the odor in the past week. This was Carlos's first glance of the complex in the daytime, and he lingered behind, curious to see what Becks saw in the place.

The backdrop of the Great Smokies sure packed a wallop. Some of the oaks and chestnuts were already covered with frost, and next month, winter would dominate the landscape. Sully Creek's flowing water provided a soft hushed murmur. Once upon a time, he and Becks had hiked all over the area, their favorite destination the top of Pine Falls. After he left Hollydale eight years ago, he'd done everything he could to keep the Smokies a safe destination with his work as a smoke jumper. As he grew older, he craved the community he once knew. His decision to return home had been the right one, just as this property should have been the right choice for Becks.

The quiet beauty gave him insight about why Becks, who'd always loved nature and outdoor sports, had purchased this land. Even so, though, the buildings had to be up to code. On this Monday, his first day of desk duty, he was tagging along with the chief and the county inspector. He'd have to break the news to Becks they'd be working together to make sure the buildings complied with regulations while setting up a realistic time frame for her complex to open.

The inspector signaled he was ready, and the three of them headed toward the administrative building, where Becks's SUV was parked. Carlos navigated around the gray slush puddles with his crutches. He stopped to caught his breath. He should have asked for more time off before reporting in, but the last thing he wanted was for anyone to accuse his father of giving his son preferential treatment.

With his equilibrium restored, he hurried and caught up with the others.

Becks spoke first. "Good morning, Chief." Her gaze wandered to Carlos's bright lime-green cast, and she arched her eyebrow. "Carlos, you're feeling better?"

"The doctor cleared me for desk duty." He'd pull his weight for the fire department one way or another. If that meant being here for the inspection, he could handle a little pain.

"That's the first good news I've had today." She ran her hand through her short hair that had been whipped around with the stiff winter wind. She looked beautiful. "This has been the Mondayest of Mondays."

"Hopefully we'll give you good news when the inspection is concluded." Roberto adjusted his hard hat. His father's tall stature might seem imposing to some with his dark wavy hair and no-nonsense brown eyes, but he was the epitome of calm resourcefulness.

Schoolchildren loved his spry self, a blend

of humor with appropriate seriousness, while more than one Hollydale resident had found solace in his firm supportive tone after a fire devastated their life.

"Shall we get to work?" The county inspector tapped his watch and handed Becks a hard hat.

"Ms. Porter, we'd like your permission to inspect the other building. Our preliminary findings of the indoor soccer building indicate an issue with the wiring. Both buildings were built at the same time." Roberto looked straight at her.

Becks granted them permission. Before long, they'd finished the preliminary tour of the administrative building, and the inspector pulled Roberto aside. Carlos opened his mouth to ask Becks about why this was such a Monday when the pair returned.

"Carlos, we'll be exploring the ventilation in the crawl space under the burned building. If you and Ms. Porter want to wait, we'll be done shortly." Roberto and the inspector went on their way, another reminder of his inability to do his job at the present time.

"What's going on?" Becks stared at him as

though he had all the answers when he was in the dark, same as her.

"Some older buildings have vents and wiring in an area between the bottom floor and the ground. They're just being thorough. How about some fresh air?" Over her protests, he led her toward the closest bench outside. He winced as he sat, happy to be off his ankle. This wasn't a good sign. After a weekend of watching television and resting, he was ready to climb the walls.

"Carlos." Becks touched his arm. "Is this too much too fast for your ankle?"

"I'm the one who should be asking if it's too soon to be back to the scene of the fire."

She stared at the mountain landscape, unwilling to meet his gaze. "I don't think I returned soon enough."

"Does this have anything to do with this being the Mondayest of Mondays?" He stretched out his good leg and made a note to ask the doctor how he could maintain the muscle tone.

Becks lowered her gaze to his leg and squinted. "You know you can do exercises with that leg that won't impact your ankle. I'd show you, but there's a lot of slush around."

"Maybe later. Come on, confide in me. What's different about this Monday?"

"This was supposed to be a new start for me. Soccer has always grounded me and helped me forge my path."

He could relate to what she was saying as he'd never wanted to do anything else but become a firefighter. "You always beat my older sister Gisele and me to the practice field."

She removed the hard hat, and her red hair was tousled in an appealing way. "How do you know it wasn't because I couldn't wait to see you?"

"And here I thought you wanted to be with me because you were after my mother's tres leches cake recipe."

"Well, that would have been an added bonus."

He'd never had this kind of easy banter with any of the women he'd dated while he lived in Tennessee. Even after becoming seriously involved with Jennifer for a couple of years, they'd never slipped into this type of fun conversation. When he chose to move back to Hollydale, they'd called it a day. Last he heard, she was now engaged, and he couldn't be happier for her, which told him Jennifer definitely wasn't the one for him.

Dating Becks had been a challenge, keeping him alive and on his feet, but he'd loved every minute. Losing her had been devastating, even if he'd been the cause of his own misery.

Now they were back in each other's lives, and earning each other's friendship again, no matter where that might lead.

The laughter faded, and he became serious. "This can still be a new start for you, Becks. You were never the type of person who let adversity stop you."

"I've always thought my twin sister, Natalie, was the one who bounced back more easily." She scuffed the ground, brown dirt kicking up where the frost and slush had melted.

"Not at all. You meet challenges with your whole self."

She looked up, her blue eyes showing some of the fiery temperament he remembered. Good. That type of spirit would get her through this hardship.

"I never expected to hear anything like that from you again, especially with the way things ended."

"Time has helped. So did clearing the air this week. Maybe we should discuss this later over a cup of coffee and a red velvet cupcake?"

The wind kicked up, and Becks shivered.

She reached into her bag for a pair of gloves. She donned one glove, then tugged on the second.

"Now's good for me. You did offer to listen the other night so don't say you weren't warned. My groundskeeper quit this morning, my ex-husband disappointed Pippa, someone's grandchild grabbed her spot at her day care for the month of December and I owe Natalie a favor for looking after my daughter."

"Isn't that what family's for? Love, cake and putting up with us when things get tough."

"I don't like to be indebted to people, whether it's my brother Mike or his wife Georgie, or even my own sister. I don't know how I'll ever repay her for babysitting Pippa for me this month." Becks attempted to smooth out her emotions, he knew, but they were there beneath the surface.

Before he could answer, Roberto and the inspector emerged from the building. Inspector Strickland hung back, typing notes into his tablet, and Roberto approached them. Becks rose to her feet and handed Carlos his crutches, watching him as he carefully got to his feet. He noticed how she provided help but hated being on the receiving end.

"Carlos, you'll get the initial notes in your

inbox this afternoon." Roberto waited for his slight nod and turned to Becks. "We've inspected both buildings. At closer glance, the thermal expansion of the steel wasn't as extensive as feared. I'll email you a list of restoration companies that can give you a quote on cleaning up the damage and getting both buildings up to code."

Becks pulled out a notebook and pen and jotted some notes. "That's good, right?"

"Yes and no. Neither building is currently in compliance as far as working sprinklers and proper ventilation." He went on about a number of other issues.

"Slow down, please. I'm trying to write everything you say." Becks's gaze stayed on the paper.

"Carlos's report will be thorough. He'll answer any questions about codes and regulations. This, along with the Firefighter's Christmas Festival, are his only duties this week."

*The festival? On his plate?* Carlos held back his groan, as that wasn't a little undertaking but rather a maelstrom. It took place the weekend before Christmas, and it was a huge community event.

"But the building itself can be saved?" Becks sought confirmation, and Roberto nodded.

"The administrative building, though, needs an overhaul. It shouldn't have passed inspection with its code violations."

"I purchased it as is." Becks placed the notebook back in her bag, that earlier gleam in her eyes gone. "I'm concerned. Insurance might not cover the modifications for the administrative building, which wasn't involved in the blaze."

"Tough times of adversity mold us into who we are, and your family's behind you. That's a huge bonus."

Carlos wasn't sure if Roberto was talking to him or Becks.

"Carlos knows the county's codebook like the back of his hand. He'll follow up with you, rest assured."

Seemed as though he and Becks had something in common, wanting to prove themselves after a setback. And now they each had a reason for ensuring the opening of this complex took place on time.

The inspector came over and pulled Roberto aside. They kept their voices low enough so Carlos couldn't make out what they were saying. Roberto returned. "There's a slight emergency. Becks, can you get Carlos home?"

"No problem."

The inspector kept his gaze glued to his phone screen. "Carlos, I'll email you the report, and we'll go over it before I sign it and send it to Becks."

Carlos bristled at how his job duties were now reduced to those of a glorified desk jockey. Still, it was better than sitting at home, wallowing.

Roberto and the inspector left, and Carlos faced Becks. "If this makes your Monday even harder, I'll arrange for another ride."

He sank back onto the bench and touched his left leg, stopping short of massaging the calf muscle.

She settled beside him. "You're not the problem." She looked at one building, then the other before returning her gaze to him. "As a matter of fact, you might be part of the solution."

"What do you mean?" He gave up and worked out the muscle cramp.

"You know about codes, and I know about injured and tired muscles." She removed her gloves and flexed her fingers. "When I moved back here, I worked at the therapy clinic as a necessity. Teaching soccer is my passion though, and I invested my life savings in this venture."

"Your life savings?" He stopped moving his fingers and whistled. "Everything's on the line for you? Same as it is for me since I have to be in top form for next year's annual firefighter's exam."

She winced and nodded. "I didn't mean to let that slip, but yes." She glanced around once more. "If I sell this for a loss, I don't know where Pippa and I will end up. The clinic already hired my replacement. To stay involved in soccer, I'd have to take a coaching job. The only one I was offered recently is in Chicago, where I don't know anyone, and Pippa wouldn't grow up with her cousins."

"Oh, Bec, uh, Becks." Her name came out with a note of compassion, and he started rubbing his leg again. "I can't wait to meet Pippa. So, what can I do to help?"

"How about a deal? You help me with the codes, and I'll help you with your physical therapy. I'll make sure you're ready for your physical exam next year." She extended her hand. "Do we have a deal?"

He wanted the handshake to linger a little longer, the contact inviting and magnetic, but that would have been awkward. "Yes, but Becks?"

That competitive gleam was back in her eyes. "What?"

"I would have helped you even without the offer of physical therapy. All you had to do was ask."

# CHAPTER FIVE

AFTER SCHEDULING A visit for an estimate from the third restoration company that Fire Chief Ramirez recommended, Becks hung up the phone in her new temporary home away from home at the distraction-free Whitley Community Center. Two weeks after the fire, a couple of companies had already inspected the premises. Now she waited for their bids, hoping one might come close to the amount the insurance company would pay out under her coverage. Somehow she'd have to find the money to cover the costs of the code updates for the administration building so she wouldn't lose everything before she began.

As it was, she was close to maxing out her savings for the opening. She couldn't ask her parents for a loan. Talking to the bank hadn't provided much hope as the fire devalued the property, and she didn't have any other collateral. The loan officer also nixed the idea of a second mortgage on her house or the land.

And Jack? Forget it. She wouldn't ask him for money.

Until the buildings were up to code, no one could work at the complex. Maybe Carlos would have some suggestions on expediting the construction and upgrades while staying within code specifications so she could still open on time?

Her phone pinged with a text from Natalie. Becks opened a picture of a smiling Pippa next to Natalie's kids, seven-year-old Danny and baby Shelby, taken at the Hollydale Botanical Garden where they'd gone to paint butterfly ornaments for Christmas presents. Of course, Natalie would find a way to keep them entertained and bring home something beautiful. The perfect twin, the happy wife, the loving mom. Was there anything Natalie couldn't do with a smile and a hug?

Becks chastised herself and clicked the heart emoji reply when an email from Kick, Goal and Score popped in her inbox. She crossed her fingers the elusive promised interview with her at Mountain Vista was finally coming through. Her heart plummeted when she opened the email. It wasn't from Wallace Key, the director. Instead, it was from his assistant, Stacy. They'd heard about the fire but still wanted to tour the facility before the company would decide on partnering with her and promote her complex. How could she schedule a tour with Stacy before the work was finished? Without their sponsorship and soccer community clout, the registration numbers for the first few months would be lower than expected.

She tapped her fingers on the small desk, wishing there were a window so she could look out at the mountains. Somehow, they always calmed her and renewed her strength, almost as much as Carlos once had. She considered her reply to the email, but none of her options seemed to line up with a good shot at the goal line. She thought about asking Dante and Amara for their suggestions. However, she was the owner. The responsibility lay on her shoulders. Besides, they didn't have any influence over the Kick, Goal and Score management.

No, but her college coach, a legend in the state and soccer community, might have some sway with the director. The only reason she hadn't contacted Tricia Weaver sooner was her mentor's impending retirement. Tricia had worked hard, breaking barriers and records along the way. The last thing she needed was Becks disturbing her, but Becks was starting to feel a little desperate. She called, but there was no answer.

Someone knocked on the door. Brooke Maxwell, the community center's director, stuck her head into the room and smiled. "Can I come in?"

"Of course. Thanks for letting me use your center." Becks pushed herself away from the small desk.

Brooke entered and plucked some imaginary lint from her immaculate gray suit jacket. The center's director always looked sharp and was on top of things. "Well, it's my pleasure. You're so quiet I almost forgot you were here." She chuckled. "I just wanted to let you know the staff room is ready for your meeting tomorrow, and we're closing in fifteen minutes."

"Thanks. It's easier to work here than at home. I love my dogs, but they keep dropping their leash at my feet. They want a walk when I need to work." Becks started unplugging power strips before taking a minute to stretch, her muscles cramped from sitting for so long. "I didn't realize it was getting late."

"Without any windows, this room is great for a cup of coffee, not so great for a long work session." Brooke waited while Becks gathered everything together before locking the door behind them.

"I appreciate you squeezing my staff in at

the last minute." Becks buttoned her winter coat. "I hate to sound greedy, but I need one more favor."

"I aim to please." Brooke opened the stairwell for Becks and nodded for her to go first.

"Is there any way I can use your gym before opening hours?" Despite Carlos's protests to the contrary, Becks wasn't prepared to accept his help without offering something in return. "During the fire, one of the firefighters injured his ankle. You might know him. Carlos Ramirez?"

"Everyone in town loves Carlos. His mom is a dear friend of mine. Fabiana credits herself and the Matchmaking Mimosas for my wedding to Jonathan."

Becks forged forward. "I want to help Carlos." Especially seeing as her place was the source of his injury. "Your gym has training equipment for his physical therapy. If you allow us early entry, there'd be more privacy. I'd only need access for a few weeks, just until I regain authorization to use the training room at my complex."

"I'm concerned about our umbrella policy since you're not paid staff."

"That's exactly why I can't take him to my old physical therapy location. That along with they'd charge his insurance company, and I want to do this for him."

"I love that Hollydale takes care of its own." Brooke sounded as though she was on the fence, and Becks held her breath since Brooke's husband, Jonathan, was a police detective in Hollydale and a fellow first responder. "You can use the gym as long as there's a staff member on-site. How early do you want to arrive?"

"I can drop my daughter off at my sister's house by seven and meet Carlos here." That was, if Carlos agreed to the plan.

"When do you want to start?"

"I'll talk to Carlos, and let you know." Becks thanked Brooke, then walked to her car.

Settling in the driver's seat, Becks hooked her phone to her charger. Natalie called, and she cringed. When did talking to her twin become a struggle? For so long, they'd had a bond no one could break, and then they grew apart. Whether it had happened naturally or not, Becks wasn't sure.

"Is everything okay with Pippa?"

"Pippa's fine. I'm just checking on your ETA."

"About ten minutes. Just so you know, I'm forever in your and Aidan's debt for this babysitting." Aidan was Natalie's husband, more of a stickler for routine than her free-spirited twin.

"It's called love." A note of exasperation sounded from her sister's normally implacable self. "But I'll be more empathetic when I return to work in January after an extended maternity leave and using all of my accrued vacation days. Between you and me, I miss my kindergarten students. See you soon!"

Silence met Becks's ear, and she gathered herself for a minute in the parking lot. She owed Nat same as she had to try to help Carlos.

Minutes later, she pulled into her sister's driveway, parking alongside her brother's classic Thunderbird. Mike waved as Becks emerged from her car.

"I swear my niece has grown another three inches overnight." Mike walked over, that familiar grin greeting her. "What have you been feeding Pippa?"

"You know, the three Cs—Cheerios, cheese crackers, and, her favorite, chicken nuggets."

Mike laughed and nodded. "Sounds like Rachel when she was that age. Speaking of my daughter, she and Georgie are expecting me home for dinner. I better be going."

"Aren't you and Georgie celebrating your second anniversary next month?"

"Nope. It'll be three years in February. Hard to believe I've been the luckiest man in Hollydale all that time."

It was great to see her brother so happy. She recalled how it didn't seem possible that he and Georgie would ever get together, especially after he arrested her on suspicion of burglary. Fortunately, that was a misunderstanding and everything had worked out in the end, including Mike being elected sheriff. They had waited until Becks and Jack could fly to Hollydale for the wedding. She and Jack had presented a happy front although their marriage was already eroding.

"Give Rachel a hug from me and tell her if she ever wants soccer lessons, her aunt would love to kick a ball around with her."

"Will do on the hug, but she's more into art and design like Natalie." Mike started the Thunderbird and pulled out of the driveway. She'd have given anything to be able to be more happy-go-lucky like each of her siblings, but Becks's competitive side brought more of an edge to her personality.

Becks entered Natalie's house, the smell of apple pie and pine intermingling for a homey feel.

"Wonderful news." Natalie clapped her hands,

her silver wrist bracelets chiming a gentle hello. Her long curly red hair complemented her floral maxi dress, paired with a chunky knit pink sweater. "Danny's counselor said that he's made lots of great progress so monthly sessions aren't needed any longer."

Nat and Aidan had adopted Danny after he'd lost his mom due to a brain aneurysm. Ever since then they'd made sure Danny had every type of support and tool needed to deal with his grief.

Nat met Aidan's sister Shelby in college, but it wasn't until her friend's passing that Aidan, Danny's uncle, arrived in town bent on taking his nephew with him back to his military base. Instead, she and Aidan fell in love that summer and pledged that together they'd care for Danny.

"That is good news."

"We're watching his favorite holiday special tonight and popping popcorn."

She collected Pippa and said her goodbyes, half wishing Nat had invited them to share the evening. Lately it seemed as though their twin bond, so strong when they were kids, was now almost nonexistent. She clicked the strap of Pippa's car seat when her daughter unclicked it again. "Pippa hungry."

"We'll be home soon, and I'll make something." She groaned upon remembering she'd forgotten to defrost anything for tonight's dinner. "It might take a while, though."

"Pippa so hungry." She jutted out that bottom lip, and it started to tremble. Was this a sign of needing to eat or the terrible twos? Most of the time Becks herself was at her most cross when she was hungry, so she'd chalk it up to that.

"How about we have dinner at the Holly Days Diner?" Her budget should be able to manage one night out with her daughter.

"Chicken nuggets!" Pippa clapped her hands together.

As long as Becks didn't have to cook or think about the mountain of problems with the soccer complex for a couple of hours, she'd go along with anything, even chicken nuggets.

FOR THE NTH TIME, the bittersweet aspect of the injury struck Carlos. If he had to break an ankle at least it was his left one so he could drive. Now that he was no longer taking painkillers, he'd been cleared for operating his car so he was no longer dependent on others for rides. Never before had he been so grateful for automatic transmission, except maybe for when he taught his younger sister Graciela how to drive.

Little mercies went a long way. Never before had he been behind a desk so much or suffered this kind of break. He groaned at his own pun as he parked his car in the Holly Days Diner gravel lot.

Many of Hollydale's residents who'd been helped by the department's services had dropped off meals at his house or the station, but even warming up the casseroles was a chore and a half.

At least the diner's parking lot was relatively vacant, making it easier to take his time with his crutches. With fall behind them, the tourists had gone. While many would return for the official town tree lighting and the Firefighter's Christmas Festival, there wasn't a crowd tonight, and he soon seated himself at one of the tables.

The sounds of a cheerful holiday song filled the air, along with the stomach-rumbling scent of grilled hamburgers and eggnog pie. This was the only month of the year Miss Joanne baked his favorite pie with the nutmeg sprinkled over the top.

"Carlos! Long time, no see." A young woman sporting short purple hair and a nose ring rushed over to his table. She wore a hot pink shirt and jeans with a white apron, and she covered her name tag with her notepad. "Bet you can't remember me?"

For a minute, he couldn't place her. Then a sprout his older sister Gisele used to babysit came to mind. "Josie? You're old enough to work at your grandmother's diner now?"

"Yep. My mom, Jolene, has a cold, so I'm filling in for her. Grandma's watching me like a hawk." Josie rolled her eyes and laughed. "If I have a daughter, I'm ending the J-O streak and naming her something without those letters."

"It's good to see you again." Josie nodded emphatically as Carlos picked up a menu from its place in the center of the table. "I'll need a few minutes."

"Take your time. It's pretty tame tonight." Josie bounced to the booth near the jukebox and checked on the only other customers in the diner.

The bell above the door jangled, and in walked Becks, the spirit of athleticism in black yoga pants paired with an aqua top and a long light gray belted cardigan. Becks held the hand of a little girl, who had a bright red mop of hair. He'd forgotten how the blue of Becks's eyes matched the depths of Lake Pine on a summer's day.

Becks met his gaze and headed his way. Funny how their paths hadn't crossed in the seven months he'd been back, but now they kept running into each other.

"Hi, there. This is Pippa."

"It's nice to meet you." He looked straight at the pair of eyes that were level with the table. "I'm Carlos, an old friend of your mom's."

Pippa stared at his hair and pointed. "That's not gray like Grandpa Carl's."

Carlos laughed and patted his head. "Let me rephrase that. I'm a *young* friend of your mom's. She's helping me with my ankle."

"I talked to Brooke Maxwell, and we can use the Whitlcy Community Center gym for your physical therapy sessions." She helped Pippa take off her coat. "Are you free to start early tomorrow morning?"

"Only if we can head to your complex afterward. I'd like to review the report there so I can show you the breaker box and go over any preliminary questions you might have. I'm most agile in the morning." Another reminder he hadn't regained his strength. Without it, he'd never make it through his physical test next year.

"See you then." Becks placed her hands on Pippa's shoulders. "Come on, Pippa, Mr.

Carlos would probably like to eat his meal in peace."

"Mommy cuts my chicken nuggets in pieces."

He contained his laughter, craving some humor after spending so much time at home focusing on what-ifs.

"Please join me." He struggled but rose to his feet, his napkin falling to the floor.

"He needs us, Mommy." Pippa ducked and scooped up his napkin and handed it to him. She turned and yanked on Becks's long cardigan. "Grandma Diane says we help people in need."

"And mothers are always right," Becks said, staring at Pippa.

The little girl pointed down and giggled. "You have a funny shoe, Mr. Carlos. Mommy, want a bright green shoe."

He should have chosen navy or gray. Why couldn't the nurse have asked him for his cast color before the blasted pain meds had taken effect. "This isn't a shoe. It's a cast."

Pippa started taking off her boot. Becks stopped her after she removed her left one. "Philippa, what are you doing?"

"If he doesn't wear shoes, Pippa not wear boots."

Oh, Becks was going to have fun with her

daughter when she was older. "I broke my ankle. The doctors put a cast on so it would get better."

Pippa tilted her head to one side while Becks replaced her daughter's boot. "Take it off?"

"I can't, but it doesn't hurt this way."

She narrowed her eyes. "Even when you sleep?"

"Not even then."

Pippa wrinkled her nose. "I like pink better."

Carlos waved his hand about the diner. "Green goes well with the Christmas decorations, don't you think?"

The Holly Days Diner went all out at Christmas. Along the long counter, elves peeked out of every corner, same as they did on the green and red tinsel decorating the front windows. Next to the entrance stood a tall tree decorated with shiny ornaments. There were hamburger ornaments, artificial bags of potato chips, and several fake pies and cakes. Giant red bells hung from the ceiling, and even the jukebox got into the act with a strand of red garland. How he hadn't noticed the festiveness before now, he didn't know.

Josie brought over a booster chair along with a folded paper kid's menu with crayons tucked inside. She faced Becks. "Where would you like to sit?"

Becks glanced at Carlos, who nodded. "Right here, I guess." She accepted the booster for Pippa with a smile and attached it to the seat next to hers. "Thanks for the invite."

"Thank you, Mr. Carlos." Pippa also graced him with the cutest smile.

Josie recited the daily specials for their benefit. "Can I get your drink orders?"

"Milk for Pippa and unsweet tea for me."

Carlos shuddered at the concept. "Sweet tea for me, thanks."

Josie departed, and Becks picked up a menu from the center of the table, knocking over the glass pepper shaker. "About tomorrow."

"How about we talk about anything else but my ankle?"

He was tired of having the same conversation with different people. He wanted to talk about anything else, although he'd lain awake every night since the fire, searching for alternative escape routes and then dwelling on his future. Getting out of the house was a necessity, and he welcomed every diversion.

Josie delivered their drinks and wrote down their orders, chicken nuggets for Pippa, a hamburger for Carlos and a Cobb salad for Becks.

Pippa smiled at Carlos. "Mommy and me didn't go up in the sky."

"Oh?" He faced Becks, who shrugged.

"Her father had something else come up." Becks reached over and side-hugged Pippa. "Which means we get to spend Christmas together."

Becks selected the blue crayon while Pippa handed Carlos a green one. "You draw, too."

"Okay. Thanks." He tapped it on the table and then drew a cat.

Pippa laughed. "Kitties aren't green."

Carlos gasped and clasped his hands across his heart as if offended. "The great thing about imaginary cats is they can be any color you want."

"Mr. Carlos is right. A little imagination can go a long way and make your dreams soar." Becks drew a cat friend for his. She then used pink for the cat's whiskers and glanced his way.

He had to admit he liked this new, mellow side to Becks. He'd be lying if he didn't want her to see a different man than the one who treated her callously nine years ago. He stopped short of asking her whether she saw him in a new light.

For one minute, his imagination soared, and he stole a glance at the beautiful woman sitting across from him. Could he dream big and see himself with Becks?

Josie delivered a basket of biscuits with a side of apple butter. Carlos and Becks thanked her. The ringing bell over the front door signaled new customers, and Josie hurried away. Becks reached for a biscuit at the same time he did. Their hands collided, and tingles traveled the length of his arm. He'd best watch out or he'd be in trouble. Becks's eyes widened, a sign she'd felt it, too. She quickly sliced a biscuit in half, slathered the top with apple butter and handed it to Pippa, who shook her head. "Brown stuff, icky."

Carlos reached over and popped half in his mouth. "Absolutely delicious."

Becks hovered the knife over the apple butter, the other half still in her hand. "Want to try some?"

Pippa glanced at him, a smidge of butter still at the corner of his mouth. "Little bit."

Becks only covered half with apple butter, leaving the other part plain, but from the look on Pippa's face, she loved it. Maybe he'd have to proceed with any type of friendship with Becks in the same manner, slow and cautious.

"You haven't aged one bit. You always did love Miss Joanne's apple butter." Becks's cheeks turned the same shade of red as the overhanging ornaments.

"Thank you." She squinted, an appraising look on her discerning features. "You're the same, although your nose is a little crooked and you wear your hair shorter."

"Training accident, and it's easier on the job if I keep it short." He smothered his biscuit in apple butter, and his gaze wandered to the selection of pies.

"You still love Miss Joanne's eggnog pie, don't you? That always was your favorite dessert around the holidays." She remembered all that about him?

Pippa tugged at Becks's sleeve. "Mommy, Pippa gotta go."

"Hold that thought."

The pair excused themselves, and the attractive redhead slipped her hand into her daughter's. Becks never looked better. Her new stylish cut complimented her, especially her porcelain skin. She carried her athletic frame with a new curviness that flattered her.

He shouldn't be noticing her attributes, or anyone's, considering his future held so many unknowns.

Friends of his mother entered and stopped to say hello. He chatted with Joe and Betty Ruddick before they proceeded to a booth. Betty was another of the Matchmaking Mimosas and loved talking about the recent developments between her grandson and his next-door neighbor.

Becks and Pippa returned. "False alarm," Becks said.

"Those are the best type. No rush, no disaster." Which wouldn't be the case if he veered away from his safety net of steadiness and fell for the risk-taking redhead again.

Again? He wasn't sure he'd ever completely gotten over his feelings for her.

Carlos picked up one of Pippa's crayons and tapped it on the paper menu. "These cats need a whole zoo of friends."

Pippa scooted into her booster chair. Carlos reached over and fastened her strap, relieved he could still do this with a busted ankle.

"Thank you, Mr. Carlos." Another smile, and his heart melted.

"About your physical therapy."

He glanced at Becks; from her tone she also seemed determined to get away from personal revelations. He went along with her this time. "Back to that?"

Becks nodded and had a long swig from

the mason jar and then sputtered out the tea. "That's pure liquid sugar."

Carlos realized she'd picked up his drink by mistake and accepted his mason jar. "Yep, sweet yet strong enough to keep me going."

Josie delivered their meals, and Pippa grabbed a handful of french fries. Becks helped her daughter with a manageable mouthful. He squirted extra ketchup on his burger and situated the toppings just so. "What time should I report for the physical therapy?"

"Is seven-thirty too early?"

"Not if I want to pass that exam next year."

"It's a good sign you're eager to get started." She laid down her fork. "I'll warn you now. I'm a taskmaster."

"Good. I'm tired of friends tiptoeing around my injury. I'm about to climb the walls or jump into Lake Pine from all the relaxation."

"You're too sensible and steady to jump into a lake. Taking a plunge isn't your style."

"From the person who always dove head-first into everything."

She shook her head and poured a tiny portion of Pippa's honey mustard sauce onto her plate next to her chicken nuggets. "Not anymore."

This from the woman who'd bought a soccer complex as is? That innate quality was still there, just hidden. Was he the person to help her reconnect with her old self?

One look at her savoring her salad and beaming at her daughter was enough to send his heart soaring, but this dinner was simply two old friends sharing a meal, nothing more. He only wished he could jump into that deep end for her.

## CHAPTER SIX

CARLOS SIPPED HIS coffee while in the driver's
seat and checked his watch. Five minutes until
seven on this Friday morning, and dawn still
hadn't peeked out from the sloping curve of the
Great Smoky Mountains. To his surprise, he'd
arrived at the Whitley Community Center before Becks for his first physical therapy session.

He tightened the lid on the thermos and then
placed it on the side of his knapsack with his
towel and yoga mat inside. He got out of the car
and retrieved his crutches from the back seat.
Already sweat dripped from his brow, same as
earlier when he'd shaved while sitting down.
This was probably a cue to cancel the session,
but how else would he pass the physical next
year if he didn't start now?

One brave Carolina wren announced the impending dawn, and hints of sunrise appeared
on the horizon, a faint trace of purple peeking through the gray dome. The chill in the air

crystallized his sweat. He managed his way across the parking lot.

The automatic doors of the community center parted, and Brooke Maxwell came into view. "Good morning, Carlos." She nodded and smiled. "How's your ankle?"

"Better every day." With Becks in his corner, the chances of that happening were that much higher. "How's Jonathan?"

"He's good. Doing well as a detective." Her smile became even wider at her husband's name. "The gym is to your right. Or you could use the exercise room. Once Becks arrives, I'll head to my office."

"Thanks, Brooke."

Carlos heard the automatic doors part. He turned and Becks was there, breathless as if she'd been running, her pink cheeks rosy with the glow of late fall. "Sorry to keep you waiting. Pippa didn't want to leave her warm bed this morning, and it took extra minutes dropping her off at Natalie's. I'd have preferred walking with you in the parking lot so I could observe you on your crutches."

She held the gym door open for him, and the light scent of apples floated his way. They entered the area together. He leaned his crutches against the wall and removed the backpack, reaching for his thermos while she hung her coat on a hook with her purse and a large, over-size tote bag.

"Coffee? I have enough to share." He extended the thermos.

"You should consider starting your day with water. It increases your energy level, and it can ease the swollenness in your ankles." She pulled out a reusable bottle from her bag.

He settled on a weight bench and shifted until he found a comfortable angle. "There's nothing like the jolt of coffee to help with those late shifts, though."

"Some habits should be broken." She went around the room, examining each piece of equipment.

"I try not to break any habits in the same months I break a bone. What are you doing?"

"I'm checking to see if I need to modify my plans for you. I don't think I will since this is the same equipment I use at the complex so I'm familiar with the specs. First, though, I'll start with a basic assessment." She glanced at him from head to toe before fetching her bag and bringing it to the bench. "I'm glad you wore loose comfortable clothing."

"I'm looking forward to getting rid of this cast and wearing jeans again."

"A bright lime-green cast isn't your favorite fashion accessory?" Becks clicked her tongue and searched his face. "What's the biggest struggle you're facing?"

"Nothing in particular. It's going well." Another bead of sweat popped out on his forehead, and she arched an eyebrow.

"Level with me." She folded her arms against her chest. "What's one area you'd like to work on to make life easier?"

He should have known he wouldn't fool her. "Balancing weight on my feet so I can do more tasks. You know, cooking and things like that."

"It takes time." She was right about that, as it seemed the best things in life required work and effort.

"At least I can drive a car again." Independence of a sort although he preferred helping others to having them give him a hand.

"I remembered how hard it was having my mother do everything for me while I was on bed rest with Pippa." She eyed his cast and retrieved a clipboard.

He zeroed in on her last words. "You were on bed rest with Pippa?"

"It was more of a precaution during the first trimester due to circumstances. On a scale of one to ten, a normal person's scale, not a big tough guy's—" she folded her arms against her chest, the clipboard under her right arm "—what's your pain level?"

"Nothing I can't handle." He reached for his thermos and stopped. "What circumstances?"

"You have to trust me if I'm going to help." She sat behind him on the weight bench.

He faced her. "Can't we do both? Learn to trust each other again while getting me on the road to recovery?"

"Only if you tell me what your pain level is." She unclipped the pencil from the top of the clipboard. "I can't help you if you evade my questions, and to answer yours, I'd had a miscarriage a few months before my pregnancy with Pippa."

"I'm sorry. Thank you for sharing that with me." A deep cramp kinked the calf of his left leg, and he tried massaging the area. "The pain comes and goes. Today, it's probably a three."

"I'll mark it as a five then." She jotted some notes. "Have you talked to your doctor about your muscle cramps?"

He shrugged and laughed. "I should have remembered you know me too well, and no, I haven't told Dr. Patel."

"Have you been sleeping?" Becks inhaled

and shook her head. "Have you found any pain management techniques that help?"

"The medication makes me loopy, so I'm hoping you'll be able to recommend something over the counter or something else altogether." Frustration tinged his voice and he clenched his hands in his lap. "Plus, if I take the pain meds, I can't drive, and if I can't drive, I can't report for desk duty."

"I see. You don't want others to think you're getting preferential treatment from Roberto."

He'd missed this level of understanding with someone, but whether he'd blocked others out or was waiting for someone like her again, he wasn't quite sure.

He was positive of one thing. There was only one Becks.

"I'll go over deep breathing exercises with you. They should help. Gentle exercise has also been known to have a positive impact on recovery." She moved from the bench to the floor, kneeling in front of him. "Especially with active people like you. Still, I'd advise you to talk to Dr. Patel. She can adjust your meds and work on a plan for pain management."

She reached for a plastic tool that harkened him back to geometry class. There was one big plastic circle attached to two long plastic movable lines like a ruler. She raised it to his leg, but he pulled back and pointed to the device. "What are you doing and what's that?"

"This is a goniometer. It measures the angles of your flexibility. Go ahead and stretch out on that mat." He did as instructed, and she bent his good leg. "This will give me a baseline so I can measure your progress over the next few months."

"You're good at this."

"Glad to hear my two years as a physical therapist after my divorce paid off."

"Why the soccer complex?"

"This will be the first of its kind in the area. The prospect of helping a child gain self-confidence through sports? That's what I want to do with my life." Her passion for what she loved lit up her face, and he missed the firehouse more than ever. Fighting fires was what he wanted to do with his life, and without that purpose?

Emptiness threatened to take over. He'd worked hard just to return to his desk at the firehouse.

"Are you there all by yourself? I've never seen anyone else at the complex."

"I have three employees. I hope to hire a

new groundskeeper at the start of the New Year and then add more staff down the road."

"You're funding it all yourself? Is the venture that much of a stretch? If so, why not take on a partner?"

She placed her goniometer back in her bag and returned with his crutches. "One question at a time. I don't know anyone who'd want to be partners. My parents don't have that type of money, and I'm not about to ask Mike or Nat for it. Soccer paid well, but my ex-husband received a windfall in the divorce, and there's no way I'm going down that road again."

She extended a hand and helped him rise. He adjusted his crutches while keeping his gaze on her.

"There are other aspects of a partnership. Someone to balance your strengths and weaknesses, help you when you fall, celebrate your joys with you."

"That sounds more like a relationship."

"Aren't strong relationships also partnerships?"

She didn't look away, the connection that had always existed forming once more between them. The air crackled, and he wondered if their kisses would still be as sweet as his favorite red velvet cupcakes.

She stepped back. "Right now our partnership centers on your recovery and my business so Pippa and I don't end up living in my parents' shed. Why don't you walk to the watercooler and back so I can assess your gait?"

He did as she asked. "What happened between you and your ex-husband?" By the time he reached the target, he was out of breath. He faced her and found her lips pursed in a straight line. Then she jotted something on the clipboard. "What are you writing?"

"I'm making notes on your balance, stability and weight transfer. Today's more of an evaluation than a full session, but I'll send you home with exercises designed for you." She clipped the pencil in place and tucked the clipboard under her arm. "Jack cheated on me. At first, he denied it. Finally, he admitted it wasn't a one-time deal. That same night, Pippa and I came home to Hollydale."

Carlos tried to find the right words but nothing came out. He'd wanted the best for her, not this kind of hurt and pain. He maneuvered into position next to the cooler and yanked a paper cup from the water tower. With a good amount of concentration, he steadied himself and tried operating the blue lever for the cold water. She rushed over, helped him and poured herself a cup.

As hard as it was, he accepted her help and let the cool liquid soothe his dry throat. "Thank you. Jack let go of the best thing in his life."

How often had he thought the same of himself. But now at least he understood why she held back whenever trust was mentioned.

"I took his recent rejection of Pippa especially hard. It's one thing to hurt me, but another to hurt our daughter. He gave away his opportunity to reconnect with her, and that's a lot to handle."

Maybe it was time to start listening to the intuition he usually only heeded when a fire was at its fiercest.

Connecting with her could be a blessing, but he needed total concentration on his recovery. Just as a partner wasn't in Becks's plans, to have someone share his life shouldn't cross his mind either.

Taking his eyes off his rehab could end up costing him more than he was willing to lose.

INSIDE THE ADMINISTRATIVE building of the Mountain Vista Soccer Complex, Becks reviewed the inspector's report with Carlos watching her every move almost as closely as she had scrutinized him this morning at the community center. She winced at the report, which didn't mince words. While the foundation was sound and the steel itself withstood the intense heat, the repair process would be draining, mentally and financially. The bottom line was she'd bought a property that wasn't up to code. She should have known better.

Carlos hadn't been joking when he claimed a few renovations were in her immediate future. Her bank account, already hanging on by a thread, was dwindling away to nothing. She hadn't wanted to admit that to him earlier.

She stopped reading the report and glanced at him. He studied every angle of a subject before committing his all. A lesson she was still learning. While the hard hat and low lighting partially obscured his face, it was hard to miss the sweat beading on Carlos's brow. He was doing too much, too soon.

Becks motioned to the chairs where their coats resided. "Have a seat and elevate your ankle. You're a firefighter. You know about R-I-C-E, and I'm not talking about the kind you buy at the supermarket."

He shook his head. "I'm fine."

"You're sweating."

"It's the hard hat."

She glared at him before plopping into the closest seat. "I've been on my feet all day and need a break." He sat next to her, his shoulders stiff, and she used her foot to drag another chair in front of his leg. "If you keep this up, you're going to be in the hospital with a case of dehydration and do more damage to your body."

"I'm fine. I'll sleep well tonight."

"No, you're not," she warned, and put her face close to his for extra emphasis.

He stared at her before fine lines around his brown eyes crinkled with traces of humor, erasing the years distancing them. "Thanks for looking out for me."

Someone knocked at the front door, and she jumped to her feet. "That must be the next construction company coming to do an estimate. This will be the fourth."

Two of the estimates came in a little higher than expected, and the third company she chose from the internet rather than off Roberto's list had lowballed it so much that further investigation showed the firm had several bad reviews.

At the entrance to the admin building, she spotted her assistant. "Sharlene?"

"Have a minute? It's important," Sharlene

called to her, and Becks hurried and opened the door, a gust of wind bringing a chill to the lobby.

"I'm surprised you're already done delivering those flyers to the schools. I thought that would keep you busy until the staff meeting at four? It's at the community center, remember?"

"We can talk outside. This won't take long."

Becks glanced at Carlos, who nodded and propped his leg on the spare plastic chair. "I'll be fine in here, jotting down some notes."

Becks slipped on her coat and stepped outside to where Sharlene was already waiting. With a flourish, she removed her hard hat and tucked it under her arm. "Hopefully this is good news. What brought you out here anyway?"

Sharlene shook her head, her brown eyes forlorn. "Honey." Sharlene's fingers reached out and patted Becks's arm. "Have you stepped back and just looked around since the fire?"

Becks nodded. "I'd have had to invest the money into these repairs anyway. Buying it as is and not hiring my own inspector was an eye-opener." Ever since the closing, she'd been doing her due diligence in regard to the estimates. Owning a business was different from anything she'd ever done before, but she'd rise to the challenge.

Sharlene wrapped her arms around herself and shivered. "I'm taking my son up on his offer and moving to Raleigh to be near my grandson. There's a job opening at his day care, and I relate better to little kids than adults."

*First Stan, and now Sharlene?* It was a good thing Dante and Amara had indicated they were in it for the long haul. It helped that Amara's grandmother was everyone's favorite ice cream shop owner, Louise Boudreaux. With such a strong tie to Hollydale, they had no intention of quitting. "Is this your two-week notice?"

"Since I just started, I was hoping you'd let me quit on the spot."

Becks never had been one to ask someone to stay when they weren't fully committed. "Text me the address where you want me to send your final check."

Becks watched as Sharlene all but sprinted to her Camaro and sped down the road without even a backward glance. She massaged her temple, wishing for the first time she had someone she could confide in. Someone with strong shoulders who she could rely on. At least she'd save on two salaries, for the time being. She texted Dante and Amara the news, and they confirmed they were still on for the staff meeting. Then she'd fill them in on her latest exchange of emails with Kick, Goal and Score. Negotiations were still underway for that partnership. The increased visibility and contacts that company could provide were more vital than ever. So was the money they'd offer for using her property for summer camps.

There was also the matter of the intriguing email from one of her college teammates, Claire Esposito. Becks would follow up with her about her new company with a different approach to coaching. Claire mentioned she wanted to focus on the whole player, not just on what it takes to win. Becks definitely valued Dante's and Amara's input about what Claire had to say.

Entering the admin building, she donned her hard hat once more and sat next to Carlos.

"Glad you're propping up your ankle." Her voice came out breathier than she'd have liked.

"Becks? Is everything all right? You're as pale as a ghost." Carlos's brown eyes showed concern.

For the first time, she missed the way he called her Becca.

"My assistant just quit. I have no groundskeeper and now no assistant." That edge was back, the one she'd noted in her voice too often when she'd returned to Hollydale after discovering Jack's infidelity. "Before she quit, she asked if I'd taken a good long look at this place."

The problem with rose-colored glasses was once they came off, things never looked the same.

Carlos reached for his crutches and maneuvered to the big window in the lobby. He motioned for Becks, and she stood beside him. He grew still and kept his gaze out the window. "What do you see?"

In the distance, the mountains stood majestically with their oaks and maples bare for the long winter ahead. The pines and the sweet gums provided a shelter break from the creek, their upper branches swaying in the wind. Her focus narrowed to the fields. Soon new sod would replace the gray ash and gashes from the fire trucks. Posts and nets would rise and her business would get underway.

He repeated his question, and her vision faded with the harsh reality of the ash and slush taking center stage. The indoor soccer building was prefab with steel tempered to withstand fire, while the contents were a damaged wreck.

It was too much to overcome. Her shoulders shook, and she closed her eyes. "What have I done?"

Gambled away her future, and Pippa's, on

a whim of independence and an unfulfilled dream.

"Look at me." His soft expression offered a glimmer of hope. "What did you see?"

"At first I saw what it could be, a marvelous soccer complex where everyone was having fun and competing hard, but then…"

Carefully managing his crutch under his arm, he cradled her chin with his hand. Those crinkles deepened, and he was that much more attractive. That look in his deep brown eyes reminded her of summer days while they were dating and when he was about to kiss her. "Then what?"

"I saw what exists, a mess of monumental proportion, a shadow of what it could be."

His fingers caressed her jaw. "It will get better. Sometimes things have to reach their worst before their best can be achieved."

Was he only talking about the complex? Or was their worst behind them? Did it take three thousand miles and nine years for their feelings to be fully realized? She stepped toward him and narrowed her gaze on his lips. Were his kisses still as toe numbingly wonderful? Another knock came, and the door opened. A man in his thirties with a thatch of dark hair and a hard hat tucked under his arm stuck his head inside.

"I'm looking for Becks Porter."

"You found her." And just in time before she'd done something she'd have regretted later. She had so much at stake already, she couldn't risk her heart as well.

"Trent Acerra." He held up his lanyard with his Ace Construction Company photo ID badge and slipped on his hard hat before his focus landed on Carlos. "Hey, man. Long time no see. What happened to you?"

"Trent! It's been a couple of years at least." Carlos used the crutches and went to greet Trent. "A firefighting injury. Not too serious, but enough to set me back for the moment. How's the family?"

"Good, we need to catch up sometime, shoot some pool at Timber River Bar and Grill." Trent pointed to Carlos's cast. "Or maybe just grab a beer."

"Sounds good to me. Are you working for your dad now?"

"Yep." He turned to also address Becks, which she appreciated. "We're based in Asheville but, as you can tell, our company has connections to Hollydale."

"Chief Ramirez says you're the best," Becks

said. "You said you can do the repairs and bring the buildings up to code, right?"

"That's right. We like to let our work speak for us. When I send you the estimate, I'll include a list of references so you can check for yourself."

To Carlos, she said, "Are you joining us on the tour or going to rest?"

"I'll rest here while you two go over the buildings. If Trent has any questions about the code violations or the inspector's report, I can answer them."

"Without proper rest at home, you won't get better." That Ramirez pride would get the better of him one of these days.

"I won't be able to get better until I see this through first. We have a deal, remember? I'm following up on my end."

No one else could make her feel this exasperated and cared for at the same time. She scooted some of the chairs together, forming a line with the backs facing the same way.

"And I won't rest tonight if you're in the hospital." Then she crossed over to her tote bag and pulled out the extra set of mittens and scarf she carried around in case Pippa lost hers. Using them for the core of a makeshift pillow, she wound her scarf around them. "If you're staying here, I want you elevating your leg until I'm back."

This time his protests didn't sound as forceful, and she left with Trent. The project manager was professional and thorough, the review taking longer than expected. On their return, they found Carlos sleeping, his face looking more like the boy's from the past but with a certain stubbornness peeking through. She wished she had a blanket to ward off the chill.

"Would you prefer a text or email with the estimates? I'll send two, one with the basic code improvements and another with add-on improvements. I should have them done by tomorrow at the latest."

Carlos awoke with a jerky motion. "You're back already? Trent, did you receive the inspection report I forwarded?"

"Yes and yes." Trent glanced at Carlos and Becks. "I haven't forgotten how you pitched in and worked your butt off eight years ago for the construction company. I've felt like I owe you for those extra projects we were able to take on, so for your friend here, I'll provide the employee discount."

With a wave, Trent left the administrative building. Carlos rubbed his eyes and glanced at his phone, sitting up with a start. "I have to go. I need to meet with my father about the Firefighter's Christmas Festival. Thanks to my new scaled-back assignment, I'm now the designated go-to person for the department."

"Is it soon?"

"The weekend before Christmas. You should bring Pippa. There will be crafts and food and Santa. All the proceeds help raise money for a new fire truck."

"That sounds like a huge undertaking for one person. You have to relax or your ankle's not going to heal. Trust me, it hurts to have your career curtailed by an injury you couldn't control."

Biting her lip, she grabbed the makeshift pillow and unwound the scarf, then replaced the chairs where they belonged, too aware she had to leave in minutes for her meeting with Dante and Amara. Carlos reached for his crutches and pulled himself to a standing position. "It sounds like you speak from experience."

"I'd just been named to the all-star team when I blew out my knee. The orthopedic surgeon was the best in the country. The damage was too extensive. I can play with the pretty good amateurs, but that extra burst of speed? That swift kick aiming for the corner of the goal? It became obvious early in my physical therapy my professional career was over." That realization had rocked her world. Dark days, but she'd made it through.

He set aside his crutches and pulled her to him, and she reveled in his hug and his strength. "Oh, Becca."

She came close to correcting him, but didn't. For a minute, she'd let herself get carried away in the comfort of his arms. Then she pulled back. "It was an accident, pure and simple, that led to my injury. I followed every instruction to the letter, but the tendons were severely damaged, and no one could bear to tell me the truth. You have a chance to regain strength in your ankle and resume firefighting if you want, but you have to make adjustments. A little sacrifice now to get what you want later."

Something close to hypocrisy roared at her as she didn't exemplify that practice. She'd always gone for what was easiest, right there for the taking.

"You're saying I need to pull back and consider what's best for the long term." He searched her eyes, his truth hitting home.

"It depends on what you want. If you want to be at a desk for the rest of your career, keep going full steam ahead. If you want something

special, something you love, it'll take work."
That Carlos stare burned into her, and her
cheeks heated. "We should go."

Her two remaining employees awaited, and
she'd best arrive on time and keep her promise
to turn this complex into a winner.

# CHAPTER SEVEN

IN THE DRIVEWAY of Nat and Aidan's house, Becks reached for Pippa in the car seat, her toddler's face still dewy with sleep.

"It's too early, Mommy." Pippa laid her heavy head on Becks's shoulder.

Even after a week of these morning drop-offs to make Carlos's physical therapy sessions, Pippa wasn't accustomed to waking up before eight. Becks readjusted Pippa's diaper bag over her other shoulder and closed the car door with her rear. The slam echoed in the silence.

Unlike Pippa, this was Becks's favorite time of day. She loved when the potential of something new threw out endless possibilities. Depending on the time of year in this small western corner of North Carolina, there was always something going on. A rousing game of soccer, a long hike to Pine Falls, a kayak ride along the Timber River. Soon skiing and sledding would fill the hours with energy and excitement. The sliver of the new moon hung low with stars dotting the sky, casting a shadow over the Great Smoky Mountains. Beauty surrounded her. And Becks hoped this day might begin a chapter with less drama and more solutions.

Taking her time on the path to the front door, Becks savored her daughter's arms around her, the sweet scent of baby shampoo still fresh. Too soon, Nat threw open the door, her index finger raised to her mouth. "Baby Shelby and Danny are still asleep. Coffee's on."

"Pippa wants to go back to sleep." Becks crossed the threshold, careful to whisper while watching out for Nat and Aidan's cat, Stormy, who wound her lithe body around Becks's legs. "Where should I put her?"

"In the guest room. Stormy, stay away from Becks. She's carrying too much at once." *As always.* Becks finished Nat's sentence in her head while her twin closed the front door with a soft thump. "Have a minute for a cup of coffee? I bought your favorite vanilla creamer."

"I'll be right back." Becks carried Pippa up the stairs to the last room on the left where she deposited her on the canopy bed. With a practiced motion, she removed Grizzie from the diaper bag and rested the stuffed bear in the crook of Pippa's arm.

With a soft snuffle, Pippa turned on her side, clutching Grizzie, already halfway back to dreamland. Becks used Nat's throw pillows for extra protection so Pippa wouldn't fall off the bed. She glanced at her watch. She appreciated the offer of a hot cup of coffee but wasn't sure she could afford the time.

She secured the baby gate at the top of the stairs and met her sister in the kitchen. "I know that look, Becks. I just want to chat. It'll only take a few minutes. You know me. No heavy discussions before noon or a third cup of coffee for me. Wait while I let Eddie back inside."

A littermate of Gomez and Morticia, Eddie, short for Edison, bounded in and rushed to Becks's side.

"Gomez and Morticia send lots of love." Becks obliged with a belly rub for Eddie, and Nat placed two cups of coffee on the table.

"Aidan's already left for work. Last-minute details still need to be sorted out for this weekend's tree lighting ceremony and all that. You're bringing Pippa, right?" Nat settled in her chair and moved the clear crystal vase with red and green colored ornaments inside.

The holiday decorations here in the kitchen alone put Becks's entire house to shame. An evergreen wreath with a big red plaid bow hung over the window at the sink. Pine boughs hung from the light fixture over the table, and signs celebrating holiday cheer brightened the room. Now that Pippa would be spending Christmas with her, she'd best start thinking about decorating her own home for the holidays. Becks raised her green plaid mug with a gingerbread figure and blew on the wisps of steam.

*Still too hot.* She lowered the cup and shrugged. "I don't know. There's so much to do at the complex."

"Come on, you can't work all the time, especially on a weekend night." Nat tapped Becks's hand with her index finger, the same cue from when they were younger and she thought Becks should change her mind.

Memories of their childhood with their secret language reminded her of the tight bond they once shared before they went their separate ways, and Nat shone at everything and Becks sought refuge on the soccer field.

That wasn't Nat's fault at all, but still the sisters had drifted apart over the years. They'd established different friends, different paths for themselves. Becks mostly hung out with Lindsay and Penelope, except it seemed like Lindsay was busy with her new husband and

Penelope was intent on solving her latest legal conundrum.

"If I don't concentrate on work, the complex will be a bust." It was no use. This cheerful kitchen was only for happy talk, and she didn't want to ruin her sister's day with her issues. "Thanks for the coffee, but I'm expected at the community center."

Becks rose and extracted her keys from her coat pocket, jingling them for good measure.

"Oh, no, you don't. You can't tease me with that kind of sentence and then run off." Nat pushed Becks's cup toward her. "You didn't even finish your coffee. Besides, what kind of twin makes her sister drink morning coffee by herself? That's a travesty."

The mock outrage from Nat, along with Eddie's plaintive plea for more attention, sealed her decision to stay. "You're more persuasive now than when we were kids."

"And you're prettier now." Nat flashed that familiar smile.

"Gee, thanks." Becks kept blowing until she took that first sip. Like everything Nat did, the coffee was perfect.

A part of her envied her sister's easy charm.

Nat cupped her mug with both hands. "I'm not going to let up about Saturday. Pippa will love it. Isn't that why you came back to Hollydale? Family and connections and a chance for happiness. You deserve that, and so much more."

"I came back for Mom's banana pudding, Dad's barbecue sauce recipe and cheap rent." She sipped her coffee, savoring the vanilla sweetness before the hard coppery truth of the past few days overtook her. Nat's concern seeped deep inside her. Having her twin in her corner meant more than Nat knew. When everything hit her about Jack, Nat had supported her and delivered a thread of hope when the night stretched out gray and dark. It was about time she made more of an effort with Nat. "Pippa and I will be there."

Nat popped out of her seat and hugged her, and even Eddie circled three times although it could have been that he was chasing his tail rather than joining in on Nat's glee.

Becks had to come up with more options; her sister's optimism was catching. As she drove to Carlos's therapy session, she wondered about alternatives. Could she ask Dante and Amara to invest in the business? That made the most sense. But they were expecting a baby soon and now didn't seem the right time. She couldn't ask them. The next most logical choice was Tricia Weaver. Yet when Tricia had returned her call, the woman had raved about her retirement. So Becks wasn't sure if Tricia would want to put that on hold for a stressful new venture.

There was no way she'd ask either of her siblings. As it was, she was taking advantage of Nat's generosity by having her watch Pippa.

A partnership of any kind was trickier than a toe kick, one of the most difficult shots in soccer only used for last ditch efforts.

Had it been too much to expect that Carlos in his early twenties with such close ties to his family would move cross-country for her? Carlos had always been so focused on his goal of someday taking over as the Dalesford County Fire Chief. Hard to do that in California.

People had let her down in the past, so as far as she was concerned, taking on a partner now was the absolute last resort.

Carlos's car was already in its familiar spot. She hustled inside and found Brooke and Carlos laughing in the lobby.

"What did I miss?" Becks unwound her scarf and placed it on a hanger along with her coat and hung them up.

"I was telling Carlos about the latest misadventures of my stepdaughter Vanessa." Brooke chuckled. "I'll be around if you need me. This arrangement has worked out well. Holidays are always extra busy, so doing this in the morning has been good."

Brooke left the area and same as at Nat's, the decorations jumped out at Becks. A giant tree with ornaments, ribbons, and paper angels for a local charitable outreach pairing needy kids with a donor who'd help their holiday wishes come true stood in the central area. A menorah was situated on the reception desk and nearby, hanging on the wall, was a sign with the principles of Kwanzaa. More indications Becks should deck her own halls this weekend, but the prospect of anything bad happening to her grandmother's Santa and Mrs. Claus china figurines scared Becks. Maybe if they were out of reach, they'd be safe from Pippa.

Was that what she was reduced to? Looking for a safety net instead of enjoying the holidays?

Carlos cleared his throat. "You okay?"

"Hmm. I'm fine. Let's get started."

She led the way toward the gym and opened the door for him. She noticed his firm arm muscles for a moment, but blinked as she wasn't going there. Soon they settled into the comfortable routine from the past week. Already his range of motion and flexibility had improved to the point where he could expand and increase his rehab once the cast was removed.

"Becks." He placed the weights on the floor. "You don't quite seem like yourself today."

"I have a lot on my mind."

"Talk to me. In case you haven't noticed, I'm here for the long haul." She met his gaze, and she wondered if that applied to her as his physical therapist, a friend, or something else.

"I don't suppose you know of any easygoing investors with money to spare?" She tried laughing away the harsh tone.

"Not offhand. But I'll let you know if that changes."

"Thanks." She sipped her water. "That's only half of what's bothering me. Places are decked out for the holidays, and I haven't even brought my decorations out of storage yet."

Carlos pushed up to a sitting position, a frown not dulling his handsome features. "Then get it done, although, you've never been one to care what others did in the past."

She retrieved her goniometer. "I never had two people relying on my business for a salary and benefits, and I'm currently down a groundskeeper and an assistant."

"What can I do to help?"

That was Carlos. Always jumping in during a crisis, same as he had when a classmate had lost her home to fire and he organized a drive among the students so she'd have touches of normalcy. That was one of the many things that drew her to him in the first place, along with that thick black hair and those soulful brown eyes.

"These sessions are about you, not me." Relying on someone else to solve her problems wasn't a habit she wanted to pick up again.

"Hey, you're more than my temporary therapist. We're friends, even though we left on not the best of terms all those years ago."

She bent his good knee and recorded the measurements. "This might hurt so brace yourself." She reached for his left leg and moved his knee. "Your range of motion is showing significant progress after a week."

She laid the leg straight and helped him to a sitting position. "I've been working on those *gentle* exercises." His voice indicated he found them anything but gentle, but she knew none of them would hurt any of his ligaments.

"Don't overtax yourself."

"Me." He snorted. "Never."

They laughed as neither of them stood by on the sidelines well. Then again, for the past few years, she'd been more likely to do just that. Buying the soccer complex was the first sign she was starting to act more like the old Becks who'd taken California by storm.

"Time for a water break?"

"If you think we need one, then yes."

He sipped from his reusable water bottle, then wiped his mouth with the back of his arm. He'd taken her advice about drinking water at these sessions instead of coffee. A little change, to be sure, but he'd put her suggestion to good use. She drank a sip from her bottle and hid a smile.

"Thanks, Becks, for today and all of the mornings this week. You're really good at your job. We make great partners."

*Partners.* Funny how she had no problem being part of a team where teammates worked together to achieve something bigger than themselves, but the prospect of being reliant on one person again scared her. Look at how badly their engagement had ended, not to mention her marriage to Jack.

Yet she and Carlos were here together this morning.

"Thanks. You're good at yours, too." One thing had been troubling her, and she wished she had more tact, but since she didn't, she'd be blunt as always. "Why did you leave Hollydale after I did? You always wanted to fight fires here in Dalesford County."

"After you left, I wanted something more daring. Guess you rubbed off on me after all. I applied in Tennessee to become a smoke jumper, and I worked for Trent so I could afford the classes. I stayed there for years, but smoke jumping involves a different set of challenges, mindset and skills. I missed being part of a community I knew well. Turns out I'm not as much of an adrenaline junkie as you."

"I don't think of myself as an adrenaline junkie. I like motion and activity. That's all. I'm quite simple, really."

"Not simple at all. Don't you know you're a hard act to follow, Rebecca Harrison?" His use of her full maiden name didn't escape her.

"How so?"

"I've dated some, even found myself getting close to proposing not too long ago, but Jennifer and I broke up when I moved back to Hollydale."

"Oh?" Something close to jealousy skittered through her veins, and that was ridiculous. They'd broken up a long time ago.

"Jennifer and I dated for a couple of years. Then Mami mentioned there was an opening in the department. When I talked to Jennifer, she said she wasn't willing to move here."

"What if Jennifer had asked you to stay in Tennessee?"

She waited for his answer, and the air crackled. "She didn't."

All those years ago, he hadn't asked Becks to remain in town. It wouldn't have mattered. Her heart had been set on accepting the professional contract.

"How long ago was this?"

"Seven months."

*Not long at all.* "What would you do if Jennifer showed up tomorrow and asked if you missed Tennessee? Or that she wanted to move here?"

She held her breath, her heartbeat racing. In all honesty, though, she wasn't sure if she was asking for his sake or hers. For some reason, being around him made her throw caution to the wind about partnerships and trust and everything that was so easy to reconcile in her mind when he wasn't in the room. When she was around him, her troubles seemed more manageable. He calmed her down and brought an excitement to her life at the same time.

"She wouldn't. She's engaged to one of the smoke jumpers on my former team."

He scooted closer to her and reached for her hand. "Missing something and having that something be right are two different things. Part of me loved a relationship, but I missed our connection. Jennifer and I weren't right for each other."

She had missed Carlos in California, knowing he was right for her, but her pride kept her from contacting him and asking if he'd had any regrets. In a way, she'd always known she and Jack didn't connect in the same easy manner either.

She couldn't really compare the two men. They weren't the same, and yet they both led her to misplaced trust and a broken heart.

The difference, though, was Carlos's innate sense of decency. Was it time to start trusting again? His face neared hers when her phone pinged a text. She reached for it, relieved for the distraction. "I want to make sure it's not Nat."

It was Trent from Ace Construction Company with his estimate. Nerves skittered through her as this would be the clincher as to whether she could move forward with her dream.

"Your fingers are trembling? Bad news?"

"It's Trent." After a few deep breaths, she was ready to open the file. "Here goes nothing." *And everything.*

Her heart skipped a beat as she absorbed the bottom line. This was right in the middle. A few thousand more than the low estimate. They'd had a cancellation and could start work next week if she could deposit one-third of the quoted price to be held in escrow pending completion of the project.

Whooping with joy, she danced around the room while Carlos grabbed his crutches. "Good news?"

"The best." She stopped in front of him. "I can afford this and open on time. As long as I can make a good impression and sign a sponsorship with a company that has extensive contacts and will use my facilities for soccer camps, I can make this work."

He placed his crutches aside and pulled her into his arms. She melded into his embrace, the smell of his sweat mingling with soap and citrus.

She leaned into Carlos for another second, enjoying the feel of his arms around her and sharing this victory with him. As a team worked together, so too had he been instrumental in her receiving the discount that helped her afford the repairs.

However, he couldn't be a full-fledged partner in this enterprise, or her life. She'd trusted him once, and he'd let her down. Once was enough.

She broke away and started placing her tools back in her bag. "Today, we both made progress. Your range of motion is improving, and I can continue this venture the way I began, solo and unencumbered."

Her happiness was apparently too effusive as a shadow fell over his face. "Friends aren't a burden, Becks."

She knew that. "I'm glad we're friends again. The employee discount for friends and family that Trent gave me because of you went a long way in my being able to continue this on my terms."

Everything was coming out wrong today. Why was she so abrasive with him when her insides were turning to mush?

"That's the issue, though. It's always about your terms. Sometimes it's nice to be consulted before you proceed headfirst. I was ecstatic for you about your offer to play professionally and would have joined you in a second if you'd asked rather than told me you'd come home at season's end."

Something akin to regret lingered in his eyes, and she rolled up the yoga mat. "That would have been nice to know back then."

How would their lives have been different had he trusted her? It was too late to go back and change the past.

Was his admission enough to risk giving him another chance now?

## CHAPTER EIGHT

"How are the preparations for the Firefighter's Christmas Festival coming along?" Carlos's mother turned her head to look over her shoulder while steering the car.

"Mami, the road!" his sister Graciela shouted from the front passenger seat, muttering something too fast and low for him to catch. "We have plenty of time to get to the tree lighting."

Mami waved her hand as if dismissing the worry, her long red nails decorated with Christmas trees. "I've been driving longer than you've been alive. I know what I'm doing."

Graciela met Carlos's gaze, exchanging a knowing smile with him. He rubbed his leg and stretched it out the best he could in the back seat. "The plans are coming along." Except the Santa Claus that always participated canceled today and the extended weather forecast was calling for a blanket of snow the day of the festival. *Fun stuff.*

Graciela asked, "Are you sure you can navigate the crowds? This event is always popular."

"Dr. Patel assured me my ankle is doing better than expected. She might even take the cast off early." During his last appointment, Carlos had asked for a referral to the Hollydale facility for physical therapy.

Seeing Becks every other morning brought too many conflicted emotions to the forefront, and he needed all his strength and focus to devote to his recovery. Carlos checked his phone once more to see if the doctor messaged him the referral, but Monday would be soon enough for a new start.

If a second chance for a genuine friendship was in their future, he needed for Becks to see him in a new light, different from the confused young adult who'd ended things far too soon.

If he crossed paths with Becks tonight, he'd broach the subject of ending their therapy sessions so there'd be no sense of obligation between them.

That still made him wonder how he'd earn her trust again.

"Roberto said I should drop you off first, closest to the tree lighting, so you wouldn't have far to walk to get there." Mami nodded.

"Thanks to Becks and plenty of rest, I'll be

able to bear weight on this ankle next week. It's no problem, Mami, I can stay with you guys and you can park wherever."

Mami shook her head, her face taut as she braked in front of the town gazebo, where the tree lighting would happen. "This traffic. All these people everywhere. I can get closer. Hold on."

"Thanks." He lowered his head. Had he forgotten how to appreciate a simple favor for fear of everyone, especially his father, thinking he was a shadow of his former self?

"My pleasure. Oh, I have good news. I forgot to tell you."

"What is it?"

"Gisele, Javier and Marisol are moving here sooner than expected. They'll be staying with us over Christmas until they find a place to rent. At last, I have a granddaughter."

Graciela grabbed her mother's arm and squeezed. "How marvelous! Everyone together for Christmas."

Carlos remained still, awed at his sister's resilience. Graciela exuded hopefulness even though she had a broken heart. Recently, her boyfriend, Jordan, an EMT, had ended their relationship. Since then, she'd transferred her energy to the animal shelter where she worked.

Family meant so much to her, and he knew there was someone out there for her who'd love and appreciate her.

He waited for Mami to ask if Gisele and her new husband and stepdaughter could stay at his place, but the question never came. He reached for his crutches and stopped. "Was there something you wanted to ask, Mami?"

"Your father's thirty-fifth work anniversary is coming up. I want to throw a surprise welcome home dinner for Gisele and family *and* a celebration party for your father. And I'd like you and Graciela to help. What do you say?"

"The shelter is so busy right now." Graciela steeled her shoulders. "But this is for Gisele and Papa. I'll make time to help organize the party."

"Actually, I was thinking Carlos could arrange the dinner." His mother turned and stared straight at him.

"Me? Wouldn't Graciela be better? She loves get-togethers and socializing." *And* she had volunteered. Didn't that count?

"You have more time. You'll be perfect. Just a few friends and your father's favorite foods."

Mami's definition of a few friends and everyone else's differed by about fifty. What was one more thing on his plate? He couldn't say no and show weakness; they'd never believe he was actually getting better. Carlos opened the passenger door. "We won't be able to keep this from Papa."

"Ha. You don't think I can keep a secret?" his mother huffed.

Graciela and Carlos shared a look and kept the laughter at bay. Their mother was the worst secret keeper in Hollydale, and everyone knew it. "Come over to my house next week, and I'll figure out the dinner. Thank you for driving and finding such a close spot to drop me off. Look for my text so you'll know where I am once you park the car."

He adjusted his crutches under his arms and made his way slowly to a bench with a view of the gazebo and downtown area. This was his first tree lighting since his return from Tennessee, and he'd missed seeing the ice cream parlor and the other mom-and-pop businesses decked out in their holiday finery. There was something about the continuity and tradition that he valued as much as Becks valued innovation and competition.

Was there a way to balance the two perspectives?

Evening descended on the town square. The mountains provided the perfect backdrop for the upcoming event. In the center sat Holly-dale's gazebo, which had seen its fair share of prom pictures, proposals and weddings over the years. Strings of white lights glowed as they stretched across the top of Main Street. More people arrived, and the owner of The Busy Bean was already doing a brisk business at her hot cocoa stand.

He heard a voice behind him and recognized Becks's pleading tone. "If you change your mind and let me hold the deposit for your child's spot in the soccer program, I'll give you a free month of lessons."

"My mind is already made up." Carlos didn't recognize the other voice.

"Can we please talk about this on Monday? I'm here with my daughter."

"There's nothing to talk about, Ms. Porter. I'm opting out of my kid's contract and expect a full refund."

Why was the woman confronting Becks here, especially when she was with Pippa? That was enough for Carlos. He reached for his crutches and turned toward Becks. Too late to help, he found the woman stomping away from the gazebo. Becks's face fought for composure, and a tear slipped down her cheek. She wiped it away with the back of her gloved hand while holding on to Pippa with her other one.

"Becks."

She sniffled and blinked. "I guess you heard that."

"Yeah. What's going on?"

"She's the fourth parent today to cancel their kid's coaching and a place on a team at my soccer complex. Everyone wants their money back." She raised her chin and tightened her grip on Pippa's hand. "This isn't the place to talk about that. I promised Pippa this is one of the best nights of the year."

"Hey, Pip." He smiled at the little girl, who had her thumb in her mouth. "Want to sit on the bench with me? What are you asking from Santa for Christmas?"

"How about you join us on the lawn in front of the gazebo?" She patted a big tote bag at her side. "I have a blanket large enough that we can all share and you can prop your leg up on the bag."

"I don't want to draw attention to my injury. I just want to be one of the crowd." A heartfelt plea, and an honest one.

"Keeping it elevated will help you get the cast off on time. That's not drawing attention, it's taking care of it." Determination sparked in her eyes, and he'd no longer take that type of loyalty for granted. Friends didn't come more fierce to their causes than Becks.

"I saw Dr. Patel today. She says I'm doing better than expected."

Becks's frown turned into a smile. "See, you need me." Her blush matched the hue of her hair and most of the red decorations. "Maybe need is a strong word. It's more like we're both reaping the benefits of our friendship."

"I'm glad I'm back as one of your friends."

Becks stubbed the bench with her boot. "Don't think you're out of the woods yet. Although, those good looks of yours do wear a person down, you know."

He laughed, enjoying himself for the first time in a month, and stood using the crutches for support. "You don't mind that my nose is crooked now? It's nice that you still notice my appearance. The feeling's mutual."

Her face became an even deeper red. "I'll quit while I'm behind."

"You're never behind in my book." He put a hand on her shoulder. "Don't let the people who've asked for their money back get to you. Don't quit."

Pippa tugged at Becks's hand. "Mommy, can I have some hot cocoa? Please."

"Good idea, pumpkin." Becks nodded.

They all walked together to Deb's stand, and Carlos soaked in the charming atmosphere of the updated brick storefronts and the quirky ambience. The lights glowed in Becks's eyes, bright sapphires that reflected all the best parts of who she was…perseverance, compassion and loyalty.

Too bad his future was too precarious to share it with anyone.

Graciela came up to them, bemusement dancing across her face. "I should have known I'd find my brother in line for hot chocolate." She pointedly glanced at Becks, and her grin grew wide. "This explains why you didn't text us. Mami and I chose a spot on the other side of the park. I can carry your cup for you."

"Thanks, but I'm going to watch the lighting with Becks and Pippa."

"Please don't feel obligated to stick with us just because I had a few rough minutes." Becks worried her lip. "I don't want to interfere with your family time."

"What happened?" Graciela joined the line.

Becks gave a two-minute version and then stepped forward to place her order, asking Deb for four cups with extra whipped cream. "Did Fabiana want anything?"

Graciela shook her head. "You didn't have to buy me a cup."

"Glad to. And hey, who can resist whipped cream?"

Graciela accepted her cup from Deb, who reached for a cardboard drink carrier and inserted the other cups.

"Well, thank you."

"You sound just like your brother."

Graciela beamed. "Thank you. That's one of the nicest compliments I've received lately."

Becks led the way to a spot on the lawn and spread her blanket on the ground. The sounds of an acoustic guitar strummed across the intercom system, the familiar chords of "It's Beginning to Look a Lot Like Christmas" sparking holiday joy deep within him. The company surrounding him also helped.

More vendors were arriving and setting up booths. "Graciela, would you like to join us?" Becks asked.

His sister glanced at Becks, then him, a sly smile overtaking her features. "I think I'd be a third wheel. I'll tell Mami you found someone, Carlos. See you later."

Even in the soft glow of the lights, Carlos could spot the shocked look on Becks's face. He lowered himself and laid his crutches beside him. Pippa stepped away from them and hid behind her mom. "There's nothing to be afraid of. They can't move on their own."

"They're big. Bigger than me."

Carlos could see where Pippa was coming from. Searching quickly, he spied the perfect booth that might alleviate some of Pippa's fear.

"Save my spot for me." He smiled at Becks, who glared back. She was taking his recovery to heart.

He didn't know whether that warmed him or whether he should be worried about her. However, this didn't feel like the right moment for those kinds of serious thoughts. He bought his intended gift and returned. Plopping on the blanket, he laid down his crutches, and Pippa inched closer to Becks once more.

"Want to help me?" He raised his voice over the singer's version of "Winter Wonderland" and removed two Christmas-light necklaces from his left pocket.

Curiosity showed on Pippa's face. "Me?"

"Yes, I need a Pippa-sized helper. Your little hands are just about the right size for this." He laid the first crutch across his lap and accidentally jostled Becks. "Sorry."

"No harm done."

He concentrated on Pippa who inched closer. "Pippa help, too?"

Carlos threaded the crutch with the Christmas-light necklace and then turned it on. "Pretty, huh?" Pippa clapped her agreement, and he handed the second strand and other crutch to her. "Your turn."

It took her three times as long, but he thanked her for a job well done and brought forth another necklace from his other pocket. "For the best helper in Hollydale. We match now."

Pippa's eyes lit up when he placed the strand around her neck. She fingered the colorful lights with awe, and Becks gave her a small nudge. "Thank you, Mr. Carlos."

The singer played the final chords of the holiday tune. Carlos drank his cocoa while the mayor began speaking, thanking the Whitley family for the generosity of the pine from their Christmas tree farm. Becks sat, looking spellbound by the night, the earlier tension dissipated for now. He hadn't seen a lovelier sight in ages.

The crowd counted down, and Mayor Wes threw the switch. The tall pine glistened with thousands of colorful LED lights glowing red, blue, purple and orange. The topper, a star formed from miniature crystals, almost looked down at the town as if guarding it, a beacon for people to find their way back home, and maybe back to each other.

He reached into his pocket and pulled out the final necklace. His cheek brushed across Becks's soft hair, the sweet smell instantly remembered, and he placed the Christmas strand with its miniature ornaments around her neck. "I didn't forget you, Becks."

He never would either. Something about her was unforgettable, and she faced him. "For me?"

The delight in such a small gift floored him. He nodded. "For you."

She reached up and touched the necklace, the wonder in her eyes a mirror of her daughter's. She opened her mouth and closed it again, staring at the twinkling colors. Then she met his gaze and mouthed the words, *Thank you*.

How had he ever walked away from her in the past?

# CHAPTER NINE

FOR THE SIXTH time that afternoon, Becks tapped her pencil against the desk in her makeshift office in the community center. With any luck, the fire chief would allow her to be in the administrative building soon, since Trent had installed sprinklers and was bringing everything up to code.

She'd been staring at these figures for too long. Something didn't add up. Math had never been Becks's best subject unless it dealt with geometry as she paid attention to angles and trajectories for goal shots, but she wasn't clueless either.

She needed a clue to crack this checking account mystery of the disappearing fifteen hundred dollars, and in a hurry, too. That money would cover Dante's and Amara's salaries and keep them on board. She rested her head next to her laptop, frustrated with the spreadsheet, the slow recovery of her complex and the lack of progress with Goal, Kick and Score.

Her cell rang. Finally something was going her way. "Hi, Tricia."

"Hello from gorgeous Rio de Janeiro. It's summer here." Tricia hadn't sounded this relaxed ever. A bundle of energy, she thrived on activity.

"That explains why it's been so hard to get ahold of you. When did you arrive in Rio?"

"A week ago. I've shopped at the Arcos da Lapa and sambaed there, ridden a cable car up Sugar Loaf, and now I'm lounging at a beach at Costa Verde." Tricia ticked off her outings like Santa checking off the names on his list.

If anyone deserved that trip, though, it was Tricia, the winningest coach in her division. "I'm happy for you. You more than earned this vacation and your retirement."

"Do you need me to talk to the director of Kick, Goal and Score on your behalf?"

"I'm dealing with his assistant."

"I know Wallace. I'll ask him to personally call you and bring up what great ideas you have for your complex. I'm sure I have his number somewhere. It's only a small favor and I'm happy to do it."

And ruin her vacation? *No way.* "Uh-uh. Tell me what else you have planned instead."

"I'm watching the fireworks at Copacabana Beach on New Year's."

Tricia's office walls had always been covered with travel posters for points around the globe. "You told us, your players, to follow our dreams. I'm glad you're finally following yours."

Becks sipped her water, waiting for Tricia to continue.

"The vacation is great, but retirement? I've never been more bored in my life. Why didn't anyone ever tell me how dull it was to do nothing all day?"

Becks choked on her water. "This is your dream. You always talked about having time to yourself."

"Dreams can change, evolve when they're not right for a person. I didn't take into account how much I need to do something, feel useful with my life. Just like pursuing physical therapy wasn't right for you in Hollydale and you made a change. What excuse are they giving about why Goal, Kick and Score is ignoring my protégé?"

"Are you sure you want to hear this?"

"Yes. Don't make me come there and ask twice."

"I keep getting the runaround. They heard

about the fire. But every time Stacy schedules a time to tour my complex, she cancels. I don't know why exactly."

"Hmm. Let me see what I can find out for you. By the way, have you heard—" Tricia paused, when a knock sounded at Becks's door.

"I've got to go. I've taken too much of your time already. I know you. You just need to process the change, Coach. Relax." Though if she was wrong about Tricia's personality, what else was she wrong about? Could people change over time?

"Stuff and nonsense. You didn't take too much of my time. I'll call the director."

"Enjoy your vacation." Becks disconnected and turned her attention to the door. "Come in."

Carlos stuck his head inside, and that attraction between them flared to full flame. She glanced down at her purse, the Christmas ornament necklace at the top. Except for her birthday or Christmas, no one had bought her a present in forever. That was something she'd forgotten about Carlos, how he'd bring her something to their soccer practices from a Snickers bar to a handmade friendship bracelet. Little things that always lifted her spirit.

And he'd acted more like a real father to Pippa than Jack. How he patiently showed her that the crutches weren't bad. How he presented her with a necklace of her own. How they giggled at each other's whipped cream mustaches.

Yet his positivity and good guy dreaminess had been all for naught once before. Could she depend on him or anyone else now?

"Carlos. What brings you by the community center?" She lowered the lid of the laptop.

"I'm sorry I canceled our morning physical therapy session."

"Things come up, especially on Mondays. Understandable." He looked like he had something else he wanted to say. "It's not anything serious, is it? You're not in pain, are you?"

"No pain. I dropped by to see if you had a logo you wanted us to use." He proceeded inside, dropping his crutches next to the other chair in the room.

She bent down and closed her purse, not ready for him to see how much importance she put into a silly necklace. "Logo? For what?"

"The banners and programs." Carlos frowned, clearly confused. "Don't you know what I'm talking about?"

"Not a clue."

"For the Firefighter's Christmas Festival. I need the Mountain Vista Soccer Complex logo, website and promo material info by five today. Your company is a paid sponsor."

"What?" She found her voice again and opened her laptop. Her heart sank. "By any chance, was the amount sponsors paid fifteen hundred dollars?"

"Mountain Vista went for the platinum level, which comes complete with parking passes and a carriage ride among other perks. Thanks for helping us reach our goal for a new fire truck and supporting our community outreach goals."

The blanket the fire chief had given her on the scene now rested on Pippa's bed, and her daughter had started tucking Grizzie in with it. She vaguely recalled Sharlene coming to her one morning and mentioning a platinum level opportunity. She'd signed off without realizing Sharlene had invested so much, and she couldn't go back on a good cause. "Five p.m. today?"

He nodded. "Sharlene promised that info in a file, but I double-checked and couldn't find anything."

She checked the time on her laptop. Five hours to go. "Can you resend me the sponsorship link?"

He pulled out his phone from his pocket and

swiped the screen several times. "There." He waited for her confirmation. "I also dropped by to see if you wanted to grab lunch while we review the inspector's latest email regarding your administrative building."

Her ears perked up at that. "What email?" She looked, but nothing from the inspector sat in her inbox or spam folder.

"You can reopen the administrative building now."

She reached over and squeezed his shoulder, her squeal of joy a happy sound. "That's great news. Thank you." A quiver of regret shot through her, but work came first. "Can I take a rain check on lunch so I can get you the logo and everything else you need?"

A glimmer of disappointment tinged his eyes. "Sure thing." He rose and waved goodbye. She called her website designer and registrar, Amara, who was now on her way to help out this afternoon with the details for the festival.

Finally, a couple of breaks. Maybe she was only down at halftime instead of being down and out with only minutes to go.

DESK DUTY WAS a mixed blessing. Carlos spent his mornings at the fire station, but he missed answering calls that much more. Carlos massaged his left thigh and listened to the latest in the long list of candidates say "no" to acting as Santa, both for the kids and the two-hour window for pet pictures.

"No, I didn't know you were allergic to cats, rabbits and guinea pigs." He caught himself before he threw a Komodo dragon onto that list. "Thanks for your time."

Carlos struck off the last name on the legal pad. Out of ten people, five bowed out because of allergies, two to other commitments at the festival, two to work schedules, and one man claimed a fear of chickens. He'd tried to convince Horace there weren't many pet chickens in Hollydale, but Horace refused to take any chances.

Roberto entered the office and sat at the edge of the desk. "How's your ankle?"

Carlos stopped rubbing his leg. "It's getting better."

Roberto's arched eyebrows seemed more fatherly than boss-like, but since they were at the fire station and Roberto couldn't grant him special consideration, Carlos refused to backtrack. "Dr. Patel and Becks are amazed at my progress."

Sometimes progress caused some pain, but

it'd be worth it once he returned to the ranks of his fellow firefighters. He felt helpless watching from the sidelines whenever they suited up in response to a call. Seeing his untouched equipment under his name caused another kind of pain every time the team exited the building.

"Hmm. If you say so."

"Is that why you dropped by? To check on me?"

"Ned's been continuing the investigation of the soccer complex fire." Roberto nodded.

"I'm looking forward to all of this being behind us." *And hanging over any future with Becks*.

Roberto pulled a folded piece of paper from his pocket. "I need you to add these supplies to our requisition order."

Carlos accepted the paper and smoothed out the creases. "I'll get right to it." He turned his attention to his laptop, but Roberto made no effort to move away. "Is there something else?"

"Everything on schedule and in place for the Firefighter's Festival?" Roberto tapped the edge of the desk.

"Except for the small issue of Santa." He hadn't even approached his father about taking the role as he knew Roberto was double-booked that day as it was.

Roberto relayed a name, and Carlos shot back that he'd already refused. Same with the next four. "Keep looking. Someone will volunteer," Roberto said.

He made as if to leave, but remained in the same spot. Carlos braced himself. Budget cuts? Physical being moved up? As long as he had a chance at reclaiming his spot, he'd give his recovery all he had. "What's the real reason you're here?"

"I don't like to mix our personal life with our professional responsibilities."

"We've set that policy since day one." He waited for the blow. His father had to do what he had to as fire chief. If Carlos was the weak link in the department, that was that. The team came first.

"But there's no way to tell you this at home without Fabiana hearing me."

If he lowered the boom, his mother would find out regardless of whether it happened at home or not. This was one of those possibilities he'd accounted for during his downtime, but now it seemed too real, too final, too forever.

"Whatever it is, I understand."

"Can you steer your mother toward her marinated ribeye steaks instead of her mojo pork?"

"Huh? What are you talking about?"

"You can drop the pretense. I know," Roberto said. "About my anniversary dinner and Gisele's homecoming party."

Carlos laughed and couldn't wait to tell Graciela they were right. Their father had found out. "I'll try."

His father thanked him and left. Someone called Carlos's cell, and he checked the screen. His doctor's office.

He answered and listened to Dr. Patel's assistant. "I'm rather surprised you want to discontinue Becks's services. She was one of the most sought-after therapists before she purchased her soccer complex. Her patients always remarked how much they loved her."

Giving up the physical therapy sessions with Becks so she wouldn't feel obligated toward him was a necessity.

How he'd explain this to Becks, though, without sounding ungrateful was something he hadn't figured out yet. He'd already turned her away once in his life and regretted it. "A fellow firefighter mentioned hydrotherapy. I was wondering if that would yield better results."

"Looking over my notes, your progress is

quite remarkable as it is. Upsetting the apple cart and changing course might prove more harmful."

So if he changed course, he might set his recovery back and risk his professional future? But he wanted to act on his attraction for Becks, one that seemed mutual. And that meant going elsewhere for physical therapy so he could ask Becks for a fresh start that didn't rely on an arrangement that resembled a contract more than friends helping friends.

"What would you suggest?" Hearing someone else assess his options might give him some much-needed insight.

"If I could stake my future with Becks Porter helping me, I'd do that." The assistant cleared his throat. "The closest place for hydrotherapy is in Asheville, and you'd have to drive at least an hour each way, which would be wearing on your ankle, unless you could get someone to do the driving for you."

In other words, the drive would eliminate any benefit he might receive from the hydrotherapy. He rubbed his leg once more, not wanting to ask anything more of his family, either. For now, his relationship with Becks would have to continue on the same footing.

"I'll stick with Becks." He asked a few other

questions about his progress and wrapped up the conversation, conscious of the assistant's time. "Thanks for the call."

He swiped the screen as the third siren of the day sounded and he heard the voices of his fellow firefighters gearing up for another call without him.

# CHAPTER TEN

BECKS'S BREATH CRYSTALLIZED in the fresh mountain air at the Stover Christmas Tree Farm. The crisp scent of pine surrounded her as did the sound of saws and the balers covering the cut trees in burlap.

She unbuckled Pippa from her car seat. With the forecast calling for a smattering of snow, Becks bundled Pippa in her sparkly pink puffy coat and pulled her rainbow knit cap over her ears for good measure. From there she held on to Pippa's mittened hand while releasing Gomez and Morticia from their crates with a firm grip on their special leash with a two-way coupler. Both dogs yipped with excitement as their paws hit the ground.

The crowd on this Tuesday morning was larger than Becks had anticipated, but that added to the Christmas spirit. Something she needed to put her business woes to the back burner. The rest of the workweek plus Saturday would be soon enough to concentrate on the soccer complex given she was short an assistant and a groundskeeper. After drowning herself in work the past few days, this morning's venture was all about her and Pippa. Happy holiday tunes were being broadcast over speakers, and employees hurling trees to the tops of cars wore jingle bells and bright red coats with the name of the farm embroidered on the back.

How many times had she come here with her family, picking out one perfect tree and a not-so-perfect one? Nat always fell in love with the smallest, scrawniest tree and would insist the Harrison family needed to have it, while Becks lobbied for the biggest, best Harrison Christmas tree ever. Without fail, her father purchased the two firs and had them tied to the roof of their station wagon for the drive home.

Now, she might be asking for trouble with two dogs and a toddler along for the experience, but last night, the drabness of the house had caught up with her. This might not be the first year her daughter remembered Christmas, but it was a foundation of good things to come.

Once she wrapped the leash around her wrist and had Pippa in hand, they followed the crowd to the entrance of the sixty-acre farm that was a Hollydale landmark. Becks stopped and admired the paint of the barn mellowed to an inviting shade of dusty red, strings of white lights brightening up the place. She recognized Mrs. Stover, who was matching pretty plaid bows to pine wreaths, and Mr. Stover, chain saw in hand, goggles over eyes, cutting the bottom off a large Fraser fir.

Recently, the Stovers had added an Elf Shop that sold homemade items. She spotted several customers emerging with jars of cider and other packages wrapped with a clothespin featuring an elf attached to the top. Pippa beelined toward the cider stand, the warm cinnamon and apple scents mingling with pine, but Becks pulled her back. "Tree first."

Gomez and Morticia preened whenever friends stopped and asked if they could pet them. Slowing down the pace, Becks heard more about Hollydale in the past ten minutes than she had in years. She stopped at a table and selected a handsaw for when they found the tree of her dreams: tall, solid and handsome. Storing the saw safely in her backpack, she led Pippa and the dogs to an area where the crowds had thinned.

"Which tree do you like, Pip?" Becks let go of her hand with an order to stay close.

Pippa ran ahead before twirling in the center of the path. "All of them."

Gomez marked one short Fraser fir with a huge bare spot in the middle while Morticia indicated she preferred its neighbor, a tall tree that wouldn't have fit in the living room. "Hmm, you two aren't any help either."

Voices came from the next aisle. "Why should I listen to you? You've already spoken your piece."

That sounded like Carlos's sister Graciela.

"Because I love you, and I thought I was protecting you when I broke up with you." It was a man's voice. Becks cringed with discomfort. Should she stay hidden, or should she let them know they had an audience?

Small snowflakes fell from the sky, and Pippa giggled. "Mommy! It's snowing!"

Just enough to make this day that much more special. Becks blinked. This was a tradition she and Pippa would share from here on, and it started now. "Watch this." She stuck her tongue out and caught a few snowflakes.

Pippa laughed and tried to catch a snowflake on her tongue. "Come on, Gomez, Morticia, it's so fun." The dogs danced like there was a party in the tree aisle.

"Becks? Is that you?" Carlos's head appeared between two trees, followed by the rest of him as he navigated through the pathway with his crutches.

"Carlos?" She stared at the bright lime-green cast and then glared at him. "You shouldn't be out here with that ankle. This isn't the smoothest terrain."

She restrained the dogs and kept a careful watch on Pippa while speaking to Carlos. Somehow every time they came in contact with each other, her heart fluttered the tiniest bit and inside she did a happy dance. This wasn't what she wanted, though. She couldn't trust him with her heart. She couldn't trust anyone with that.

"I got official clearance to up my activity level, within reason. As long as I don't try to climb the walls of my house, which is exactly what I was doing when Graciela thankfully came by and rescued me, I'll be fine." Carlos smiled, which made his dimples stand out. Could he get any more handsome? "And now I need someone to rescue me from my sister."

"Why? What's happening?" Pippa darted around trees, and Becks rushed after her, pulling the dogs along until Gomez spied Graciela talking to a young man in his early twenties and yanked himself and Morticia toward him. "Gomez!"

"No, name's Jordan." The man, who was probably about ten years younger than Becks's thirty-two, stepped forward. "I'm Graciela's boyfriend."

Graciela pursed her lips. "I didn't take you back. Why should I take you back? I've cried for hours over you."

"I'm sorry, Graciela. More sorry than you'll ever know."

Carlos emerged through the tree line, pulling himself up to his full height even with the crutches. "Jordan, this might not be the right place or time to talk. If Graciela doesn't want you back, you'd best be on your way."

"Actually I do want him back." She sniffled, her big red knit cap bobbing up and down. "I really, really do."

Jordan slipped his hand into Graciela's and smiled. "I promise. I won't make that mistake again."

"Carlos," Graciela said to him, but her gaze never left Jordan. "Could Becks drive you home? This one and I have a lot of talking to do."

"I'd be more than happy to take you home," Becks said.

The young couple didn't need any extra prodding and hurried away.

Becks glanced at Morticia who guarded Carlos as if he was her personal mission. "You've made a friend."

Balancing with his crutches, he used his right hand and petted Morticia's head. "I'm glad." He glanced at Pippa, running circles around the closest tree. "Are you okay with my cutting in on your time with your daughter?"

Becks's head was almost spinning from Pippa's speed and agility. "The more the merrier."

His smile widened, and those dark brown eyes melted into a rich toffee color. *Uh-oh.* She was noticing his eyes. Best to back away. They were only hanging out together so he could pass that physical next year and she could understand what the hired company was telling her about county construction code. It was more confusing than any soccer play she'd ever attempted. Once he was back on the fire crew and her soccer complex was operating at full steam, they'd return to their separate lives.

Except they seemed to keep running into each other, and every time it made her giddy.

Pippa planted herself in one spot and pointed to a small tree. "This one."

Carlos made his way over and examined the tree. He patted Pippa's shoulder. "Hmm, this one needs a few more years to grow, just like you."

Steeling herself for a meltdown from her

daughter, Becks breathed out a sigh of relief when Pippa skipped to the next tree. "This one."

Now Becks understood. The novelty had worn off, and Pippa wanted a tree, any tree. Why look at trees when cider stands and live reindeer were more enticing? Becks went over and squeezed Pippa's hand. "It's hard to take our time, but we need to take our time."

Carlos guided Pippa to the next tree, which was too large, the next too scraggly. Becks somehow managed Gomez and Morticia, who loved all the trees. "Our yard's too small for all of them," Becks stated matter-of-factly.

Carlos's robust laugh reached her, warming her toes that were starting to feel nippy despite her thick wool socks. "What about this tree?" he asked her.

Pippa jumped up and down as she rushed over and hugged the fir. "My tree! My tree!"

Carlos invited Becks into their circle, and she gave the Fraser fir the once-over. It wasn't the biggest. It wasn't the fullest. And yet it exuded charm and personality, something she never associated with a plain old tree before. She rested the backpack on the ground and pulled out the saw. Pippa burst into tears.

"Don't hurt my tree!" Her wails brought a

man in a Stover Christmas tree coat running in their direction.

"Is everything okay?" The man took one look at Pippa and gave an apologetic smile. "I see the problem."

"Pippa." Her daughter stopped sniffling and looked at Carlos, whose voice exuded calm authority. "We have to cut it down so it can spend Christmas with us." He glanced at his cast and scuffed the ground. "Or, at least, your mom will cut it down."

"Why don't you, and your wife and daughter, have a cup of apple cider and pose for a picture by the sled?" The man smiled at Pippa while Becks waited for Carlos to correct the guy's mistake.

"Apple cider?" Pippa rushed over, her excitement clear for everyone to see. "Mommy, please!"

"What do you say, Becks?" Carlos asked.

As much as she wanted to stay and cut down the tree, she wanted to spare Carlos any further pain involving his pride.

This was bad. Her career had stopped them from getting together once, and now it was the only thing keeping them together. How would she feel after the therapy sessions and their time together ended?

Pippa's bright eyes were only matched by Carlos's glistening ones. "Sounds good to me," she said.

THE SMELL OF fresh fir filled Becks's living room along with mellow instrumental holiday music. Carlos loved the coziness of it all. While he didn't see any other decorations around her home, the trimmed tree occupied center stage in front of her picture window. Becks lifted Pippa, who placed the star on the top.

Maybe tonight was the start of something new, the next phase of both of their lives. The guy at the tree farm had thought they were married. He'd thought about correcting him but hadn't, content in the moment and liking the idea of being Pippa and Becks's family.

Becks danced and twirled Pippa in time to the music. A genuine sense of belonging and caring filled his heart, and the thought of kissing Becks before he left would make this evening complete.

"Again!" Pippa giggled.

Becks shook her head. "Dinnertime. We have to wash your face and hands."

"Pippa not dirty." She landed with a thump on her bottom, and Gomez rushed over and licked her face. "All clean."

Becks swooped her up. "Nice try, but doggie kisses before dinner warrant a trip to the bathroom." With Becks's high spirits on full display, that rush of emotion swirled in him once more. "Is minestrone soup okay for dinner? That's what I made in the slow cooker this morning."

"Sounds great."

"Make yourself comfortable. We'll be back."

He settled on her couch, and Morticia jumped up next to him and snuggled close. Somehow every road he'd ever traveled in his life led to this moment, and for once, he only saw one path forward. A road with Becks and Pippa.

Becks ran back into the room, her face ashen, her hands shaking. He stumbled to his feet, upsetting the dog. "What's wrong?"

"It's Amara. She's one of my employees, and she's pregnant. She's having stomach pain, and she and Dante are headed to the hospital." Her fingers trembled as she clutched the phone. "I have to call my mom and see if she can watch Pippa. I'm sorry, but I have to cancel our dinner."

Not as sorry as he was. Becks couldn't seem to catch a break. "The soup's already made, right?" He waited for her nod. "I can watch Pippa and feed her and the dogs. Then we'll watch holiday cartoons until she either falls asleep or you get home, whichever comes first."

Skepticism was written on her face. "That's a lot to ask of anyone."

"It's no problem, and you drove me here. While Pippa watches television, I'll arrange for a friend to drive me home once you get back."

"You already have five people in mind for that ride, don't you?"

He chuckled while Pippa returned to the living room. "You know me too well."

"When I get there, I'll text my mother. She can relieve you."

"Becks. Trust me."

She went over and kissed the top of Pippa's head. "If she's not okay…" She shuddered, a shadow of sadness passing over her features. "I hope she is."

"Pippa and I will be fine."

Becks muttered something while she grabbed her coat and bag. "Text me if you need me to call in the reserves."

She disappeared in a flurry, and he was alone with the two-year-old dynamo. Everything crashed in at once. He often couldn't fix his own dinner and headed to either the Holly Days Diner or the new Asian bistro on the rare occasion his mother didn't conveniently drop by with a covered dish. His fingers itched to call Mami, but he could do this on his own.

He reached over and grasped his crutches. Once steady, he headed to the kitchen, feeling like the Pied Piper with Pippa, Gomez and Morticia following him in a straight line.

"Where does your mommy keep the dog food?" Pippa stared at him as if he'd asked a question in a language other than English. He'd worry about the dogs once he and Pippa were fed. "What about you? What do you like with your soup? An apple? Plain crackers? Bread?"

"Cheetos and chicken nuggets." Pippa grinned.

He wasn't born yesterday, and he clicked his tongue. "Not on my watch, Pip. Try again."

"Grilled cheese?"

That he could handle. He opened some cabinets and found the dog food before locating a pan. Persistence paid off, and he made the sandwiches.

After dinner, he and Pippa settled on the couch, and he congratulated himself. While the kitchen was a mess, four stomachs were now full, and the dogs had done their business outside. He only hoped all was going well for Becks. He hadn't heard from her, not even a text checking on Pippa.

Morticia placed her snout on his left leg while Pippa snuggled against his side. He could get used to this. *Fast.*

They watched one holiday cartoon special, then two. His eyes were starting to droop, he noticed. After what felt like only seconds, he heard a soft crash and a "Uh-oh." He shot awake and spotted the tree tilting precariously sideways.

Every ornament that had been on the bottom half of the tree now lay scattered around the carpet. Only the star and colored strings of blinking LED lights remained in place. Pippa sat in the middle with Gomez on one side and Morticia on the other.

"They did it." Her little thumbs pointed at the dogs, whose tongues were lolling.

Carlos's shallow breaths came out faster. Pippa and the dogs could have been injured or worse on his watch had the tree fallen. Becks would never trust him if she found out about this.

He didn't know how much longer she'd be gone, but it would take a good hour to hook every ornament back in place. Unconvinced about Pippa's reply, he sent her the closest thing he had to his father's stern look, which he'd seen so often in his childhood. She squirmed and jutted out her lip. "I did it." Then joy came back to her face, and she clapped her hands. "Now we have fun again."

*Fun?* He groaned as the why behind her actions kicked in. "No, you're going to sit on the couch while I fix it. You can't do this again. The ornaments have to stay on the tree this time. All. The. Time."

"Pippa help." She folded her arms, and her green eyes gleamed with determination.

"Not now."

"I want my mommy. You're no fun." Pippa went over and grabbed an ornament. When she tried placing it back on the tree, it fell off again. She began to cry.

He hobbled to the couch and waved her over. She climbed next to him, leaving enough of a gap for Gomez to jump up.

"Mr. Carlos mad at Pippa?"

"No. You and your mommy are…" He hesitated and searched for what they meant to him. The word everything came to mind, but he held back. "Special to me."

She yawned and leaned into Gomez. "I'm sleepy. I want my mommy."

"You can sleep in here, so you'll know when she's home."

"I'm sorry, Mr. Carlos."

Were some relationships in life as easy as that? Looking up at someone with great big eyes and apologizing for mistakes?

"I know. Just make sure the ornaments stay on the tree from now on." He waited a few minutes until sleep finally overtook her. Then he rose and surveyed the mess before him.

Should he apologize to Becks for the chaos? He might as well see if he could set things right first. He tested the weight of his ankle and stood without crutches. Nothing seemed out of joint. He was relieved.

With a sigh, he picked one ornament up and found the process easier this time although he marveled at how Pippa undid a whole afternoon's worth of work in such a short time. Connecting the last ornament to a branch, Carlos lost his footing and a twinge of pain shot through his calf as he fell back on the couch, disrupting Gomez who yelped. He and Morticia ran to the front door. The sound of the key in the knob alerted him to Becks's presence, and he leaned against the cushions, rubbing his thigh.

How he was going to get off her couch without alerting her that anything was wrong was a mystery. The throbbing lessened, and he felt relieved. He only needed a few minutes recovery time, and he should be good to go.

Becks stopped short in the archway, and his breath hitched. He realized he wanted to come home to this sweet, beautiful face every day. She'd taken on a business that would build up kids as they pursued dreams. As a teenager, she'd always been after the brightest, the new trend, the hot shot, yet today showed she cared for her community, for her home, for her daughter. He really had thrown away a treasure all those years ago.

As much as he wondered if Pippa was onto something with a simple heartfelt apology, he didn't dare try that tactic as far as a potential relationship was maybe in the balance. Not when his career might have taken a permanent nosedive with no hope of following in his father's footsteps. Without a steady ankle and profession, he had little to offer. Instead, he concentrated on his foot, wiggling his big toe while making sure he didn't break something.

"How's Amara?" Carlos asked.

"Fortunately, it was a case of indigestion. Better safe than sorry. She's fine, and the doctors don't see any problems with the pregnancy." Becks smiled, her relief evident. She called for Gomez and Morticia. "I'm going to take them outside before I put them in their crates and grab some dinner. Do you mind staying for a few more minutes? I'd love to eat before Pippa wakes up."

He couldn't resist. Besides, he'd have to come clean. He couldn't keep Pippa safe and out of trouble for one night.

Pippa and Becks were a formidable team. Was there a place for him here? He soaked in the family feeling, the same happiness surrounding his childhood home, the same contentment from his teenage years whenever he and Becks were together.

*Tell Becks.* Confiding in her the worst aspects of himself? That his leg was throbbing but not as much as his heart had ached when she flew to California and he'd immediately known he had made a terrible mistake? Admitting his flaws to someone? Big time bad idea. He never liked to show his weakness.

Becks appeared in the archway, a bowl of steaming soup in her hands. The backlight from the kitchen provided a glow around her.

"Sit down and eat. I have plenty of time to stay until you're finished." Some days it seemed like he had nothing but time while he rested his leg. He picked up his phone. "I still have to text my friend Mason who's giving me a ride home."

"Let me carry Pippa to bed, and then we can talk."

Pippa stirred and snuggled close to Becks, a beautiful sight.

They left the room, and he texted Mason, who'd be there in forty-five minutes after he finished reading his stepdaughter a bedtime story. Carlos smiled at Mason's selfie of him and Chloe in matching feather boas. Carlos was happy for his friend, the perpetual bachelor paramedic, who'd found love with the girl next door. He and Lindsay were perfect for each other, starting out as neighbors and ending up as husband and wife.

"What's so funny?" Becks came in and curled her legs under her on the oversize chair. Then she picked up her bowl and stirred her soup with her spoon.

He held up the phone and she laughed at the picture of Mason and Chloe. "He'll be slightly delayed in driving me home for good reason. How's work going on the complex?"

She leaned back and rested the bowl on her thigh. "Trent texted me today's evening update while I was at the hospital. There's been another setback. He needs my authorization to install a new electrical panel with a dead front and increased voltage supply, adding another couple of thousand dollars to the cost. Have to have it so I'll be in compliance with code regulations. At this point, though, that extra four thousand might as well be forty thousand."

Her voice choked up, and she transferred the bowl to the coffee table. His heart twisted for her. "Becks. Is there anything I can do?"

She held up her hand. "No sympathy, please. I'm the one who bought the place as is. I'm the one who has to live with that."

"But not alone. We all make mistakes." The air became charged, and a muscle spasm in his leg reminded him why he couldn't speak up. What could he bring to her team? A busted ankle and a career up in the air? No, he'd stay in his lane and keep from reaching out and comforting her. Maybe even kissing her.

"Some bigger than others." She winced and sat next to him. Her hand landed on his knee, but he kept himself from asking her to examine his painful leg. "I'm sorry. This mistake was a big one. You're hurt because I didn't do my due diligence."

Her cheeks paled, and she raised her hands to her face. "Becks." She began sobbing, and her body shook as everything with Amara and then Trent must be hitting her at once. "It was an accident. You didn't set the fire on purpose."

He'd fought far worse fires than the one at the complex. Maybe that split second of indecision on his part had led to his fall, debris or no debris. They'd never know for sure.

He put his arm around her shoulders, wanting to console her and tell her how he was feeling. Her body stilled, and the moment was here. She stared at him, but then turned to the tree. Her head tilted slightly as if she was trying to figure something out. A slight tremble turned into a fit of giggles.

"I see Pippa was a handful."

He didn't move a muscle. "What makes you say that?"

"The ornaments are in different places, and you improved on that bare spot I couldn't get rid of." Using the back of her hand, she wiped away the tears and smiled.

He smiled back. "Hopefully she took my words to heart that they stay on the tree this time."

They looked at each other, and the laughter started. Like that, the comfortable ease was back, but then she met his gaze, and the chuckling stopped. Her blue eyes widened as if she was aware of something changing between them. Her tongue touched the corner of her mouth and he leaned forward but pulled back. The last thing they needed was to complicate their new friendship.

She sensed his retreat and reached for her dinner. "Pippa's good about not making the same mistake twice. That's smart, don't you think?"

"It is." Part of him knew he was doing just that. Making the same errors all over again. However, her message was clear. In her book, he was a mistake, his choice to break up with her a permanent loss in her column. The doorbell rang, and Becks flew off the couch with a little too much exuberance.

She returned with Mason following. "Lin took over nighttime duties. Are you ready to go?"

*Now or never.* Carlos stood and tested his leg. He stumbled a bit before he regained his bearings. It wasn't as bad as he first feared. Reaching for the crutches, he stopped bearing the weight on his left ankle. "Yep. Thanks for the ride home." He inhaled the piney scent of the tree and faced Becks. "Glad Trent is being honest with you about what's happening with the complex. You're in good hands."

Knowing that didn't make his leaving any easier. Yet she'd made herself clear about him, and he respected her choice.

## CHAPTER ELEVEN

CARLOS WINCED AT giving into pride last night at Becks's house. This morning, the pain upon waking was severe enough for him to call Dr. Patel's office for an emergency appointment, and here he was in the waiting room, flipping through a magazine but not seeing any of the pictures or reading any of the words.

The nurse called his name. He replaced the magazine on the table and rose, nerves jangling about whether he'd lost any chance at resuming his firefighting career. At this point he'd take that even if someone else followed in his father's footsteps as chief.

In the exam room, worry bore down on him as he flipped through a magazine. But he couldn't focus. If he couldn't fight fires after his injury, what would he do for the rest of his life? Giving something back to his community was a part of who he was.

It wasn't long before he found himself in Dr. Patel's presence, her wrinkled brow not a positive indication of recovery. "Give it to me straight."

She swiped the tablet and placed it on the counter next to a clear jar of tongue depressors. "Mr. Ramirez, I know telling you to slow down is like telling a bird not to fly."

His shoulders sagged, the wind knocked out of him. "A friend of mine had an emergency…"

"I know you well enough to know you can't resist a friend in need, but you might have caused ligament damage. The cast will come off in a few weeks, and we'll know the full extent of your prognosis then." She tugged at both ends of the stethoscope hanging around her neck.

"Not any sooner?"

Dr. Patel shook her head, the blunt ends of her black bob bouncing with her. "No, but maintaining an active pace and not resting and elevating the ankle will damage your prospects for a full recovery. You have to take it easy." Her voice took on a serious tone. "Repetitive strain or impact at the site of the break could result in a stress fracture. At that point we might even be discussing surgery. R-I-C-E is your friend."

"Rest, ice, compression, elevation." He could repeat that in his sleep. He'd check with his father to see if he could do his desk work from home. Barring that option, he'd make sure to always elevate his foot at the station.

"I want to see you back here in one week, and I want you to start using a mobility scooter rather than crutches. If you're still in this much pain," she said, and held up her hand, "I know you're putting up a strong front, but you have to be open with me."

One week? That was an eternity. And he'd do anything to not give everyone at the station pause about whether they could depend on him or whether his ankle might give out once more.

"What about physical therapy? Should I switch to hydrotherapy or continue the gentle exercises with Becks Porter?"

Dr. Patel hugged her tablet to her chest. "Hydrotherapy might help your muscles." She swiped the screen on the tablet. "But I'd prefer you scale back on the physical therapy. Take it easy. Your ankle needs rest."

Carlos ran his hand through his hair, already thicker and fuller as he hadn't visited the barber on the first Tuesday of the month for his standing appointment. "I still have to pass the physical next year. How do I make sure my arm muscles don't atrophy?"

"Without two fit ankles, you don't have to

worry about your arm strength. I'll see you in a week." She nodded and left the room.

He rubbed his neck, worried about this latest setback on several fronts.

BECKS SAT ON Nat's tree swing, savoring a moment of peace, a heavy weight on her shoulders. Today, she'd received a call from a local businessperson and philanthropist, Frederick Whitley, with an offer to purchase the land and buildings for the same price she paid if she accepted before Christmas. After that, the offer would go down by 25 percent.

She stared at Nat's house, the rambling Victorian perfect for her sister and her family. Natalie dreamed big, and Aidan loved finishing one fixer-upper and moving on to the next on his carefully planned list. It helped that her brother-in-law loved her twin more than he loved his lists.

She and Nat were so different. Thoughtful Nat would never hurt anyone or make a monumental mistake like Becks. And not just any mistake, but one that left Carlos in a bright green cast with a chance his career could be over. If Carlos didn't regain full mobility in his ankle, she'd have to live with that regret.

Maybe she should accept Whitley's offer and

be done with the whole matter. That was what a responsible businessperson would do. Cut their losses and move on. After a defeat, her soccer team would watch game footage and figure out what they could and should have done differently. Sometimes, the hard truth was they were outplayed and they had to accept the loss and concentrate on the next opponent.

Selling the property and concentrating on the next stage of her life might be best for everyone. A tap on her shoulder snapped her out of her reverie, and Becks found Nat standing there.

"Hi." A color riot in a puffy purple coat, yellow gloves, pink cheeks and a bright orange knit cap that covered her ears, Nat motioned for Becks to move over and sat beside her. "I saw you out here. Aidan is watching the kids so we can go for a walk."

They stood at the same time.

"I'd hate to put him out like that."

Nat wound her arm around Becks's and moved toward the sidewalk. "Nonsense. My husband has plans for them, and knowing Aidan, we'll come back and find they're all expert painters and decorators."

Becks wouldn't put that past Aidan.

"I need to go home. I have a lot on my mind." Why could she be frank and honest with everyone except the two people she cared most about?

When did she place her affection for Carlos on the same level as her love for her twin?

"Then this walk is what we both need. You need to talk to someone, and I need to listen." Becks separated from her, but Nat kept them going forward. "You were so deep in thought sitting on my swing you didn't even see me. I stopped short of performing a cartwheel on my front lawn to get your attention."

"And yet you thought of tapping me on my shoulder, and it worked." The wryness in Becks's voice was unmistakable.

"Am I reaching you?" Nat stopped, and Becks followed suit. "What happened to us? You used to confide everything to me, and I do mean everything in great detail, that was bothering you. Suddenly one day, snap! You shut me out just like that."

Becks set out at a brisk pace. "Life happened. I accepted a college scholarship, and then you surprised me by applying and accepting an offer from a different university."

Nat matched her stride. "You shut me out way before then. It was like one day we were the picture postcard of identical twins with our own language and everything, and the next you cut off your hair and signed up for soccer camp."

Becks rarely gave her sister enough credit for her perceptiveness. "You didn't seem upset at the time."

"Upset? Not really. *Hurt?* Absolutely. You shut me out and didn't look back."

Becks wished she could say she didn't know what that felt like, but the way Carlos had made the decision to break their engagement without talking or listening to her had wounded her to her core. "I didn't think you noticed. You never said anything."

And once Carlos ended their relationship, she hadn't said anything either. She'd distanced herself on social media and hadn't asked about him.

"You practically lived on the soccer field. Hard to talk to someone who isn't around."

Becks bristled, and that old armor of defensiveness protected her. "Says the person who found another best friend in college."

To her surprise, Nat smiled and wound her arm around Becks's shoulder. "We're finally talking again. This is beautiful."

Nat would always find the silver lining no matter the disaster.

"We're different, and we have separate friends, separate lives to a degree." Speaking of which, she needed to rally Lindsay, Penelope and Kris together after the New Year. She'd lost touch with her friends.

"I think neither of us has fully appreciated the other. Don't you know? No matter where we are or what we're doing, no one will ever take your place." Nat pulled Becks closer. "You can never have too many people in your corner."

"But you always had everyone in your corner." Becks blurted out the words too late to take them back.

"Is that what you thought? And why we grew apart?" Nat stopped walking. "Because you thought life is a competition, and I won the lion's share of attention? That's not a reason to shut yourself off and make all your decisions by yourself."

That was the exact reason, and Becks almost stumbled. Carlos had jumped to the same conclusion about her and their relationship. She'd never given herself a chance to appreciate how Natalie shone and was true to herself, too afraid she'd fall into the shadows and lose

Natalie's love. Although she hadn't lost her sister's love, she sure missed out on a closer friendship and weakened their bond.

In that same way, Carlos must have been scared about her future, her moving on without him and chose to distance himself. Just as she didn't give Nat the option of letting them find their way together so too did Carlos run away due to fear.

"Everyone loved you. Loves you." Becks started and stopped. Nat was extending an olive branch, and the only way it could grow into a thriving tree was honesty and respect. "But, you're right. We lost sight of what was best about each other. How we could encourage each other's strengths and help us to be the best people we could be."

The fluttering in her stomach eased, and she could breathe easier.

"You're beautiful inside and out, you know." Nat nudged her head toward Becks until the two touched.

Becks laughed. "And your sense of humor is second only to mine."

Nat's giggles were like echoes of her own. "Sounds like we're starting the mutual fan club again. Want the first meeting to come to order and center around what had you so contemplative on the swing?"

"Only if the next meeting takes place at The Busy Bean over coffee, and we talk about you."

Nat squeezed her tight. "That's a date. I'm asking because I love you, you little lug."

That love radiated from Nat's whole self and Becks felt it clear through to her heart. No halfway measures for Nat, something they had in common. "Love you, too. And the truth is Frederick Whitley made me an offer for the land, at the complex, and it's too good to refuse, but…" Her throat clogged.

"But what? I sense you don't want to sell."

"It feels like quitting."

"How so?" Nat prodded, but in a good way that Becks needed.

"There are situations where you walk away and know it's right—" Nat nodded, and Becks continued "—but this doesn't feel like one of those times. I feel like I have unfinished business."

Nat hugged her and squealed. "It's called intuition, and it means you're listening to yourself. Isn't it wonderful?"

Becks cringed as a little bonding went a long way in one night. "It might be wonderful if I only had myself to consider, but there's Pippa."

"Don't worry. It'll…"

"All work out in the end." Becks finished her twin's sentence for her, and they laughed.

They rounded the corner and found themselves on Main Street. They'd been talking so long, Becks hadn't even realized how far they'd walked. The glittering white lights strung overhead twinkled in the darkness. Nat strolled beside her, and they paused outside Miss Louise's Ice Cream Parlor. "I love milkshakes in December." Nat smiled at the storefront.

"I prefer hot apple cider."

Natalie hugged her twin. "I know. Isn't that perfect? We like the same things…"

"Just in different months." Becks finished another of Nat's sentences, and it was as if the years had melted away. If time could bring a new dimension to her relationship with her twin, was it time to start afresh with Carlos?

"That brow just became very serious. What else is wrong?" Nat lingered at the menu posted on the window for another second. She licked her lips and then resumed walking. "Unless I miss my mark, I'd be willing to bet a peppermint milkshake against a hot apple cider this has something to do with a certain firefighter who's sporting a lime-green cast."

The twinkle lights gave way to antique bronze lamps that gave off an ambient glow, the perfect backdrop for the rugged mountaintops surrounding the small town. They headed back toward Nat's house now, the silence comfortable yet pointed until Becks found her voice again. "I owe you a milkshake."

"I'll hold you to that, but what's going on between you and Carlos?"

"After last night, nothing."

"What happened?" Nat squeezed her arm reassuringly.

Becks kicked a pine cone off the sidewalk and halted, not believing her eyes. Some people decorated with lights and wreaths, but Hyacinth Hennessy not only did up her house but also covered her lawn with an assortment of holiday bird feeders and wind chimes, creating a nature's playground. They stopped to enjoy it before continuing their walk. Becks's grin faded at how her evening with Carlos ended so badly.

"I'm having a hard time letting go of how he ended everything." When he asked for his grandmother's ring back, Nat had returned it for her along with a good chunk of Becks's heart. It wasn't until Becks had seen Carlos at the soccer complex in his firefighting gear that she realized she'd never resolved her feelings for him.

"I can see where that would be hard for you."

"He's not as easy to get over as I thought."

Her sister's house was once again in sight, and Nat pulled her back to the rope swing Aidan connected to the large oak in their front yard. She and Nat sat side by side. "Maybe it's not that you have to get over what he did as much as you need to ask yourself if you want him in your life now and in what way."

The porchlight flickered on, and Nat jumped off the swing. "That's our cue although I'm sure Aidan already had everything in precise military order, better than when we left."

Nat's observation penetrated deep and opened something Becks would have preferred closed. Last night, Carlos had come close to kissing her, and yet he backed away, a furrow of confusion and hurt on his brow after she brought up how Pippa rarely made the same mistake twice. Becks grasped the rope attached to the swing and twisted it until her hands burned. He thought she'd called him a mistake.

Good thing he was scheduled for a physical therapy session in two days, a perfect time to clear the air.

# CHAPTER TWELVE

IN THE HALLWAY of Hollydale Middle School, Carlos bumped his mobility scooter against the row of gray metal lockers outside the classroom where his new brother-in-law Javier was substitute teaching. He and Gisele were currently living with Mami and Papa along with Javier's preteen daughter, Marisol.

Talking to students about Christmas lights with frayed cords and pet safety wasn't what he had in mind in terms of scaling back on his commitments. Earlier today, Carlos entered the fire station with every intention of broaching the subject of strategic long-term planning, or even inventory, along with an update on Ned's investigation. Instead, Roberto recruited him for the holiday home safety lecture. He couldn't say no.

Javier stuck his head outside the classroom door and waved Carlos inside. "The kids are so ready for the holiday break, and having a substitute doesn't help, but they should cooperate."

Carlos smiled and connected his laptop so his PowerPoint slides were projected onto the whiteboard at the front of the class. Over the next fifteen minutes, he drew out some of the students. By the end of the presentation, the students were laughing and voluntarily answering his questions. The bell rang, and they started pouring out of the room, ready for the long day to end. Javier dipped his head at Carlos.

"Are you sure you're not a teacher? You handled the class today like a pro."

"Thanks, but this is part of my job. I do this every year."

Javier gathered the textbooks on his desk. "I'm not saying this off the cuff. You have a real rapport with middle school students. That's an accomplishment in and of itself."

*Teaching.* Was that another way of giving back to the community if his ankle didn't heal? The prospect of quitting firefighting left a sour taste in his mouth, just like when he was a kid and his mom warned him about being a better brother. Back then, he'd thought his mother's request was taller than Mount Mitchell, the highest point in North Carolina. His and Graciela's relationship became stronger when he listened to her and put the time in to understand her hopes and dreams. Maybe it was time he got back to his old habits.

Three girls headed his way, and he lowered himself back into the uncomfortable hard plastic chair. He recognized his niece Marisol but didn't recognize the student with the long brown hair with purple nail polish, although she looked familiar, or her friend with the short blond hair.

"Thanks for sticking around," Carlos said. "Do you have any questions for me or for Mr. Lopez?"

"I'm Vanessa, and my family has the cutest labradoodle named Daisy. She's the sweetest." The blonde kept talking about her pet until the brunette nudged her. "Sorry, Firefighter Ramirez. Everyone says I tend to talk a lot, but I wanted to know more about what you said regarding dogs and poisonous stuff. Can you repeat what's bad for dogs?"

"Poinsettias get a bad rep, and they're mildly poisonous, but you need to really watch out for holly berries and rosemary plants. Those wouldn't be good for Daisy." Carlos could recite the list in his sleep and smiled at the trio. "And if you have cats, try to leave some space on the tree so they can't chew the ornaments or the electrical cord. Any other questions?"

"Thanks, but Rachel and I have to run. We're taking a babysitting class at the community center where my stepmom works." Vanessa pulled on Rachel's arm and dragged her toward the classroom exit.

"Hi, Aunt Becks," Rachel said.

Carlos's ears pricked up at the sound of the familiar name.

In less than a second, he registered Becks's presence at the archway. Her gaze met his, and his chest tightened at how beautiful she looked even in the harsh glow of the school's fluorescent lighting. He was drawn to that red hair the way a moth was to a flame. They'd had so much fun decorating the tree this past weekend, and that type of happiness didn't come along every day.

"Becks." While he wanted to jump to his feet and run over to her, that wouldn't be wise in light of his doctor's advice.

"Ms. Porter." Javier turned off the overhead projector and opened the desk drawer, pulling out a woman's black handbag. "I believe this is yours."

"Call me Becks." She sent a warm smile his way. "Thank you. I've been to four classrooms looking for it."

Marisol went up to her, an awestruck look

on her face. "I can't believe Becks Harrison lives in the same town as me."

Javier handed Becks her purse and pointed at Marisol. "My daughter and I just moved to Hollydale to live closer to my wife's family. Marisol and I saw you play in California."

"It was the first professional game I ever attended." Marisol had a happy but slightly dreamy look in her eyes.

That awestruck look resembled how Carlos felt whenever he was near Becks, but if he let himself, this flickering attraction could maybe grow into something real and substantial.

But Becks thought being with him was a mistake. Could he change her perception of him so she could see the man he was now? Someone who wouldn't be so foolish as to throw away the best thing in his life.

"I hope my team won." Becks's blue eyes glinted with amusement before her mouth formed an O. "You must be Gisele's husband and stepdaughter. It's a pleasure to meet you."

Javier nodded. "Yes to both."

"Hey, Marisol," Rachel yelled from across the classroom before turning bright pink. "Georgie's waiting for us in the car line since she's driving us to the community center. Come on."

Marisol turned toward Becks. "Do you accept payment plans for soccer lessons? I'm taking a babysitting class and once I find some work, I'll be able to pay you, but I spent my money on Christmas presents."

"I'm sure we can work something out. Let me talk to your father." Becks waved at Rachel. "Hey kiddo, give Georgie and your dad a nudge from me."

"Will do, Aunt Becks." Rachel smiled, showing off her braces with purple bands. "Can I practice babysitting on Pippa?"

Becks laughed. "That sounds ominous, but send me a text and we'll arrange something."

The Harrison family was as close as his although at times when he and Becks dated in high school and college, his family had ruffled Becks's feathers from how close they were. Now the more mature Becks was embracing her family. It was good to see.

"Thanks." The three girls left together, giggling and chatting.

"Ms. Porter." Javier faced Becks. "I wouldn't mind knowing if you offer any type of payment plans. Marisol loves soccer, and this would make a wonderful Christmas present."

Carlos hadn't known what to get his new

niece, but Graciela and he could surely go in together for the gift. He opened his mouth, but Becks beat him to the punch. "I'll work something out with Amara, she's the registrar, and get back to you. Having Marisol at the academy would be awesome."

Javier opened his laptop and sat behind the desk. "You're coming to our welcome dinner that Carlos is organizing, right?"

*Good grief.* This surprise party was the worst kept secret in Hollydale.

Becks pushed her purse strap to her shoulder before turning to Carlos. "I wouldn't want to intrude on a family dinner."

Her blue eyes clouded, and he reassured her. "You're more than welcome at the party, Becks."

She nodded and backed away. "I'll think about it. Oh, and I'll see you tomorrow for our session. No canceling this time."

Before he could update her on the newest setback, she left the classroom, and he no longer could say what needed to get out into the open.

If they agreed hydrotherapy was the best route for him, they no longer had a common purpose holding them together. Tomorrow that connection would come to an end. Part of recovery was a strong support system. While his family was the foundation, Becks was becoming the part of the support that held him up.

Without her, his heart would be as damaged as his ankle.

And same as his ankle, the damage might be permanent and irrevocable.

WITH AN HOUR until she was due to pick up Pippa at Nat's, Becks lingered at the soccer complex. The pitch at the middle school earlier today went better than expected, but dread crept into her stomach at the upcoming conversation. She'd known Dante and Amara since college, each standout athletes with Dante a star midfielder on the men's soccer team and Amara a gifted gymnast. They'd moved to Hollydale for these jobs and to deepen Amara's connection with her grandmother, Miss Louise. It was one thing when her pride got the better of her and it only affected her; letting her coworkers and teammates down, however, left a deep wound.

She only had a few days remaining on Frederick Whitley's offer that would reimburse her original asking price. Her employees and friends deserved to know she was leaning toward accepting it.

She paused when a text chimed on her phone. Up on the screen popped the date and time of the Ramirez family get-together, taking place next week. A second later, another bubble popped up from Carlos, adding how much he wanted her there.

Her heartbeat accelerated, and her skin warmed as she reread the text. Everything was happening so fast. All those years ago, she'd fallen in love with him the minute he brushed the black lock of hair off his forehead and introduced himself on the soccer field.

Two years older than her, he'd been the epitome of calm unlike her more impulsive self. She tended to kick first and think later whereas methodical Carlos was always calculating angles and would gladly sacrifice glory for the good of the team. When they started dating in high school, she fell for the way he valued tradition while she tended toward whatever was shiny and new.

And yet he'd been the one to break up with her, going from happily-ever-after to a cold future in mere minutes. And she'd never been quite the same. His recently mending those pieces of her broken heart felt a little overwhelming, like the pace of their new friendship in light of everything swirling around her, most of it a direct result of the fire.

She walked from one room to the other in the administrative building, cleared for business once more. The indoor fields, concession area and party zones in the prefab steel building were progressing, but the construction crew had taken the afternoon off since the electrician couldn't be here until tomorrow. At least they'd made progress with the smoke damage, the reports encouraging, but not enough to stop her from considering Whitley's offer.

Amara greeted Becks. "Hey there. We've had three new registrations today, and me and Dante found out we're having a baby boy. I received a clean bill of health after that indigestion scare."

"That's great." Her spirits soared and she hugged Amara.

Then Becks returned to earth. She still had to tell them. Anything else would be unfair.

"Except we also had four cancellations." Amara rubbed her belly, the swell more noticeable with each passing day. "Sorry this little guy isn't older or you'd have one more on your roster."

"I'm guessing she's told you the news." Dante smiled and approached Amara to slip an arm around her.

"Since you're both here, I have some news."

"Let me go first." Dante smiled and settled into a chair next to Amara in the conference room. "While Amara updated the website, I contacted sportswriters I know in Asheville. As soon as the indoor complex is ready, they'll feature it online and in print. Today, I cranked out press releases and we updated our session schedules with Amara's new numbers."

"They're better than they seem, and with this new push for publicity, we'll be back on track for the spring session, right before this little one makes his appearance." Amara concluded with a flourish.

"We've picked out his name. Keon Louis Jones." Dante gave Amara a fist bump, then held out his fist to Becks. "Teamwork at its best."

She inhaled, not wanting to ruin the holidays, but they needed to know. "I've had an offer for the land."

Dante withdrew his hand, his gaze critical. "You can't throw in the towel without even really trying. You were relentless on the field. You should be that way about the complex. That's why we jumped at your job offer. We've put our hearts into this place for the past few weeks."

"I am trying. And I do love the changes you've made." Becks wanted more than anything to be a responsible employer, to be a responsible everything and show she'd turned a new leaf. That she'd quit her leap first and ask questions later rule. If she couldn't, selling would be her best option.

Amara rubbed her baby bump. "We can make it through this. We've experienced hard times before."

"But soon the coffers could be empty, and I'd never want to miss paying your salaries. You deserve to have some security, especially with the baby coming. There only seems to be one way to salvage a win at this point. Sell the complex to Whitley. I have to decide right away."

Amara pulled Dante away, and they departed. Becks followed and felt like an interloper watching them hug while they stood next to their car. To have someone through thick and thin, that was everything. Someone to discuss the easy times with along with the rougher patches.

Dare she trust Carlos and tell him about the offer, factoring his advice into her decision, let alone into her heart.

The last time she spoke to him about major life changes, though, he'd called off their engagement. In the past few weeks, though, she'd seen another, different side of him. This time might be different.

Dante opened the door for Amara as another car, a red sports car she didn't recognize with a red ball for Rudolph's nose attached to the front bumper and brown fuzzy antlers attached on each side window, appeared out of nowhere. Dante stilled, and Becks headed outside with the express intention of sending the driver on their way. The complex was closed, most likely for good.

The Ferrari pulled in next to Becks's car, and a woman in her sixties with cropped silver hair emerged. Becks rubbed her eyes. "Tricia?"

"Retirement's overrated." Trim and tanned, Tricia smiled and shut her door, her aviator sunglasses masking her eyes. "Becks, you look terrible."

The irony of Tricia's pronouncement wasn't lost on Becks. "Says the woman who looks fabulous after how many hours in an airplane?"

"Eleven, but who's counting?" Tricia waved her hand, her rainbow scarf complementing her navy coat. She turned her attention to Dante and Amara. "I never forget a soccer player. Dante Jones, right?" After his nod of acknowledgment, she tapped her forehead. "Wait a second, and it'll come to me. You were on the gymnastics team, right? Amara Boudreaux? Your vaults were expressions of beauty."

Amara dipped her head in a sweet show of modesty. "That's one amazing memory there and thank you for the compliment. I'm Amara Jones now. Dante and I married a few years ago."

Tricia glanced at the buildings, then the soccer pitches and frowned. "I thought you were further along with your business."

Tricia never did waste time mincing words.

"Let's see. A fire, two employees down and half the sign-ups canceled." Becks winced at the bitterness in her voice. She'd fought so hard to dial that back the past few years.

And now after another disappointment, she was falling into her old habits.

Tricia whipped off her sunglasses and sent

Becks that same look that inspired fight in her players for the past forty years. "So, what have you done to set it right?"

That wasn't the question she'd expected to hear. Then again, Tricia also didn't believe in sugarcoating a situation. "I'm entertaining an offer for the sale of the complex."

"Bah, humbug." Tricia shook her head and kept that glare red-hot. "Good thing I arrived when I did. After I disembarked, I talked to the director of Kick, Goal and Score, and he'll be here next week."

Tricia strode toward the grassy playing area, and the three others followed her. "But I have to accept an offer on the land by Christmas, or the price drops," Becks said. That sentence left a vile taste in her mouth.

"Once a Mountaineer, always a Mountaineer." That was their college nickname. "You're made of strong stuff, Harrison. We have a week to set to impress. When will your indoor facility be able to open?"

"Not until after the New Year. The crew's eliminated the smoke residue, but the code updates and partitions aren't finished yet." As it was, one more overage on the estimate along with the prospect of the fines from the final report were enough reasons to accept Whitley's offer. "But Kick, Goal and Score won't be able to look at the indoor fields."

"We can work around that." Tricia bent down and felt the grassy fescue mix in her fingers. "Once they see you and hear how determined you are, I'm confident they'll agree to sponsor Mountain Vista by next week."

"You can't be sure of that, and they haven't been forthcoming with me." Especially, given how it had taken someone of Tricia's stature for the company to finally agree to a visit.

"That's distressing to hear. What about Team4Life?" The dynamo straightened and started back toward her car, and Becks was almost suffering from whiplash from Tricia's speed. "Considering your teammate Claire Esposito started it, you should consider it."

"We've been in touch. She's explained her philosophy and I like the idea of a new alternative soccer league that takes a holistic approach to sports. That a coach and team should focus on mental health, nutrition and competition." Relatively new, Team4Life didn't have the connections or sponsorship potential to fund more intensive summer camps and other competitive opportunities as Kick, Goal and Score. Reluctantly, Becks had glossed over the details Claire had sent her. "I like the approach, but Kick, Goal and Score is a proven entity with a traveling league and alumni who've competed at the highest amateur levels and on professional teams. Affiliation with them will bring us lots of clients."

Tricia pressed her key fob and retrieved a brochure from her purse. Amara stuck out her hand and grasped it before Becks could. "Claire's expecting your call."

*Of course she was.* "You're making my decision hard."

"Good."

"I like this approach. Look, Dante." Amara pointed at something, and Dante squeezed her shoulders while looking at the brochure.

Tricia yawned. "I'm staying at the Eight Gables tonight and leaving for my home in Durham early tomorrow morning, but I'll be back after that. It's only a three-hour drive. Listen to Claire with an open mind."

"This could be the start of something good," Dante said.

Amara nodded.

"Another facility will booster Claire's efforts, and the two of you can help each other grow and bring in needed revenue," Tricia said.

Becks smiled and realized how good it felt to have hope again. A few weeks ago as she watched the flames of the fire lick at the complex, she'd felt overwhelmed as her dreams went up in smoke. Now, though, there must be something about the holidays bringing a new sense of excitement. That, along with this group supporting her, caring about her and the complex. Something dangerously close to the hope embraced her once more. "I'll set up a meeting with her."

"Good. You do that."

They all said their goodbyes since Tricia insisted she wanted an early night with no fuss and no dinner out at a restaurant. Her jet lag had caught up with her. Ready to head to Nat's, Becks headed to her office for her purse and work tablet. Cutting her losses and selling would still be the smart and sensible decision, for her and Pippa.

Mixed up and confused, she needed to consider her options.

First, she'd best let Nat know she was running a few minutes late. Picking up her cell, she stared at Carlos's text. If she accepted Whitley's offer, she'd have to decline the invitation to the Ramirez family celebration. She wasn't sure she could face Gisele and Javier considering how she'd be letting Marisol down. Regardless of what happened with the complex, she wanted to help Carlos rehab his ankle.

But could she? If she let his family down, how would he feel about seeing her so often? Her head pounded with the decisions around her.

As if on cue, Carlos texted, asking her once more if she was coming.

Rather than sending messages back and forth, Becks called him.

"Hi, Becks." He sounded happy to hear her voice. "You have perfect timing. I've been working hard on the final details for the Firefighter's Christmas Festival and need a break."

"Sounds like you wanted a distraction more than an answer about the dinner." She reached for a binder with a new set of plays and threw it into her tote bag.

"You're never a distraction."

She realized she was smiling thanks to him. "Is everything coming along with the festival?"

"Thankfully Ned Grayson and his wife stepped up at the last minute. It wouldn't have been the same without a visit from Santa and Mrs. Claus. Your ad looks great in the program. I have a special copy for you."

"I'd stop now at the fire station to pick it up except I'm running late to get Pippa, and I promised we'd decorate our gingerbread house tonight." She chuckled at the memory of Pippa covered in flour when they'd baked the gingerbread. "I'll see you tomorrow for your PT session."

"Hold on a sec. I texted you for an answer. Can I mark you as my plus-one?"

His buoyancy lifted her spirits, lightening her load and making her laugh. *His plus-one.* There was something romantic and anticipatory about that phrase. Like she was his date for the celebration. Being his plus-one on a permanent basis? A quiver shivered down her spine at the joy that would bring into her life before she quashed it cold. Pippa and she were a team, and she'd never be flying solo again. "That was the reason I'm calling, but I'd be a plus-two at this point, and that wouldn't be fair to your family."

He laughed. "Have you met my mother? She'd love to have Pippa there. She wants me to settle down so she can spoil grandchildren."

Jealousy at Carlos ending up with someone else sparked something deep in her, and she quickly diffused the flame. "How's the weather? I hope the streets are clear for driving."

She waited until she could bear the silence no longer. "Carlos?"

"I was hoping to tell you this in person."

Apprehension crept into her. "Tell me now."

"I want a partner, Becks, and not just a mother for any future children. Someone I can trust and who can, in turn, trust in me. I want someone who knows I love red velvet cake, not someone my mother chooses with a perception of my twelve-year-old self."

The heartfelt emotion in his voice floored her.

"Sounds like you know exactly what you want." That type of certainty had always been her hallmark. When did she lose sight of herself? More to the point, was she finally regaining that sense of self gone for too long?

"Spending a lot of time at my desk lately has given me the time to map out every path and reflect on each of them." A short pause and they both seemed to need a beat.

"I'll give the dinner some more thought." Reflection was never her strong suit, but Carlos had a way of getting under her skin and thinking in terms she'd never considered before.

Hanging up, Becks considered calling him back and inviting him to join her and Pippa for the decorating. She stopped herself. Trust was hard to win back once lost. They hadn't made it all those years ago, and he'd damaged her heart. She had also lost trust in herself, leading to a series of bad choices.

Protecting her heart was a must while she made the best possible decision about the property, for her sake and for Pippa's.

# CHAPTER THIRTEEN

CARLOS HELD HIS cell in his hand, unsure of whether to call Becks back again. She expected him for his session tomorrow where he'd have to come clean about Dr. Patel's new prognosis and that it'd have to be scaled-back physical therapy until further notice. He adjusted the pillow so his left leg was elevated a touch more.

His reticence over telling Becks ate at him. He had to let her know about his appointment at the therapy clinic, but this type of news wasn't something he should communicate over a phone call. The shiny program for the Firefighter's Christmas Festival stared at him from the desk. Now, he had the perfect excuse to stop by Becks's house tonight.

A knock made him glance up, and Ned stuck his head around the training room door. "Got a minute?"

"Yes, sir." Carlos kept from wincing at how hard his cast hit the industrial beige floor, but the anticipation of finding out the investigation results overtook the twinge of pain in his stubbed toe. "Is the investigation concluded?"

"Almost, but not quite." His boss frowned, and Carlos pushed away any dread about the report's conclusion.

"Then let me give you a quick update on what I've been doing. I started the review of the Hazardous Material training guide yesterday. I should have my recommendations for changes done by the middle of January."

"Not a small task, but a necessary one." Ned walked in and settled in a plastic chair.

"Yes, sir."

"That's not why I stopped by. Leigh and I are heading to Richmond tomorrow. Leigh's grandmother is in the ICU. We planned to fly out Sunday after the festival, but the only flight she could get leaves in the morning. I'll be returning on Monday for the holiday shifts and for the final touches on the investigation."

Ned's words hit Carlos, and he stared at the battalion chief. "Then you won't be able to play Santa, and Leigh can't be Mrs. Claus." And the report wouldn't be concluded before then either.

Ned nodded, his forehead creasing. "Sorry

about the short notice, but Leigh's grandmother is eighty-three, and…"

"Say no more. Family first." His gaze landed on the program. "And I have the perfect replacement in mind for Mrs. Claus."

Now if he could only convince Becks of his idea.

FOR THE SIXTH time in a row, the walls of the gingerbread house collapsed, and Becks planted her face on the table. Pippa giggled and clapped her hands. "Again."

Somehow Becks lifted her head for one more try. She couldn't let Pippa down, and she had something to prove to herself as well, even if it was gingerbread.

Becks reached for the bowl of royal icing when the doorbell alerted her to someone at the front door. Gomez and Morticia barked and ran to the foyer. She frowned, not expecting anyone this Thursday evening. "Stay here, and guard the icing and the gingerbread house."

She hurried to peek through the peephole and found Carlos waiting on her front porch. Her heart did a funny leap at how his black sweater set off his tawny skin and black hair, taking on more of a slight wave with the longer length. She opened the door, and he gazed at her like she was the most important person in Hollydale, if not anywhere. The feeling was mutual and so strong that it nearly took her breath away.

"You have something in your hair." He entered using a mobility scooter instead of crutches. Before she could sneak a look in the closest mirror, he reached up and pulled out a glob of white royal icing from her hair.

So much for her assumption about that gleam in his eyes. "Thanks. What brings you by tonight?"

"I have your program."

"You could have brought this to me tomorrow at your PT session." She flipped through the pages until she found the complex's ad and squealed before it hit her. People might see this and sign up. She'd disappoint them when she pulled out of the venture. This only complicated her decision, and the deadline was looming. "It turned out fabulous. Thank you."

Gomez and Morticia crowded around her, and she invited Carlos in rather than risk having the dogs run out onto the street.

Carlos sniffed and headed toward the kitchen. "Something smells delicious."

"I'm baking a pork chop and sliced apple casserole while Pippa and I are building a gingerbread house, except I can't get the walls to stay up. Don't suppose you know anything about building gingerbread houses?"

"As a matter of fact, I'm an expert."

Pippa spotted Carlos and clapped. "Mr. Carlos!"

"Pippa!" He navigated his way to the chair next to the toddler, and she hugged him. Then he sat, pushing his scooter under the table. Morticia wagged her tail and nudged her head under his hand for some attention. Gomez stayed closer to Becks and Pippa.

He studied the four walls of the gingerbread house, flat against the silicone mat near the gumdrops and other decorations.

He reached for a wall and stopped. Becks sensed his hesitation and tried to keep the mood light.

"I was just about to check my phone for gingerbread experts, but since you claim to be one, you've saved me from choosing someone who might turn out to be a dud."

Carlos laughed and shook his head. "You don't need me to save you. You never have."

Their gazes met, and that might have been a reason they never worked in the past. She didn't need saving. That wasn't her personality. Never would be, and yet Carlos lived for duty and helping others. They mixed together like oil and water.

But didn't the strongest relationships flourish by not taking away from the other's personality but supporting one another? Look at Natalie and Aidan. Her twin and her brother-in-law were opposites with his stiffness in staunch contrast to her sister's sunniness. Same with her brother Mike, who was more gregarious than his wife, Georgie. Becks wanted a real relationship like that, if she dared to take a chance and trust someone again. If she let him, Carlos could provide the cornerstone of such a foundation.

Memories of the past haunted her once again, and she questioned her judgment. There was so much at stake now. She'd accept his help with the gingerbread house, and that would have to be all she could accept from him.

The silence drew out, and she reached for a wall, intent on one night of merriment. "Well, I need your help saving this gingerbread house and letting it fulfill its holiday destiny."

He flexed his arm muscle, the slight bulge attracting Becks's eye. That building attraction roared to life. "Then I best put this to use." He then tapped his forehead. "Along with this."

While the pork chop and apple casserole baked in the oven and the dogs played outside, she, Carlos and Pippa laughed and assembled their version of a gingerbread house. Carlos hadn't exaggerated, and the finished product was pretty and colorful with icing swirled on the rooftop holding the gumdrops and hard candy in place. Becks let the dogs inside, and Gomez and Morticia darted for their food dishes.

During dinner, she couldn't remember the last time an evening had passed so quickly. *Oh, wait.* It was the night a few weeks ago when Carlos helped decorate the tree. She loaded the dishwasher and returned to the dining room. "Are you sure you don't need to be somewhere else?"

Carlos met her gaze, those brown eyes deep and telling. "I'm right where I want to be, Becks."

Sparks flew across the room, warming her skin, and she stilled.

They couldn't make it when life was easier, back when she didn't have a business to get off the ground and there were no broken ankles casting doubt over an uncertain future.

So far, she hadn't seen anything to indicate this time would be different.

She gulped and switched her focus to Pippa, royal icing in her child's hair and a smidgen of pork chop casserole on her cheek. "Bath time, Pippa." She faced Carlos. "I'll be at the community center at seven, if that still works for you."

She swooped over and pulled Pippa into her arms, nuzzling her daughter's stomach with her nose, making raspberry noises. When she looked up, Carlos was still there, his gaze guarded as if he was holding something back. Self-conscious, she blinked. "Do I have icing in my hair again?"

He glided over on his scooter and touched her hair, Pippa in between them; her breath caught in her throat. His warm fingers gave her goose bumps as he pulled at something and then held it out. "A gumdrop."

"I always liked to be different."

"I know."

The air felt charged with electricity, and she wanted to prolong this minute, this connection, but a squirming Pippa got in the way. "It's getting late, and tomorrow will dawn bright and early." She cringed at how she was stating the obvious. Was he making her this flustered?

Was that a bad thing?

"If you have a few minutes after she goes to

bed." He tickled Pippa's tummy. "I'd like to stay and talk."

"Sure."

After Pippa's bath, Becks read Pippa a bedtime story while Gomez and Morticia hovered at the edge of the bed as if listening. She kissed Pippa good-night and was about to turn out the light when she caught sight of Carlos at the doorway, dark circles smudged under his eyes.

She joined him before switching off the light, Pippa's half-moon night-light transmitting a golden glow. "Make yourself comfortable while I tend to the dogs and settle them for the night."

She let Gomez and Morticia outside one last time before they went into their crates. When she could stall no longer, she found Carlos in the living room, staring at the tree, the scent of pine filling the air. The twinkling LED lights bathed the room in a whirl of bright color.

"Have you checked the water today? Real trees are a safety hazard if precautions aren't taken."

Becks nodded. "Yes, and we didn't overload the lights." She sat on the couch, and he unstrapped his mobility scooter before settling next to her, his citrusy aftershave complementing the aroma of the Fraser fir. She reached for his hand. "Thanks for being concerned about Pippa and me."

The ambience of the holiday season heightened her awareness of him, not as Carlos the teenager, her first love, but as the Carlos who'd stepped in and helped her and Pippa find a tree, who'd laughed over another gingerbread wall collapse, who smelled wonderful. A potent combination of strong masculinity and sweetness.

She shivered and stared at the fireplace, the hope of the holiday season creeping in, making her believe this time they would thrive even in the midst of all the chaos around them.

He must have thought she was cold as he curled his arm around her. Should she correct his misperception? These shivers had nothing to do with her surroundings and everything to do with his nearness.

Then he stiffened and moved his arm away. "Becks."

He sounded ominous like he wanted to revisit the past again. She wasn't sure she wanted to rehash that anymore, not with an unsettled future ahead of both of them. She kept her tone light. "Yes, oh wise gingerbread architect."

"I need a favor."

*All you had to do was ask.* His words came back to her. Out of that earlier tension came a slow burning friendship, and the thought of something more terrified and excited her at the same time. "Is that why you brought the program over?"

"Seeing you is motivation enough." He smiled, and her heartbeat sped.

Would his kisses be as potent now as when they were younger? There was no denying the pull between them, and she reveled at his features. The slight bend of his nose, the thick stubble, the wide-set eyes that had seen devastation she didn't even want to imagine yet still held a quiet strength and determination.

She licked her lips and nodded. "Yes."

"Will you be my wife on Saturday?"

Her eyes widened, and her mouth slackened at the question that was far more than a favor. *Carlos's wife.* She never saw herself married again, but wasn't as opposed to the idea as she thought she'd be. Then she realized there was no ring, no bending down on one knee like the first proposal, not that he should kneel with a broken ankle anyway. Something wasn't right. "Isn't that the day of the Firefighter's Christmas Festival?"

His cheeks reddened, and he hung his head. "Santa and Mrs. Claus had a family emergency. Everyone I've asked has other commitments."

*His wife on Saturday.* Acting the part, not living the part. Her heartbeat started returning to normal. He wasn't asking to marry her. She willed away the disappointment she shouldn't be feeling, considering how little time they'd spent together. "Let me see." She pulled out her phone and checked her schedule. "I'm working at the soccer booth in the morning, and then I promised Pippa a carriage ride in the afternoon."

"Can't blame a guy for trying." He smiled and reached for his scooter.

With the complex's future up in the air, she shouldn't even be setting up the booth, but somehow the thought of selling Mountain Vista, without giving every drop of sweat and spirit into the venture, ripped her apart. Besides, she didn't have to take anyone's payment until she was sure the academy was a go. Maybe she hadn't accepted Whitley's offer yet because doing so would be admitting defeat. For too long, she'd let circumstances and others affect her. Starting now, she had to take a stand.

That should begin with putting her best foot forward period.

"Hold on a second." She started texting. "Let me see if we can make this happen."

In seconds, she heard back from Nat, who agreed to take her shift at the soccer table. "One problem solved, and I'm sure my mom will watch Pippa."

"I'll need breaks because of my ankle. There will be plenty of time for you and Pippa to get your carriage ride." That mischievous glint returned. "So you'll be Mrs. Claus?"

"I'll even memorize the names of the eight reindeer and twelve days of Christmas by Saturday morning. I see why you wanted to ask me tonight. I might have worked your ankle so hard tomorrow morning, you'd have forgotten to mention it."

That glint faded, and he leaned back on the couch. "I can't make it tomorrow."

"Then what time works better for you? Or is the festival the problem? You're swamped with last-minute details. We can have an informal session right now. I'll just make some room." She pushed the coffee table closer to the wall, leaving an open space between the tree and couch. "I'll grab a couple of exercise mats. When I get back, we'll start with relaxing breathing techniques for when everything gets a bit overwhelming."

Come to think of it, maybe the person she needed to practice those calming techniques on was herself.

"Becks."

He ran his hand through his thick dark hair. "I visited Dr. Patel this week, and she's recommending I scale back on the physical therapy for now."

"Why?"

He massaged his left leg. "I might have ligament damage."

That was the second time in the past five minutes he'd knocked the wind from her sails.

"You don't know that for certain, though. You can still come through with flying colors and be back at full duty next year." She'd found solace when her orthopedist delivered similar words during her presurgery consultation, but then the op was a bust and she'd had to end her professional career.

"How do colors fly anyway?" He stopped and collected himself. "I let my pride get in the way. I did something to impress a special someone, and it backfired."

Jealousy rose deep in her throat until his gaze captured hers. He was talking about her. She was that special someone, and his injury must have happened while he was watching Pippa.

The lights from the tree deepened the circles around his eyes, and she longed to give this man who dedicated so much to others a little happiness. "You don't have to hide from me. I know you love red velvet cupcakes and how much you love your work."

"Having a strong sense of our career choices is something we've always had in common. You were good enough to follow your dreams into professional soccer, and I always wanted to follow in my father's footsteps." He tapped the lime-green cast against her textured carpet.

"And I know what it's like to have it disappear in an instant." When it happened, she didn't know which was worse, the physical pain of a failed knee surgery or the emotional pain of her dreams ending. "If we're going to keep talking, you need to elevate your ankle." She dragged the coffee table over for just that purpose and grasped the stack of photo holiday cards. "Mind if I start putting these in envelopes?"

He reached for half. "Only if you let me help."

"You'll save me a stamp if you take yours

with you." She pulled out his envelope and handed him a photo holiday card.

"Thanks. Cute picture of Pippa." He set it aside and glanced at her, his hands still busy at work. "You changed the subject when I brought up the end of your playing days. I remember what you said about the surgery taking a bad turn."

Everything had collapsed on her within a few months. "At first, the surgery seemed to have helped, there was only a small chance that it would, but I had to take it. All the physical therapy sessions really strengthened my knee, but my career was over."

Her knee stiffened, and she rotated it. He stopped stuffing envelopes and squeezed her hand. "And now my firefighting days might be over."

*Because of the fire at her complex.* If he did lose his job, how could she forgive herself for that? How could they build anything with that cloud always hanging over them?

He let go of her hand and stuffed another envelope. "How did you get through the uncertainty? That feeling that you're leaving something unsettled and unfinished."

"You have your family to help you through

this rough patch, and don't cut yourself short. You'll recover." Was it selfish to hope he did not only for his sake, but for hers?

The air around them was so quiet she could hear their breathing. He leaned in, and she worried he could hear the hammering of her heart.

Putting the cart before the horse so to speak wasn't the way to start anything substantial, and she knew he wouldn't settle for anything else. Neither would she.

She scooted away, and he searched her face. "What's happening between us?"

Funny he should ask that when she was always the impulsive one, the fiery one. They'd almost gone over the precipice just now, before reason and caution had intervened. "You and I never had a problem with chemistry, but there's too much left unsaid still."

"And you don't want to make the same mistakes we did when we were younger." He ran his hand through his hair, the dreamy look replaced by one of exasperation. "We have to move beyond our past."

"I thought we had."

"No, you think I'm a mistake."

"I never said anything like that." Now she was exasperated too.

"You said Pippa's good at not repeating her mistakes."

"That's exactly it. I was referring to my daughter, not me." She waited until his face relaxed.

"You were really talking about Pippa?"

She nodded. "Believe me. After you left, I realized my words had a double meaning, and I've been meaning to clear this up. Now you know I wasn't talking about you, right?"

"Yes, and I also realized something. I've never apologized to you. I'm sorry I ended it the way I did, Becca."

His nickname for her. The sound was still as sweet as the first time it fell from his lips. "You're still the only person who calls me that."

"Do you mind?"

"Not from you. Apology accepted."

"Thanks."

He gave her a smile and reached for his mobility scooter.

"See you Saturday, Mrs. Claus."

"Until then, Santa."

She watched him head down the driveway, making sure he was safe until the headlights of his car faded from view.

If Santa were real, would she ask him for another chance with Carlos? She shook her head, too aware she needed to shut down a second chance with the firefighter who was staking a claim on her heart.

# CHAPTER FOURTEEN

"I'M GOING TO freeze out there." Becks stared at the red velvet dress with the flared skirt that only came to her knees.

In the tent for the organizers at the Firefighter's Christmas Festival, Graciela stepped back and tilted her head. She grabbed three safety pins. "You look fabulous. If I had your legs, I wouldn't be complaining."

Graciela placed two pins in her mouth and reached behind Becks, pulling the fabric together.

"If I had your coat, I wouldn't be complaining. I don't think the cold weather will keep anyone away from the fun today." A pinch at her waist made Becks cry out, "Ouch!"

"If you'd quit moving, I could pin this. You're about three inches taller than Leigh, and I need to tuck in the waist. There, all done." Graciela moved to her side and nodded. "Besides, I've been an elf at Santa's Workshop before. You run so much you don't have time to get cold. Hollydale's always busy the last week-end before Christmas."

Becks touched the fuzzy white angora trim. "What happened to a long dress with an apron and a gray wig?"

"I'm merely the seamstress. Leigh Grayson ordered this and left it with me before she departed for Richmond. All she said when she handed me the box was that she wanted a more contemporary feel." Graciela tapped her watch. "I have to get to the shelter to bring over the pets for fostering opportunities. That's something new I've implemented. I'll be taking over Santa's Workshop from twelve until two for pet pictures with Santa. Carlos said your parents are bringing Pippa and Gomez and Morticia for photos." Her face scrunched up and she frowned. "Oops, that was supposed to be a Christmas surprise."

As Becks waved her thanks and then strolled away toward the gazebo, she wondered what else Carlos had said about her to Graciela.

Then she caught sight of Hollydale's downtown merchants pulling together to make the most of the season and she let herself be carried away by the holiday spirit. The Firefighter's Christmas Festival had grown into an all-day community event. This year the theme was Santa's Workshop, and there were three huge displays of mannequin elves working on toys, snowmen helpers delivering toys to sleds and animatronic reindeer about to take off with a countdown clock behind them.

Vendors were finishing last-minute preparations. She passed a cookie decorating booth, and next to it, her friend Kris was helping her mother Deb with the final touches on their beverage stand. Becks waved and kept walking. The information booth hawked a scavenger hunt and promised a prize to those returning a completed bingo sheet. Brooke waved from the Whitley Community Center table where visitors could add their names to a giant stocking using glue and glitter that would hang in the center's main foyer.

All the money raised went to a great cause. They'd met their goal for a new fire truck with all the latest add-ons and improvements to replace the thirty-five-year-old standard that was marked for retirement. Additional funds would cover the cost of a special program for handing out basic supplies, as well as blankets and even teddy bears to those in shock at the scene of an emergency.

Nearer the gazebo sat the older utility truck,

ready for kids to climb on board it and have a fun time.

With a smile, Becks kept walking until the sight of the whole gazebo itself took her breath away. Overnight, volunteers transformed it into a gingerbread house that resembled the one sitting on her dining room table. Inside the gazebo was Santa himself surrounded by plump holiday cushions on a special wide bench seat so children would sit next to him rather than on his lap. Behind him on one side stood an enormous decorated tree with gold balls and silver stars. On the other side of Santa was a huge wooden display with names etched into it and teddy bears with firefighter hats at the bottom.

If she didn't know it was Carlos in that costume, she'd have had to check twice. "Look at you!" Her spirits rose in the presence of Santa Claus.

Maybe the magic of Christmas would bring joy into her life, and a little bit of trust, too.

His deep brown eyes gleamed. "I'd rather look at you."

A warmth filled her that had nothing to do with the weather or physical exertion. Instead, it had everything to do with Carlos. He looked at her as though she was special, like she could trust him with her heart.

"Anything for the kids." Carlos gave a loud "ho ho ho."

"They'll love you." And with that Becks gave into the fact she was falling in love with him. How could she not? Carlos cared deeply for everything and everyone around him, and he'd worked hard at expressing his feelings the past few weeks. Opening up was hard for him, and he was now doing just that.

Before she could tell him how proud she was, a young woman wearing an elf costume complete with pointed ears and curly black shoes entered, carrying a large box. "Here's the first batch of stockings for the kids. Hi, you must be Mrs. Claus. I'm Livy, chief elf and photographer." Her curly black hair peeked out from her striped cap. "Since Carlos, I mean Santa, can't walk, your job will be to pass him a stocking when the child, or children, sits down. I snap the picture, and then they confide in Santa what they want for Christmas. Once I get the all clear from the big guy, it's the next child's turn."

"Got it." Her job seemed simple enough, but concern for the strain on Carlos's ankle still niggled at her.

Carlos waved her over and pointed to the large green cloth bag in front of his left foot on the gazebo floor. "I see that look on your face," he said. She tried to relax. "Mason Ruddick brought this over. On the outside it looks like a sack of toys, but inside there's a shelf so I can elevate my ankle during breaks."

"See, I told you your friends and family are behind you." Before Becks could add anything else, the chief elf cleared her throat.

"They're already starting to line up. You might want to get the first stockings ready to hand out. My cousin Jordan, his girlfriend and I stayed up late last night filling them."

Becks turned to Carlos, who shrugged. "Graciela and Jordan got back together."

"Tell me about it." Livy grinned and checked her camera. "All ready here."

The morning passed by in a blur. There were a few grumbles about Santa having to feed his reindeer every fifteen minutes each hour, but Becks and Livy united and made sure all went well. Most of all, though, Becks couldn't help but be impressed at how Carlos handled himself as Santa. He listened to every child with genuine joy while they chatted. He even soothed the toddlers who burst into tears. Whatever he murmured to them in reassurance worked most of the time as those quivering lips almost always turned upward in a huge smile before their parents escorted them away.

Becks reached down for another stocking when two familiar faces entered Santa's Workshop, Pippa's and her father's. Her father sent her a thumbs-up while Pippa ran over to her and hugged Becks's leg before climbing on the big bench by herself.

Then Pippa's eyes widened. "Mr. Carlos! You're Santa Claus?" Her face contorted, and Becks didn't know if she was about to laugh or cry.

"Santa's at the North Pole getting everything ready for the best Christmas ever." Carlos looked around, his gaze narrowed as if he was a spy about to impart top secret information. He leaned over to whisper in Pippa's ear. "I'm his special helper with a direct line to Santa."

Pippa nodded, her features breaking out into a grin. "You're Carlos Claus!"

Becks chuckled, her anxiety disappearing in a flash. *Carlos Claus*. The name suited him as much as his surroundings. He'd find a way to help the community whether or not it was as a firefighter or doing something else if his ligament damage was too serious for him to continue at the station. Perhaps teaching? Today and last week proved he had a rapport with children of all ages.

Carlos handed her daughter a stocking, and reached out for Becks. "You should be in this photo with your daughter."

Normally Becks would only want Santa and Pippa together, but the Mrs. Claus outfit changed everything. "One with Mrs. Claus, and one without me."

Livy snapped both pictures.

"What do you want for Christmas, Pippa?" He smiled while Becks moved close enough to hear whatever Pippa might mention.

Her daughter tapped her fingers against her chin. "Bones for the doggies."

Carlos nodded, and his gaze met Becks, who gave a slight smile. "What about for you?"

"I want you to be my daddy."

Becks's mouth dropped open, and her father moved in, ready to whisk Pippa away if necessary. Carlos held up his hand. "Santa tries his best, but this involves just your mommy and me. Santa stays away from those decisions."

Becks held her breath.

"I love you, Carlos Claus."

"I care about you, too, Pippa." Carlos wrapped his arm around her and gave her a hug.

He gazed at Becks, and her heart melted.

Her father reached for Pippa's hand. "I left Grandma Diane taking care of Gomez and Morticia. We better go find them." He turned to Becks. "And Natalie said to tell you she's spread the word among her students, both former and present. You have fifty new sign-ups between her kids and their siblings."

Becks's mouth dropped open again. Her dad and Pippa left Santa's Workshop. Livy turned to address the crowd. "Santa has to feed his reindeer, folks. He'll be back in fifteen minutes." Livy drew the curtain around the gazebo, giving them privacy.

A murmur of groans reached them as Becks settled beside Carlos on the bench. Then again, she almost wished she hadn't. Her tender feelings for him were growing.

"Thanks for what you said to Pippa."

"Anytime, Mrs. Claus. Part of the job, you know."

*No.* That went above and beyond with the same dedication and kindness she'd remembered from him. These traits were even more important now considering she knew not everyone kept their promises. Letting go of the past was hard, but not letting go would be worse for her heart.

HOURS LATER, CARLOS REMOVED his Santa hat, the white wig and beard staying in place. He wouldn't take that off until he was at home so none of the kids would wonder why Santa suddenly had curly black hair. Let the magic take root.

He glanced at Becks, her cheeks rosy red and her blue eyes bright. Unlike him, whose pink cheeks came courtesy of Graciela's expert application of cosmetics, Becks's were from the heat of the close quarters and her natural exuberant self. Though he'd roped her into the task, she'd given her whole heart into smiling at the visitors and making them welcome with kind words.

He'd missed this type of teamwork while he'd been assigned paperwork and school visits, but his heart rate had accelerated in a different way here than on calls. Becks brought an element of fun into everything from his physical therapy exercises to days like these.

She met his gaze with a smile. "Santa's Workshop was a great success. The firefighters outdid themselves this year from what I saw while I manned the soccer table for an hour. Plus I did get my carriage ride with Pippa. My parents are keeping her until later."

*Ask her to dinner.* That inner voice blurted the suggestion as he glanced at the black boot hiding his bright lime-green cast. Out of sight but not out of mind. Maybe it was time to test the waters where Becks was concerned.

Before he could say any more, however, his sister rushed in, carrying a clear bottle with liquid as well as a sad expression.

"Graciela? Is something wrong?" Becks beat him to the query.

"I forgot to give Carlos this spirit gum remover for when he takes off his beard." She handed him the bottle and then faced Becks. "Can you and Pippa help him remove his beard and makeup tonight?"

"What's happened?" Carlos asked. Calm and collected, his sister rarely seemed this disheveled. He placed his hands on his hips and went into big brother mode. "Did Jordan…"

"No, we didn't break up again. We really talked. You know, the type of talk that goes beneath the surface and we cleared the air, but that's not why I'm upset." Graciela sniffed and wiped a tear from her eye. "I brought six dogs from the shelter, hoping to place them in foster homes."

Becks placed her hand on Graciela's arm. "I'm sure they'll find homes after the holidays."

"Five of them did." She lifted her lips in a slight smile until they formed a straight line again. "But I have to take the sweetest of the group back to the shelter. Tinsel's a darling, and I thought someone would open their heart to him today."

Becks said, "I'd volunteer except Gomez and Morticia are so close, and I don't think I could handle a third dog."

Graciela waved away her objection. "That's sweet of you, Becks, and I'm sorry if I made it sound like I expected you to take him home."

"Can I say hello to him and take his picture? See if Mike and Georgie have room for him? Or maybe one of my friends? I don't think Penelope has a dog." Becks reached into her pocket and pulled out a handful of miniature candy canes. "Oops. I kept a stash to offer the kids while they waited in line. Where should I put these?"

"Take them home to Pippa." Carlos reached for his mobility scooter then started for the ramp. "I'll come with you. Maybe one of my fellow firefighters can open up his or her home for the holidays."

At the booth where the shelter had camped for the day, the last of Graciela's volunteers waved and slung a backpack over her shoulder. "Glad you're back. Gotta run."

Graciela neared the crate where a large short-haired golden retriever mix reclined. "Hey, there, Tinsel." She reached in and patted the dog.

As soon as Tinsel stood, Carlos saw what probably held people back. Tinsel only had three legs, the front left one missing. Becks seemed to take it in stride. "Mike and Georgie have experience with dogs, so I'll start by texting them."

Tinsel's large brown eyes stared at him, and Carlos felt an instant connection.

"I'll foster him."

Graciela adjusted the scarf with a snowflake print around Tinsel's neck. Tinsel waited patiently.

Carlos repeated himself, and Graciela glanced his way. "What was that, Carlos?"

"You heard me." He stepped toward Tinsel, whose muscles seemed to relax as if he sensed he was supposed to be with Carlos. "He's coming home with me."

Graciela chuckled. "I have to screen everyone. Any other time, I'd jump at the opportunity for you to foster Tinsel, but I can't let him go home with you."

Carlos bumped his mobility scooter against his sister's knee. "I have a fenced-in yard, and I'll hire Marisol to take him on walks. If she can babysit, surely she'll jump at the chance to earn a little money walking a dog, as long as she feels safe around him and they get along."

Tinsel laid at his feet, panting but content. Carlos knew he couldn't give up on this dog. It'd be like giving up on himself.

Graciela looked torn, and Carlos sent a silent appeal to Becks. She stepped forward. "I'll walk Tinsel in the morning." She must have understood him, their connection still alive and strong.

Graciela folded her arms and rolled her eyes. "How can I say no to Santa and Mrs. Claus?" But then her gaze narrowed. "You don't have any dog food, Carlos, and I'm not sure your house is dog friendly."

"It'll give me added motivation to throw away the pizza boxes next to the sink."

"And I have dog food. I just bought an extra bag for Gomez and Morticia." Becks knelt beside Tinsel and held out her hand for him to sniff. He licked it immediately and allowed her to pet him. "Carlos, if you come over on your way home, I'll help you with the spirit gum remover and make sure you have everything Tinsel needs before my parents drop off Pippa."

He appreciated her help. Most of all, Tinsel needed a secure place in the world. Even Becks sought security, returning to her hometown and investing in the soccer complex. Watching Becks with Tinsel gave him hope she might be there when stability once again entered his life.

"It would feel great to have Tinsel placed in a home today," Graciela told them. "If you have regrets tomorrow, call me and I'll pick him up."

*Regrets?* Carlos had those over the way he treated Becks all those years ago, but he'd apologized and they were finally moving on. He didn't want to regret losing this opportunity to make a difference in Tinsel's life.

"You hear that, Tinsel? You found a home." Carlos bent down and gave his dog a pat on the head. Tinsel soaked up the affection.

"A temporary foster home," Graciela reminded him. "Nothing's written in stone."

Whether he had Tinsel for a short time or the

dog had found his forever home, he intended on making every minute count. Glancing at Becks, he wondered whether their friendship was a true lasting bond or if it too was as seasonal as those candy canes in her pocket. One thing was for certain. He cared for Becks much more than just as a friend.

## CHAPTER FIFTEEN

BECKS ENTERED HER house and waved Carlos and Tinsel inside while carrying the garment bag for the Santa suit, which also held his change of clothes. Without the dogs barking and Pippa's laughter, peace and quiet dominated her little home on this Saturday night. Usually, she relied on that noise to drown out the emptiness inside her. She waited for that familiar ache to surface, and nothing. Sometime in the past few weeks, her life had become full and rich, partly due to the man standing behind her but also by accepting help and working hard at the complex.

Suddenly, an empty house wasn't something to be feared, but something comforting and tranquil. Something that could renew her inner strength and sustain her through anything.

Carlos closed the door behind him and Tinsel. "Are Gomez and Morticia in their crates? Normally they bark by now."

"They're at my parents' house too. They'll

come home with Pippa later. Speaking of dogs, look at this sweet fellow."

The minute she'd laid eyes on Tinsel, she knew he and Carlos were destined for each other, with Tinsel gazing at Carlos with adoration and unconditional love.

"Becca."

One little word, two syllables, five letters with a wealth of emotion. Tinsel circled then rested on the carpet, his gaze not leaving Carlos, while Carlos stepped toward her. She gave a slight nod, and his lips met hers. She savored this moment, his kiss sweet and full of hope of wonderful moments to come. It was everything she remembered and so much more. It wasn't every day a girl kissed Santa Claus.

The fake beard and mustache tickled, and she laughed when they separated. "That was something, but I have that spirit gum remover from Graciela. Let's get that beard and mustache off before Pippa comes home. Why don't you keep Tinsel company in the living room, and I'll gather the supplies to change you from Carlos Claus to Carlos Ramirez again?"

"I don't know. There's something nice about being Carlos Claus."

"Yeah, but Carlos Ramirez has to show me he kisses just as well. I'll be a few minutes while

I change my clothes." She laughed and headed for her bedroom.

They should have just enough time for another kiss, a special moment for the two of them before the world crashed in around her. By tomorrow night, she'd have to make a decision about the complex. With the positive reception at the festival, she'd regret selling even if she ended up on the losing side. She didn't need extra time. She'd call Frederick Whitley tomorrow and tell him no.

Once she's swapped the velvet dress for sweats, she gathered a basket of cotton balls, a bowl and a trash bag before returning to the living room where Carlos and Tinsel presented the picture of domesticity. In the time it had taken her to hang up the Mrs. Claus outfit, Carlos had also changed and removed the Santa wig. Now he was elevating his ankle with Tinsel resting at his right foot, obviously having decided that Carlos was someone he could trust. Maybe she should also allow herself the luxury of trusting again.

*Oh, great.* Now she was taking her cues from dogs.

"Is this going to hurt?" He eyed the basket with a degree of caution.

"From the man who has a broken ankle?"

It was Carlos's turn to laugh. "Point taken."

With caution, she gave his cast a wide berth. "Did you overtax yourself today?"

"No." He reached over and caressed the edge of her jaw with his thumb. "Honest. Making all those kids happy energized me. I feel great."

She melded into his touch before pulling back and gripping the bowl.

"That's adrenaline." She soaked the cotton balls in the spirit gum remover. "Pippa and I will come by tomorrow morning to see how Tinsel is adjusting."

"Is Tinsel the only reason?" Mischief laced his question, and she dabbed the treated cotton ball on his chin.

"Maybe his owner is part of it." This knowledge rocked her world. Since the fire, Carlos had become integral to her life again. As scary as the fire was, the thought of trusting him, letting him inside her world terrified and excited her.

"I'll look forward to starting the morning with welcoming a beautiful woman to my house."

She silenced him with a kiss, the Santa beard not getting in the way of the intensity. Threading her fingers in his thick black hair, she relished the closeness, no space separating them. Seconds ticked by, and the world whirled around her. His scent, his Santa beard, him. The kiss deepened, and she lost all sense of time. With reluctance she pulled away, relieved the weight of the past finally seemed behind them.

"Do you always interrupt like that?"

"Only when I have to yank a Santa beard off such an attractive chin." She laughed before cringing at his wincing when the first segment came off. "Sorry about that. Will another kiss make it better?"

"There's one definite way to find out."

He kissed her this time, but who was keeping track any longer?

She blotted the skin where the mustache connected with his upper lip and the other two beard segments. "You made a very attractive Santa, and you're going to make a great foster home for Tinsel."

"He already seems happier, don't you think?"

Tinsel wasn't the only one. Carlos made her happier as well. The calm personality she remembered had matured into a man whose steady composure urged others to do what was right. In the middle school hallway, she saw the kids hanging on his every word. A pillar of strength, this man would never betray a trust. Allowing him into her heart was as natural as breathing. She opened her mouth to tell him just that when her phone rang. She checked the screen, and her stomach sank. "It's my ex-husband. The dog bed is in the garage. I'll run and get it while I talk to him."

"I can leave…"

"This won't take long." Especially considering it must be the middle of the night in Europe.

She pressed the green Accept button on her screen and then opened the door to the garage. "Hello, Jack. What time is it in Europe anyway?" For all she knew, he was calling her by mistake.

"I wouldn't know since I'm not there."

Her lips formed a straight line. "Where are you and why are you calling me?"

"I'm proposing to my girlfriend, Steph, and I want Pippa there." How had she never noticed how much Jack sounded like a petulant child?

"She's two, and you've already disappointed her this holiday. I don't think it's in her best interests to see you whenever you happen to have a whim to be a part of her life. Next time have your attorney contact my lawyer, and they can talk about how you were a no-show and went to Portugal when the court authorized your visitation." Maybe this was pent-up frustration talking, but Becks wasn't going to let him railroad her into letting him take Pippa.

"I know. I was wrong." Becks blinked at Jack's admission. "Steph has let me know that in no uncertain terms over the past three weeks."

Becks leaned against the wall for support. This Steph sounded like she might be a good influence on Jack. The concept of a woman becoming Pippa's stepmother crossed Becks's mind, and her stomach tightened. She'd never actually considered this possibility as Jack had a roving eye and, for so long, he hadn't been involved with raising Pippa. Accepting Jack and Steph in her life was hard, but she had to for her daughter's sake.

"She sounds like she might be the right one for you then."

"You'd like her. We're in North Carolina. She convinced me to spend Christmas here, and we're renting a cabin about an hour from you before we head back to Lisbon the day after New Year's. We want Pippa in our lives." His pleading tone caught Becks off-guard.

What should she do? This wasn't a game where there was a winner or a loser. Earlier today, Pippa had wanted Carlos to be her daddy, and now her actual father wanted to be involved in her life. A low groan came out of her, and she gripped the phone. "I swear, Jack, if you're going to disappoint Pippa again, you and Steph can turn right around and leave us in peace."

"I knew you'd say yes. That's why I waited until we arrived at the Charlotte airport. I'd rather not get the attorneys involved, and I want Pippa to meet Steph."

She couldn't deny Pippa a chance to know Jack. One more chance, and if he blew it this time, then she'd consult Penelope about her options.

"If she gets homesick, you'll bring her back, right?"

"Steph is great with kids, and she's planned out adventures. She'll be great for Pippa."

Becks's teeth clenched at the thought of some woman she'd never met, and only learned about a few weeks earlier, spending Christmas with her little girl, but Jack was her father, and he did have a court order allowing him custody over the holidays.

"That might be the case, but Pippa's only two. If she wants to come home, I want you to let her do just that. Promise?"

"Spend the day with us tomorrow, and once everything's fine, you'll feel better about letting her stay with me."

Jack sounded too confident, same as always. That type of enthusiasm transferred well to coaching where he pumped up the players, but it wasn't working with her. Instead, she went a little numb, but accepted what would be best for her daughter. They sorted out the details before she ended the call. She'd pull herself together until Carlos left, then she'd start packing Pippa's clothes.

Carlos and Tinsel waited on the other side of the door, and Becks pasted on a fake smile, trying hard to convince herself this was for the best.

"What happened?" Carlos, his chin now free from Santa's whiskers, greeted her in the living room where the Christmas tree lights had lost some of their luster. "Why did Jack call?"

"He wants Pippa for the holidays again."

"Did you call your lawyer? What did Penelope say?" Carlos touched her arm, providing comfort. "Someone needs to look out for you in all of this."

That almost undid her, and she struggled for composure. "He and his girlfriend are already here in North Carolina, and they'll be spending the holidays an hour away. The four of us are meeting tomorrow in Asheville, so Pippa can get to know Steph. They want to talk to me and go over their plans. If everyone agrees, Pippa will stay with them at the cabin they rented." She choked out the words.

His arms, warm and solid, drew her in as her tears dampened his black T-shirt. She let it out, and somehow they found themselves kissing once more, the saltiness of her tears blending with the pure sweeter taste of him. At the same time, they pulled away from each other.

"I don't—"

"We shouldn't—"

Their voices overlapped, and the thinnest chuckle came out of her. He motioned for her to go first. "I have to pack for Pippa."

"Maybe Pippa will want to come back with you, and she'll be home tomorrow night." Carlos reached for her hand and stroked her thumb.

"Jack plays to win."

"Pippa's not a game." Carlos pursed his lips, and Tinsel raised his head at the tone as if checking to make sure everything was all right before resting again.

"I know. That was a poor choice of words, but Pippa deserves a real relationship with her father. That's why I agreed to this, and why I'm asking you to go now so I can get ready."

Her mind registered a sense of déjà vu. Those were almost the exact words she'd said to him all those years ago. This time, however, he clasped her hands in his. "Becca…"

"I'm tired, and my heart hurts." The truth slipped from her, and a wave of fatigue washed over her.

"It's okay to have these feelings. You're a good mom, Becks." He squeezed her hand, and a sense of calmness came over her, something she wouldn't have felt even a month ago.

He was helping her build a sturdy foundation for a house made of something other than gingerbread, and yet tonight showed her how a situation could turn in the blink of an eye. He must know that better than almost anyone as he'd responded to fires that could devastate a life in a matter of minutes.

As much as she wanted to turn to him, she held back, her trust in people once again eroded. "Good night, Carlos."

"You're still coming to my dad's dinner, right?" He met her gaze, those steady brown eyes a beacon of strength, but wasn't it better to rely on herself?

"I don't know. If everything goes well for Jack and Pippa tomorrow, I'd be lousy company."

"That's what friends and family are for. We're not just window dressing for the good times." He brushed her cheek, and tingles stayed there while she collected the dog bed, kibble and supplies for Tinsel.

After she loaded the trunk of his car, she walked to the front porch without looking back. What started as a beautiful day and promising evening had turned into a Christmas calamity.

CARLOS UNCLIPPED TINSEL'S LEASH. It was as though the dog exhaled a sigh of relief at coming home. "Don't get too used to me, Tinsel. According to Graciela, if someone better comes along, that's the place for you."

So many years ago, he'd let Becks go and someone else had come along. Tonight it was as if he and Becks hadn't moved forward at all thanks to her ex's actions. Her eyes had lost their luster, and he found himself with no answer about how to rebuild better than before.

He shouldn't have left her alone with all the packing for Pippa and her preparing to say goodbye for the first time, and yet he didn't have any right to stay. He hesitated, torn about whether he should go back over there and say everything he'd held inside. Tinsel thumped his tail. Was it a sign? His doorbell rang. It was Gisele and Javier.

He rolled his eyes at them. "Let me guess. Graciela sent you."

Gisele entered and squealed. "You're every bit as cute as your pictures."

"Thanks, sis. Every younger brother longs to hear that." Carlos joked as Gisele made a beeline for Tinsel.

Javier entered with a thirty-pound sack of food and a tote bag on his shoulder. "Sometimes your sister confuses me with a pack mule."

"I know you love me anyway." Gisele sent her husband a blinding smile.

Sassy and confident, his sister had always been quick with a comeback, just like their mother. Carlos had always taken after their father, calm and steady, whereas Graciela was a blend of everyone, the crusader with a soft heart. His sisters had his back, and he'd go to the moon for either of them. From what he'd seen of Javier, his new brother-in-law was cut from the same cloth.

"Where do you want his new dog dish?" Javier pointed to the tote bag.

"Wow, Tinsel, Christmas came a week early for you." He started to strap his leg to the mobility scooter, but Gisele pointed a stern finger in his direction.

"You sit and bond with that dog. He needs somebody," Gisele said.

He nodded. "I'm surprised Graciela didn't hit you up for a home for him."

Gisele started pulling items out of the bag. "She did, but Marisol owns the cutest little pair of bunnies."

"They're going on eight, which is almost ancient for rabbits, and we don't want to risk anything happening to them. In a couple of years, we'll be ready for a dog. Maybe a sibling for Marisol as well." Javier returned Gisele's smile.

Carlos hoped the two would never leave their honeymoon phase. "Thanks for the supplies. I stopped at Becks's house, but everything's still in the trunk."

"Do you have what you need for the party on Thursday? Last I heard Mom had invited twenty more people today at the festival." Gisele held up a bottle of dog shampoo. "Where do you want this?"

"In the bathroom." He felt the blood drain from his face. "Twenty people? I thought it was a family affair."

He'd need extra plates and flatware, more bottles of champagne, and a dog sitter.

Was it too late to rent a heated tent and six-piece band? Maybe send out engraved invitations?

"You know Mami. Nothing is ever small with her. All three of us weighed over eight pounds at birth." She faced Javier and grinned. "I was the cutest."

Carlos collapsed onto a chair. "I only planned for nine people."

"Wait a second." Gisele ticked off her fingers and listed family members, one by one, stopping when she reached seven. "Who were the other two?"

"Graciela's boyfriend, Jordan, and Becks Porter."

Gisele arched her eyebrow in Javier's direction, some unspoken words obviously being exchanged between them. "Could you unload Carlos's trunk for him?"

"I'll make as many trips as I possibly can." He bussed Gisele's cheek before facing Carlos. "Where are your keys?"

Carlos reached into the pocket of his sweatpants and threw them Javier's way. He braced himself for what was coming next. "There isn't that much stuff, so you might want to be quick about whatever you want to tell me."

Gisele held her arms up as if she was surrendering. "Mami wanted me to tell you it's no longer a surprise party. She rented the pavilion at the Whitley Community Center."

"Why did she even ask me to help if she intended to do everything herself?"

"She wants you to feel useful."

Like he was supposed to stop being useful on account of a broken ankle? "I'm keeping busy with station stuff, and I played Santa today."

Tinsel came over and nudged his hand, and Carlos obliged with a quick scratch behind his ears. The fellow was so happy to have a home. How would the dog handle it if Graciela pulled the carpet out from under him once she found somewhere else for him to live permanently? Would he be happy? Or would Tinsel's eyes mirror Becks's when Jack announced Pippa would spend the holidays with him?

Gisele huffed. "Most of this just happened today. Word's gotten out and more and more people came up to Mami at the main booth expecting an invitation, and you know Mami."

"I also know how hard it is to stay upset with her."

They laughed, and Carlos settled on the couch with Tinsel curling up on the carpet at his feet. Gisele eyed Tinsel with a degree of suspicion.

"Will you be able to manage Tinsel on your own?"

"He's worth the effort."

Javier entered, lugging the thirty pounds of kibble on his shoulder. "Are you two done talking or should I leave this somewhere and wait in the car?"

Gisele walked over and bussed his cheek again. "Put it in the kitchen pantry, and then I'll introduce you to the Timber River Bar and Grill since we don't have to pick up Marisol from her friend Rachel's house for another two hours." She wiggled her hips. "There's a dance floor."

"If I recall correctly, it's line dancing night. I thought newlyweds preferred romantic slow dancing," Carlos said.

"Spoilsport." Gisele stuck her tongue out and then looked at Tinsel. "Maybe we should stay, though, and keep you company."

Carlos shook his head. "Thank you for bringing in the dog food and other supplies, but I've kept myself alive with my broken ankle. I can keep a dog alive, too. Tinsel and I will be fine." Then he shooed them out of the house. "Go have fun until it's time to pick up Marisol."

Javier helped Gisele with her coat, and she sent Carlos a worried glance. Javier cleared his throat. "I'm an expert at line dancing." Javier winked at Gisele, and Carlos coughed loudly.

"That's my sister so please take the flirting to the bar and spare me the details." They laughed and left him alone with Tinsel, who snuffled a sigh of contentment as if relieved he found a home.

Whereas he felt the opposite. Frustration clawed at Carlos. Broken ankle, broken relationships, broken career. What should have been a happy time considering those amazing kisses with Becks and fostering a dog who oozed love was turning into one lousy evening. It seemed as though Tinsel sensed something was wrong and shifted closer to him, his warm body covering Carlos's right foot, a reminder good things came when patience prevailed.

A good fit was a good fit whether by chance or by careful deliberation. Tinsel had waited in the shelter for something better, a new chapter in his story. As much as Carlos didn't like sitting on the sidelines, sometimes waiting for a jewel was worth it. Another kiss from Becks and a relationship like his sister found with Javier would certainly be worth the wait.

He summoned his patience and let it seep into his soul. He'd wait for Becks. Those kisses were only part of it. She understood him in ways he didn't share with others. A younger Becks would never have agreed to spend the day with Jack without exhausting every legal avenue, but now, she put Pippa first. And how she stepped in and played Mrs. Claus might just be the icing on the proverbial gingerbread house. The word smitten wasn't strong enough. Maybe it was time to sit back and expect something good to come from resting his foot and reconnecting with Becks. In this case, inaction seemed the best course of action.

# CHAPTER SIXTEEN

Mountain Vista Soccer Complex had consumed Becks's every waking moment in the four days since she had spent the afternoon with Jack and his girlfriend, Steph. Legalities aside, Pippa needed her father in her life, and Jack seemed to have changed for the better with Steph around. As hard as it was to admit it, Steph was pleasant and genuine, and her face lit up when she talked about Jack and Pippa. They both promised Becks that they'd bring Pippa to Hollydale if she was homesick. Pippa was excited to stay at their cabin with them, and Becks agreed to the plan.

At the end of each day, though, she had a video call so she'd see her daughter's face and hear her voice. Happiness registered in Pippa's eyes when she talked about their trip to the zoo one night followed by the description of ice skating the next. On this Wednesday before Christmas, Pippa, Jack and Steph were heading to a farm with real reindeer while Becks waited for Carlos in the lobby of the administrative building.

And not that she was counting but five days, eight hours and fifty-two seconds had passed since she and Carlos shared their first kiss in nine years. They'd exchanged texts, but their paths hadn't crossed since then. That would change when he arrived with the county inspector for the final inspection and walkthrough with herself and Trent.

Impressed didn't begin to convey the admiration for the job Ace Construction did on both buildings. All traces of the smoke damage were gone, and they'd installed a new sprinkler system and breaker boxes. This morning had been their last scheduled day of work. All she had to do now was wait for the others to arrive.

Butterflies pooled in her stomach as she stared at the outdoor soccer fields, all ready for tomorrow's meeting with Tricia and Wallace Key, the executive director of Kick, Goal and Score. What if the damaged building didn't pass inspection? How much more money would new repairs set her back? For the first time since she'd passed on Whitley's offer, she wondered if she should have accepted it. When she called him on Sunday, he expressed his dismay but said he'd found a contingency backup property that would suit his needs. It was too late for regrets now. Besides, those consumed too much energy. The future was what she had to focus on; it was full of possibilities. She and Dante had spent long hours installing goals and painting lines on the fescue for the six outdoor fields. She went outside and retrieved her favorite soccer ball from her car's trunk. Bouncing it on her bent calf distracted her until cars turned into the parking lot.

*Now or never.*

She placed her ball in her trunk and slammed it shut. The county inspector and Carlos piled out of one car while Trent slid from the driver's seat of his truck. Everyone shook hands, and Carlos sent her a wink. Somehow, he always managed to find a way to ease her fears.

Inspector Strickland asked Trent a few questions, and Carlos glided over to her on his mobility scooter.

"Look at you, maneuvering that scooter like a pro."

"How are you? Your texts were too…" He paused as if searching for the right word.

"Long? Short? Businesslike?" she suggested.

A slow, deliberate pause was more like him. "Cheerful."

Her laugh filled the air, and Inspector Strickland and Trent looked their way. Her cheeks grew hot even with the chill of the day. "Inside joke."

"We're ready to start," the inspector said.

He was all business as he should be. Carlos stepped back and indicated Becks should go first. "Official approval for you to open comes from the county on the advice of the fire department, so that's why we're both here to check the buildings."

Suddenly, it was as if Carlos had donned his work mask, giving no clue to the warm kisses they shared the other night. Then again, she expected nothing less from him as a firefighter and inspector, and she'd accept no less from herself. She never wanted another scene like the one that greeted her three weeks ago. Accidents were one thing, but sheer negligence was another.

Trent led the way to the HVAC system in the administrative building before crossing to the circuit box. "This is the latest model on the market and meets every code. It comes with a built-in protector that will prevent an electrical surge in case of a lightning hit or a brownout."

Inspector Strickland and Carlos nodded, and the inspector checked off something on a clipboard. Becks yearned to look at it, but he kept his paperwork out of her line of sight. This was more than her livelihood.

They proceeded to the main ventilation shaft. Inspector Strickland pointed a flashlight into an area while Carlos asked several technical questions.

"The air change per hour exceeds code, and during occupied hours, all interior spaces are continually ventilated. My company utilized the latest in green energy conservation measures, which will improve efficiency and save Ms. Porter costs in the long run." Trent pointed out the new posted signs for fire escapes. "And the automated sprinkler system is integrated with the overhead water pipes, and they're set to deploy in case of fire."

She could recite Trent's speech word for word as he'd walked her through this yesterday afternoon. Unlike her former unprofessional self before the closing, she had interrogated Trent about every facet of smoke removal and code compliance.

The inspector checked more boxes, and Becks considered that a good thing. Then they ventured outside where Trent reviewed the rules and regulations for the pitches, parking lot and even the landscaping. Inspector

Strickland took measurements and made calculations.

Becks searched Carlos's expression for an answer as to how the inspection was going, but it gave away nothing.

Still, she was proud of what she'd done here.

As hard as it would be to wait for the inspection results, she had no alternative. She held the door of the administrative building open while Trent and Inspector Strickland barreled forward. She hesitated for a second as a gust of chilly air swirled around them. Carlos hung back.

"You okay, Becks?"

"What if the place fails inspection?"

"Ace Construction never cuts corners. Trent and his father always insisted a job worth doing was a job worth doing right. You'll pass."

His confidence gave her the boost she needed. "Thanks. I thought Trent did a phenomenal job. I understand why you worked for Ace Construction."

They went inside.

"I wanted an extra job so I'd fall asleep at night and not rehash how I treated you. I stayed on Trent's futon when I wasn't working for him and at the fire station during my shifts.

Between the two jobs, I earned the money for the smoke-jumping course."

He'd suffered after their breakup, and her heart went out to him. She'd known how hard she'd taken the loss of their relationship, but now she knew how he'd reacted. It didn't make her feel better, and Becks read between the lines. They both tended to throw themselves into work whenever something difficult crossed their paths.

What if they turned to each other instead?

Inspector Strickland and Trent waved them over, and the inspection concluded. Trent pulled Becks aside. "Carlos and Inspector Strickland are being thorough, but I'm confident in my team. If you don't pass inspection, we'll follow through and fix it. If it's on our end, we won't charge you. That's part of our warranty. If you run into any issues during the first ninety days, I'll handle the repair personally."

She was extra glad she'd hired Trent. "Thank you, and please add me to your list of references."

He chuckled. "You say that before you see my final bill."

"Your crew is worth every penny." His warranty lifted her spirits, giving her a boost of much-needed confidence. "You have my email for the final invoice?"

He nodded and checked his phone. "Your deposit covered about 40 percent, but you already authorized the overage for the electrical issues. I didn't want the increase coming as a surprise."

Performing the math in her head, she would have enough to cover that and this month's paychecks for Amara and Dante before the registration fees for January came due and money rolled in again. "Sounds good."

Becks caught up with Inspector Strickland and Carlos. The inspector wrote something on a business card. "This has the inspection report number, and I'll post it as soon as possible."

"I have a business meeting scheduled to take place here tomorrow. Can I go ahead with that?" Without the report, she might run into issues during tomorrow's interview with Wallace Key and Tricia. "I'd like to show the indoor facility to a potential sponsor."

That interview was crucial for extra funds on the balance sheet.

"You can do that. I still have to file the paperwork, but everything appears in order. Still, I want to double-check my notes one last time.

Tomorrow's my last day before the holidays. I'll have the inspection results up before I leave, but it looks good on my end." Inspector Strickland slipped his tablet and clipboard into his attaché case.

"Thank you for that assurance. I appreciate your finishing this up before Christmas." A wonderful present indeed. He proceeded to the door. "Ready to go, Carlos?"

"I'll catch up with you in a minute." Carlos removed his knapsack and pulled out a water bottle.

The inspector waved and headed for the car while Carlos swallowed a long sip, giving her enough time to screw up her courage. "About the party tonight—"

"Marisol has talked nonstop about it. The highlight of her evening is going to be you."

This revelation was a blow to her resolve to cancel. "This is a happy occasion, and I don't want to spoil it. I haven't been the best company this week."

He placed his hand over hers. "A certain redhead is teaching me about balance. That concentrating on my sadness only compounds the pain rather than my overcoming it. I'd like a chance to return the favor."

Something sizzled in the air, the attraction

between them more vibrant than ever. "But your father deserves a fun night. So do Gisele and Javier."

He caressed her cheek. "And you deserve a night out."

"My dogs—"

"Will be fine for one evening, and that headache you're about to claim doesn't really exist, does it?"

"No, it doesn't." She leaned into his touch before stepping away. Too often she trusted people and ended up burned. "I miss Pippa."

He slipped the backpack over his shoulders. "So do I. If nothing else, talking to Marisol will do you a world of good. She's been walking Tinsel for me. She's a sweet kid. Javier's a great father, and she's warming up to Gisele as her stepmother."

"You'll let me off the hook once I talk to your new niece?"

"By then, there might be other reasons for you to stay." He winked and started for the door.

That promise scared her more than the possibility of a bad interview with Wallace Key.

CARLOS STEPPED BACK to admire Marisol's and Graciela's help with transforming the pavilion into a winter wonderland. The room sparkled with colorful lights, and illuminated stars of every shape and size hung from the ceiling. In one corner, poinsettias, Mami's favorite flower, surrounded a tall Christmas tree decorated with red and blue ornaments. Lively salsa holiday music played over the speakers.

"Are all your family celebrations like this?" Marisol's mouth formed a giant O. "I'm so glad we married Gisele."

Graciela hugged her new niece. "I'm glad you and Javier married Gisele, too. Let's check on those steaks."

He sent them off and made his way to the main table where Mami and Papa would hold center stage. Every table held photos of Javier and Gisele on one side and a memento of his father's thirty-five years of serving the community on the other. Firefighting was such a big part of the Ramirez family. Would his father look at him differently if Carlos had to submit his resignation?

The place card with his name caught his attention. He was seated between two of his mother's best friends, who were part of the Matchmaking Mimosas. Nowhere did he see Becks's place card. On a hunt for it, he finally found hers at the other end of the pavilion, seated next to Max O'Hara, one of his father's best friends who co-owned the local auto repair center with Becks's sister-in-law, Georgie Harrison. Considering Carlos invited Becks, this wouldn't do at all. A little change was good for everyone.

He switched Hyacinth's card with Becks's, placing his mother's friend at the table seated next to Max, who was the same age as Hyacinth. Both of them were single. Hmm, this could work. His mother wasn't the only one who could play matchmaker.

Now he was right where he wanted to be. Next to Becks.

BECKS SEARCHED FOR her place card on the tables at the pavilion. She expected to sit at the table with her brother, Mike, and his wife, Georgie, along with her sister-in-law's auto shop co-owner, Max, a sweetheart of a man who'd recently lost his sister to cancer, but her card wasn't there.

She should have texted Carlos her regrets after getting confirmation Tricia and the director of Kick, Goal and Score were arriving tomorrow, but she didn't have the heart to cancel. Since she was here, she might as well have fun. There wasn't any more festive spot in Hollydale tonight anyway. Her foot tapped along with the lively music while she searched another table for her place card without any luck. Someone brushed against her and the woman apologized. Becks murmured a quick "don't mention it" just as she caught sight of Carlos.

She felt breathless at how his plaid Oxford shirt stretched across his broad chest. Dressy yet casual, he was the most handsome man here, and she couldn't take her gaze off him. He made her way to her, using his knee scooter.

"I wasn't sure if you'd make it, Becca." The noise fell away and his voice, whiskey smooth and fathoms deep with emotion, glided over Becks like it was the sweetest thing in the world.

"I almost didn't come." She rubbed her sweaty palms against the side of her velvet dress. "I couldn't resist the food."

"Is that the only reason you came?"

She looked away, unwilling to meet that smoky gaze and all the implications of the dreams written on his face. "No, but it was a great selling point."

"You're here, and that's what matters." Carlos winked and rolled around to her side, guiding her to the table, front and center. "You look beautiful tonight. That bright shade of red suits you."

"Thank you." She and Natalie had often been told growing up that redheads should never wear pink or bright red. They grinned and wore what they liked anyway.

She glanced at his leg and her mouth dropped open. "Did you slit your pants?"

"Shh. You're the first person to notice, or at least the first to mention it, but it's the only way to get around the cast. I wasn't about to wear sweatpants with a jacket and tie."

"It'll be our little secret." Like the time in college when she played hooky with him, and they'd driven across North Carolina to the Outer Banks to spend the day surfing and building sandcastles.

At the top of the Cape Hatteras Lighthouse, he'd proposed. Saying yes, she hadn't believed anything would stand in the way of living out all her dreams. Yet a harsh reality crept in, and she couldn't have her dreams and Carlos.

She blinked away the memory and spotted her place card at the main table next to Carlos. "Oh."

"You sound surprised." He reached over and squeezed her hand. "You shouldn't be. I want you next to me."

*For tonight or for always?*

One look at his face and she wasn't sure of anything anymore. This time she wondered if there was a way to braid her life together so she could reach for her dreams and have Carlos, too.

She needed time to think. Carlos's prudent cautiousness was rubbing off on her, and that wasn't a bad thing. So far everything about him since they'd reconnected proved he was worthy of her trust, from the way he cared about Pippa to how he went above and beyond to help her with the code statutes for her complex.

Maybe it was time to give in to her growing feelings.

"Carlos, sit down and rest your ankle." Fabiana approached from behind.

"Hello, Fabiana." Becks moved forward and they exchanged a hug. "Thank you for your hospitality this evening. It's wonderful Gisele and Javier have settled in Hollydale." She took her seat next to Carlos's and drank from the goblet of water beside her place card.

Fabiana's brows furrowed. "Wait a minute. What's—"

"Becks, could you please go to the buffet

line for me? I don't want to bump into anyone." Carlos positioned the scooter nearby.

"Of course." Becks rose and glanced at Fabiana. "Is something wrong?"

"Graciela and I reviewed the seating chart a few minutes ago."

Carlos coughed and thumped his chest. "Make sure you add a dollop of that horseradish sauce to my plate. That'll clear out my sinuses."

That cough was phony. Becks had a sneaking suspicion something had gone awry. Hyacinth approached their group. "Fabiana, darling, thank you so much for placing me next to the most enigmatic man." All of a sudden, Max appeared beside her, and if Becks wasn't mistaken, the military veteran's cheeks were bright pink. "We've been having the nicest conversation, and I look forward to talking to him more after we sample your delicious cooking. I can't believe we've lived in the same town and have only passed the time of day. Aren't the holidays so wonderful? A time for dear friends while expanding one's circle to include new ones."

"Hyacinth, there's been a mistake…" Fabiana's nostrils flared as she arched an eyebrow toward Carlos.

Hyacinth reached out and gave Fabiana a hug. "There are no mistakes tonight. Everything is coming together so beautifully. Celebrating new additions to your family is an absolutely delightful way to start a busy week of holiday festivities." Hyacinth looped a long sparkly scarf around her neck and reached for Max's hand. "You must have some fascinating stories about your automobile repair shop."

"I fix cars, and Georgie restores them."

Hyacinth led Max away, asking multiple questions while Max beamed and nodded. Carlos faced his mother once more. "Yes, Mami. I changed the place cards."

Tension laced the air until Fabiana smiled and patted Carlos's cheek. "As long as everyone is happy tonight."

Someone called Fabiana's name, and she rushed away. Marisol ran up, excitement shimmering in her dark eyes. "Ms. Porter, you made it, and we're at the same table. Can you tell me what it was like playing professional soccer? How many hours did you practice each day? What age did you start playing? I want to know everything."

One look at the buffet line, and Becks knew she'd have plenty of time to talk to Marisol. "How about I tell you while we wait?" She faced Carlos. "Do you want a little of everything?"

He nodded, and they excused themselves.

In the line, she answered Marisol's questions, but was stuck on Fabiana's reaction to her sitting at Carlos's table. What had she done to hurt Fabiana's feelings? Her gaze landed on Carlos's mother laughing and holding on to Roberto's arm. The spitting image of his father, it wasn't hard to imagine Carlos twenty-five years from now, active and dashing. However, Carlos's career was up in the air, and his mother was probably worried for the cast to come off to see if the fire at Becks's complex cost him his future as a firefighter. When Becks considered it like that, the mystery of the snub became clear.

Fabiana must blame Becks for the injury to Carlos's ankle and subsequent desk duty. Even if she and Carlos had a chance at building a relationship that could withstand their past, the fire would always be between them.

Especially if Carlos could never work as a firefighter again. She glanced at someone patting Roberto's back. All Carlos had talked about as a teenager was following in his father's footsteps.

Just as she'd had to admit Pippa needed a relationship with her biological father so too did Carlos need firefighting and his family like he needed air and water. She stiffened and went through the motions, intent on getting through this evening. Later she'd figure out how to put some much-needed distance between herself and the man who'd brought back her feelings.

SOMETHING WAS WRONG with Becks. Since he'd admitted to his mother he'd switched the place cards, Becks had acted so formal around him although she'd been great with Marisol, who basked from the attention from her idol. While Becks had warned him she might be bad company on account of Pippa's absence, he'd glimpsed another side of her when she arrived. He'd wager whatever was bothering her had nothing to do with Pippa and everything to do with the place cards.

"Why don't we head to the Holly Days Diner after this and see if Miss Joanne has any eggnog pie left?" He whispered his idea to Becks, who shimmered tonight in a bright red velvet dress that matched her fiery nature. She was easily the most beautiful woman in the room.

"I should go. I have to get ready for my meeting tomorrow." She grasped her clutch just as Javier clinked the side of his water goblet with a fork.

"You can't leave during the speeches," Carlos said, and someone at the table shushed him for his efforts.

He turned his attention to his parents, sitting together, holding hands. His mom's brown eyes glistened with joy and pride. His father looked at her as though she were the only woman in the room. Happiness radiated from them, and that was all Carlos had ever wanted, and who better to emulate than his father, a man who'd worked hard as a fire chief and enjoyed the bounty of riches around him.

Javier finished his toast, thanking everyone for the warm welcome extended to himself and Marisol, and Carlos glanced at Becks over the side of his goblet, her face stony and impenetrable. He shouldn't have insisted she come tonight. Not with her heart so entwined with Pippa and her mind on the inspection. Far from helping, this night was only widened the chasm between them. He couldn't break through. No matter what he did, she always pushed him out. You couldn't build a foundation out of flimsy gingerbread.

Gisele stood and accepted the mic from her husband. A signature sassy smile marked his sister's pretty features. He watched as Becks slipped away, and he didn't stop her.

His father nudged his ribs. "You can hear us any old time. Go after her."

With nimble fingers, Carlos adjusted his boot scooter and smiled his thanks to Papa. He caught up with Becks in the courtyard, a veritable winter wonderland. "Becks." She kept walking and he called out again. "Becca."

She stopped and turned around, her fingers trembling as she tried buttoning her coat and gave up the effort. "You should be in there with your family."

He'd loved her too long to give up without trying. "So should you, but we're both outside. Why?"

Her throat bobbed, and something akin to pain crossed her face. "There's too much in our way, Carlos. There's a reason we didn't make it back then. We're just too different."

He glided toward her, the scooter rolling along the sidewalk. "Maybe the reason we didn't make a go of it was lack of communication. We've both matured a lot. Sometimes the best things in life are worth getting right, not mention waiting for."

A glimmer of a smile lit up her face, the encouragement enough for him to close the distance between them, enough so he could smell apples and sunshine.

"That speech was longer than your proposal at Cape Hatteras."

"See? We have shared memories, and we could make more. New ones, special ones." Too often he'd thought of her as the fiery one to his cool self, but there was something about her that brought out the heat in him. He liked that side of himself as much as he loved her.

Her fingers steadied, and she buttoned her coat. "Carlos, the sprinklers didn't go off. Your injury is a direct result of my negligence. You might lose what you love most in this world because of me."

"You owned the property for less than forty-eight hours."

"But I didn't do my due diligence."

*Four buttons to go.*

"Firefighting means everything to you and your family. That's partly why we're here to-night."

"So this doesn't have to do with Pippa or the complex, but whether my family will accept you?"

"Your mother was deliberate in her seating arrangement."

*Two to go.*

"She's right. I'm the reason you're wearing that cast."

"It was an accident, pure and simple, and you're wrong. There are things I love more than firefighting." *Like you.* "It's a part of me, an integral part, but people also occupy my heart."

"I can't be one of them. It wouldn't be right." With the last button fastened, she knotted the belt at her waist for good measure. The courtyard's tiny white lights reflected in her eyes along with pain and regret. "You can't even tell your mother you like red velvet cupcakes more than her homemade cake. I won't put a wedge between you and the people who mean the most to you."

"You're the person who means the most to me." He came closer and held her hands. "I don't want to let you go this time."

He leaned in and kissed her, her lips sweet and luscious and everything he'd wanted. This was the kiss that relaunched the feelings she'd awakened in him. He closed his eyes, absorbing the moment. Leaning his weight on his knee, he wrapped his arms around her. Lightness and goodness surrounded him and he poured his heart into the kiss, into what they could have if she dove deep and accepted the happiness he offered.

He opened his eyes and broke away, seeing so much in her expressive eyes.

"But your family."

Those weren't the words he wanted to hear so he kissed her one more time. He knew the minute she released her doubts and threw herself into the kiss. This. A complete sense of being alive. This was what he'd been missing all these years.

He broke away once more and cradled her face in his hands. "We both have families who love us and want what's best for us. Mami will accept you because I accept you. I—"

Before he could utter the words of love in his heart, she kissed him again and then stopped, stepping back and touching her lips. "Let's go back inside before you catch your death of cold. That would be something your mother would never forgive me for."

He wasn't finished, not by a long shot, but this was a start, and that was more than he'd ever thought possible.

## CHAPTER SEVENTEEN

IN HER OFFICE at Mountain Vista, Becks hummed music from last night's party and swayed her hips in time to the rhythm. She didn't usually tango or salsa at work, but that wasn't a bad thing.

For the first time in a while, life was going her way, and her relief was palpable.

She hadn't talked to Pippa last night, but Jack had texted he and Steph had made arrangements for the three of them to go snow tubing today, and Steph had forwarded pictures of Pippa in her parka and snow pants. Although Becks was still adjusting to another woman holding a special spot in Pippa's life, Steph seemed on the up-and-up. She hoped Jack appreciated the treasure he'd found this time.

Already this morning she'd had her appointment with Tina Spindler, a bookkeeper and accountant who delivered good news. Tina came highly recommended from Brooke at the community center, who had nothing but praise for the accountant who was friends with Fabiana. All morning, Tina regaled Becks with stories of her friends, the Matchmaking Mimosas.

Even with the extra electrical work, the discount Ace Construction Company had given helped keep costs under control. Becks would make payroll for this month and next.

And Carlos? For the second time since the fire, they'd shared an incredible set of kisses, and there was no sympathy or gratitude or anything of the sort behind them. That kiss changed everything. Hope replaced her fears about his family's approval. They were building something real, not temporary like a gingerbread house destined to be consumed by the end of the holidays.

With a smile, she picked up the nearest soccer ball and headed outside. She was far along the trail to Sully Creek before she even realized that had been her destination. Was her fledgling relationship with Carlos like this creek? Winding water that made its way around rocks and crevices before reaching the clear blue depths of Lake Pine? Maybe she just needed to trust herself and enjoy the journey.

Behind her, she could hear rustling along the

path, and then came a familiar voice. "Dollar for your thoughts?"

"Big spender." She faced Carlos, surprised to find him here of all places. He was back on crutches. "What are you doing here at the creek? How did you get here? Where's the scooter?"

"Whoa! That's a lot of questions. It's easier to walk with my crutches on the rocky terrain." He grinned, the boyish features shining through his mature masculinity. "I saw you heading this way."

"You shouldn't even be walking period, so this must be something more important than a simple hello, right?"

"It's official, and I had to tell you right away." She braced herself. "You passed inspection. The paperwork is official and online."

Those words were as much music to her ears as the imaginary chords she'd heard earlier. Gray clouds parted, revealing the bright sky, and sunshine streamed down to warm her cheeks. She whooped for joy until the dark clouds obscured the sun once more and she stilled. "You traveled down this path just to tell me that?"

"I'd go anywhere for you."

She believed him.

She shielded her eyes and saw cars arriving

in the parking lot. "My appointment's here. Now that the approval's online, it's all behind me?"

He pivoted and faced the same direction. "Yep."

"Come on." She started up the path and waited for him, making sure he navigated the tricky slope. "Gentlemen first."

They made their way back to the parking lot where Tricia stood talking to a tall bald man, who appeared to be in his late forties. Tricia turned toward Becks and nodded. "Here she is. Becks Harrison, meet Wallace Key, the director of Kick, Goal and Score."

The man smiled warmly. "We didn't recognize your application since you signed your emails and correspondence as Rebecca Porter, but believe me, Becks Harrison is a name in the soccer world."

Tricia folded her arms. "That's not very sporting of you. You should afford everyone the same respect."

Wallace nodded. "That's why I'm here to talk terms."

Becks gulped. This deal was supposed to benefit her. They sponsored her and paid her money for being an affiliate of their program. "Stacy and I discussed terms," Becks said.

"You'll be our primary sponsor and use our facilities for your summer camps."

"That was before I knew you're a professional soccer player. I have new ideas to capitalize on your former success. Stacy and I came up with a new proposal, a partnership that will be mutually beneficial."

Becks looked at Carlos and saw his skepticism mirrored hers. Still, she'd best hear Wallace out. "Go on."

"We created a whole campaign revolving around you and what you'll bring to our travel leagues and summer camps across the state."

"You want Becks to be a spokesperson for Kick, Goal and Score?" Tricia said, her disdain clear.

He nodded at Tricia. "I want her to be a presence for us, play up her stellar record and experience. She'll travel more and talk up our camps and other complexes while keeping this as her home base." He turned to Becks. "You'll be coaching and mentoring the best of our best. The same as Tricia did for you."

That gave Becks pause. Mountain Vista was based in Hollydale. Her home was here, and this was her community. This facility was for the residents of all ages to learn more about the sport and enjoy it. More to the point, she wanted every child and adult who signed up for her program to be more than a name. To learn drills and strategy from her and everything she could pass along that she'd learned. Games would encourage teamwork and be fun, same as when she started playing. In the past few weeks, she'd been reminded of how much Hollydale had played a role in her development and how the town came together for the Firefighter's Christmas Festival and Roberto's anniversary celebration.

Becks introduced Carlos and as a group they all toured the outdoor fields. Becks sent a mental note of thanks to Dante for all his hard work getting the complex in shape. They proceeded to the indoor soccer fields where Wallace laid out the specifics of his offer. "The contract is already in your inbox, Becks. Next month, we'll work on a promotional campaign where you'll travel to Charlotte and Raleigh, all expenses paid, for exclusive seminars with the state's premier players. I'd like those to happen at least three times each calendar year. You can look over the substantial compensation package this afternoon and sign it in the presence of a notary then. Once Tricia explained who you are, well—" Wallace shrugged and waved his hand dismissively "—that was a mistake I won't make again."

What he was saying would be a big boost to Becks, but her complex? She wasn't seeing her business benefiting from her absence or the extra pressure to produce results.

What Key wanted was for her to make another choice that would put her career first without talking it over with the people she loved.

"Thank you for your time."

He beamed as the group walked to the small concession stand where water and healthy snacks would be sold to people visiting and watching the games. "I'm looking forward to getting our contract signed and starting the promo by New Year's. You'll be a feather in our cap."

This was everything she'd wanted for the past month, but why did it feel so wrong? The thought left a sour taste in her mouth. She wanted each child in her academy to feel special, to learn about the game and become a whole person who could lose with grace and win with humility. A glance at Carlos made her wonder how much those soccer lessons where Roberto stressed teamwork and joy had helped form Carlos into the strong man he was today.

Once Wallace departed, Becks inhaled a deep breath of fresh mountain air and released it. She faced Tricia, finally understanding how Carlos had never been able to tell his mother his favorite dessert was red velvet cupcakes rather than her homemade cake. How could she express her reservations about this company she'd wanted on her side for so long to her mentor who'd done so much to bring about this meeting?

"I have a confession." Tricia shielded her eyes. "I asked Claire Esposito to come this afternoon to pitch Team4Life. While she can't offer the monetary compensation package of Kick, Goal and Score, her program has real merit. It concentrates on the whole player. Coaching youth to their full potential while also teaching the benefit of good nutrition and teamwork."

It was clear which approach Tricia favored.

At that moment, a plain dark blue compact came into view. Claire emerged from her car and sent a warm smile toward the three of them. Suddenly, Becks had choices, and people in her corner. She counted Carlos among them. With the promise of him waiting for her, and more kisses in their future, the air seemed that much sweeter.

WITH HIS KNEE scooter helping him along, Carlos held on to Tinsel's retractable leash. The dog was thriving, learning to trust Carlos more each day. Carlos had to admit there was something special between them, but he couldn't let himself get attached to Tinsel. Graciela had made it all too clear Carlos was only to foster the animal.

Tinsel had so much love to give someone someday, but Carlos wasn't that person.

Just as the other day had driven home that Becks had so much love to give, but Carlos wasn't the person for her. His innate nature valued harmony, and Becks's lifestyle with its emphasis on competition and winning didn't mesh with his more practical, down-home self.

From the opposite direction came a dog walker with two bouncy, energetic charges. Becks all but glowed beneath the warm streetlight. The antique lamps were only one of the charming touches that set Hollydale apart from other towns. Her jaunty tartan beret sat at an angle covering her short red hair. Gomez and Morticia spotted Tinsel and bounded toward him, and a smile widened across Becks's face.

"Carlos." Her husky voice reached out like a blanket. "And look at Tinsel. What a handsome dog!"

Tinsel seemed to preen under the attention of the beautiful woman although the retriever stood resolute due to the onslaught of two excited dogs who wanted nothing more than to make his acquaintance. Gomez and Morticia quickly accepted him into their fold, but Tinsel seemed hesitant to join in.

"He's perfect for you." Becks wrapped the leash around her hand. "Can we join you? If I didn't know better, I'd think you were avoiding me."

"Gomez and Morticia might be too rambunctious for Tinsel." Carlos went for the obvious excuse.

Becks commanded her dogs to sit and still, and they did so, albeit with mournful looks in their amber eyes. "Problem solved." She slipped each dog a treat. "Can I give Tinsel one?"

"Go ahead." The dog gobbled it up and appeared to love the attention from Becks even more.

"Are you headed downtown?" Becks turned her head from one direction to the other. "Maybe the takeout window of the Holly Days Diner?"

"I'm finished and was returning home. I just

needed some air." The last part slipped out, and he instantly regretted saying that aloud.

"You need air when there are too many options ahead of you or something is bothering you." She slowed her usual pace and walked alongside him. "You've been my third ear lately. Time for me to return the favor."

How could he let her know everything on his mind when she was the everything?

She laid her gloved hand on his coat, and he halted along with the dogs. Tinsel tried to keep his distance, but Gomez and Morticia weren't having any of that and kept including him in their pack, especially Morticia who was obviously the alpha among them.

"I finally opened up to Mami."

She hugged his arm. "Was it as bad as you thought?"

He shrugged and kept her close while he could, the sweet scent of apples tantalizing and reassuring. "When Marisol walked Tinsel earlier, she reported that Mami had her sampling four red velvet cupcakes, each from different recipes."

Becks laughed, a deep, rich sound that resonated with him. "Fabiana never does anything in half measures."

"Especially this close to Christmas."

"I know. I have all these decisions, and it doesn't seem like there's much time to make them."

Those were words he'd never have heard from Becks all those years ago. He started moving at a slow pace once more. "Claire seemed nice. Sorry I had to leave early."

"Don't be sorry. Claire, Tricia and I talked for a long time. I really like her approach."

"I hear a but in there."

"Dante and Amara like paying their mortgage and will have another mouth to feed soon enough. Kick, Goal and Score would make everything so much easier. It would be the winning move."

Had Becks changed or would the thrill of competition always come first for her?

"Life doesn't always revolve around winning."

This time she was the one who halted and grasped rather than squeezed his arm. "Give me some credit, Carlos. I'm trying to think of what's best for everyone—my daughter, my staff and the complex's future players."

He scrubbed his free hand down his jaw, the stubble thick and rough against his calloused fingers. "Wallace was persuasive, but I felt like he was capitalizing on what's best for his company rather than your complex."

"That's why I haven't signed that contract. Unfortunately I can't go with him and Claire. Not with such different approaches to their coaching styles and life balance." Exasperation entered her voice, and she nodded at Hyacinth and Max who stopped to chat for a minute and admire all three dogs. Hyacinth and Max continued their stroll.

A few minutes later, he and Becks drew closer to his house, a small ranch befitting his bachelor status.

"Are you going to sign with Wallace?"

He waited anxiously for her answer. The Becks of old signed the contract with the professional team without consulting him at all. Talking with him about her choices was progress. Trust was something else, however. If they had any chance of being together, he had to trust her intuition.

"In a perfect world, I'd sign with Team4Life. I loved Claire's presentation and holistic approach. With that program, I'd feel like I was making a difference in every person's life who signed up for Mountain Vista." Her voice became almost raspy, the emotion and stress of the decision clearly weighing on her.

"But there's Dante and Amara, Pippa, and all the expenses you didn't expect." He finished her sentence for her.

They reached his front gate and he crossed into the yard. She stayed where she was on the sidewalk. "Yes, those have to be considerations. This isn't just about me."

With that came the revelation this was a new Becks, different from the person who'd traveled to California on what seemed like a whim. The spirit and determination were still there but now she thought of others and reflected on every decision with that mindset. The fire changed everything. She'd grown in the knowledge that she needed to take steps to protect what she loved, and she'd done just that.

"I see."

"Do you? It sounds like you're assuming my signature on the Kick, Goal and Score contract is a done deal."

He stilled because he'd thought just that.

She looked at him and her face paled. "You think I made another life changing decision on the spur of the moment. And without thinking about how it would impact everyone around me."

She was right. "Uh…"

As if on cue, her phone buzzed and she

reached for it before looking his way. "Pippa's calling in ten minutes. I have to go."

She trotted down the road, giving Gomez and Morticia their lead, which they accepted with glee judging from their long strides.

Tinsel shot him a look that seemed to indicate even his dog knew he'd blown that conversation.

# CHAPTER EIGHTEEN

CHRISTMAS EVE ARRIVED with all of its gloriousness, and Carlos wanted to revel in that feeling. He gazed out his parents' bay window. The sky promised a white Christmas, rather unusual in the Great Smokies of North Carolina but still a welcome joy.

He wrapped his hand around the cup of hot cider and scooted to the couch where Tinsel curled up at his feet. His mother loved Christmas, and her house was decorated to the hilt. The eight-foot artificial tree sparkled with colorful lights and ornaments, some of which came from Cuba courtesy of his maternal grandparents. Poinsettias of every color lined his parents' hearth. Mami did love her favorite flower.

Tonight the family would go caroling. His mother had already distributed maps of every house where the family would be singing on the way to the midnight service.

Despite all the trimmings, something seemed off, but he couldn't put his finger on what.

"Jordan wishes he were here, but he and Mason are the paramedics on duty." Graciela settled next to him. "Wish I could say the same about you."

"What? That I was on duty?" He rubbed his leg, too aware of his fellow firefighters and first responders who sacrificed today and tomorrow with their families to do their duty. "While Mami wouldn't want to hear it, I agree. I'd give anything to be at the station in my gear."

"No, that you were here *here*. You're a million miles away." Graciela lifted her cup of cider to her mouth and blew away the wisps of steam, the cinnamon stick bouncing out of the way. "Ankle bothering you?"

Carlos shifted in his seat at how his sister was only half-right. "It's doing well. I saw Dr. Patel yesterday. The cast will be coming off next week." Tinsel snuffled and he reached down, the dog's soft fur providing an outlet for his edginess. Then again, he warned himself not to get too close to the sweet dog. "Any nibbles on Tinsel's permanent home?"

"I have a lead. Are you that anxious to get rid of him?" Graciela lowered her drink, mimicking the expression on his mother's face with that same arched eyebrow.

"Not at all, he's an absolute angel." And he was, as day by day he was trusting Carlos a little more.

"Then what's bothering you?"

Carlos sipped his cider, the apple crispness reminding him too much of Becks. "Aren't I supposed to be the one who asks about his little sister's life? How are you and Jordan getting along these days?"

A starry look in her eyes was her response, and he considered whether he'd better have a talk with Jordan about treating his baby sister well. At the Christmas tree farm, however, she'd held her own, so it was time for him to step back. She could more than handle her personal life.

"You changed the subject, so you must have blown it with Becks again." Blunt and to the point, his sister never pulled a punch.

He swirled the remaining cider around his cup. "I wouldn't say I blew it." Okay, he had, and he knew it.

"Then why isn't she here with you?" Graciela's perceptiveness weighed on him.

"When did you get so smart?"

"When did you get so stubborn?" She kept that eyebrow high, but her grin snuck through.

"Didn't you hear? It runs in the family." He grinned back, happy to have returned to Hollydale.

Graciela sipped her cider. "Everyone around here would appreciate it if the two of you acknowledged your feelings for each other already."

He frowned and shifted on the couch, Tinsel stirring and giving Graciela a disdainful look for having his slumber disturbed. "Becks doesn't have feelings for me."

A short burst of laughter from his sister brought Tinsel to full alert, and he barked. "Even Tinsel knows you're fooling yourself." She placed her cup on the table and faced him. "I see what you're doing."

He blinked, unaware he was doing anything. "I'm trying to enjoy my Christmas Eve and relax before the grand night of caroling." But was Becks enjoying hers? Without Pippa, she'd have the Harrison family supporting her, but Carlos should also be there for her. The way they'd left everything, though? No, better to stay here and make sure she enjoyed her Christmas Eve.

"You're brooding. Why don't you go talk to her?"

This time the laughter came from him. "Were you elected to do this or did you volunteer for the job?"

She rolled her eyes and shrugged. "I'll never tell." She reached over and rubbed his arm. "I'll watch Tinsel for you. By the way, I saw Becks at the gazebo with her sister ten minutes ago on the drive over here."

The dog rose as if he knew they were talking about him. Somehow, Carlos realized he wouldn't be the same once Graciela found the dog a new home. Just like he'd never been the same after Becks left for California. He'd gone through the motions as far as his career and friendships were concerned. Yet he'd never attached himself to anyone the way he had with his Becca.

Carlos stood and nodded. "I'll make sure she's okay with Pippa spending Christmas Eve with her father."

"If that's the only thing you're going to say, send a text." Graciela leveled him that same look again, and let out an exasperated sigh. She whapped him with a furry red pillow with white snowflakes. "Carlos, I love you, but you're rather dense sometimes. It took you years to tell Mami you don't like ice in your water and that tres leches cake isn't your favorite. Don't take years to tell Becks how you feel."

Out of the mouths of little sisters.

BECKS ARCHED HER leg and bounced the soccer ball on her calf, counting along with the motion. "Eighteen, nineteen, twenty." She stopped and handed the ball to her nephew, Danny. "Your turn to get to twenty while I talk to your mom. And this ball and lessons are one of your presents from me."

Danny beamed and embraced her in a tight hug. "Thanks, Aunt Becks." He pulled back and frowned. "I only made you a drawing for your present."

Becks hugged him back. "That's exactly what I wanted. Refrigerator art."

She gave him a high five and made her way over to Nat, who handed her a thermos. "Thanks for the lessons, Becks. I'll practice with him in the backyard."

"So, why'd you want to meet at the gazebo? It must be important if you didn't want to bring it up at Mom and Dad's house." Becks watched Danny bounce the ball off his bent knee.

"It's so pretty here with all the decorations, I thought we should hang out. It's chilly but not that cold." Nat waved at a group crossing the main square, her silver bangle bracelets chiming softly in the breeze. "No talk of work. No life-changing discussion. No strings attached. I wanted to spend some time with you. Just you."

"It is beautiful." Christmas Eve in Hollydale. There was no other place she'd rather be. She was happy.

"And look at you. Sitting still and watching the world with me." Natalie smiled.

Maybe that was what this holiday season represented, new hope for relationships she thought had fallen by the wayside. Warmth filled Becks's chest in spite of the dropping temperature. She squeezed Nat's hands, covered with bright pink gloves. "Love you, Daffodil."

It had been too long since she'd used her special nickname for Nat.

"Love you, too, Fireball."

And too long since she'd heard hers.

Nat's gaze narrowed as if she found something interesting in the background. "And now I think it's time I took Danny back to Mom and Dad's before he becomes an icicle."

Becks turned, wondering what had set Nat

off, and found Carlos heading their way, his knee scooter helping him make quick time. She placed her hands over her mouth, trying hard to keep from laughing too hard at his ugly turquoise Christmas sweater with bright green poinsettia leaves surrounding a group of dancing Santa firefighters with axes. She gave up and let the laughter flow out of her.

Nat and Danny waved their goodbyes while Carlos approached, and the chuckles gave way to one last giggle. Quickly, awareness of his steady calm demeanor made her feel anything but silly. His vibes of warmth and security created a safe space in her chaotic world. He was what she'd needed all along.

She couldn't deny what was in front of her any longer. While trust would never come easy for her, and maybe it never had like it did for her twin sister and her brother, Carlos had earned her trust and then some. He put out a fire for her at her complex and stoked the fire within her. Since then, she'd worked alongside him at his physical therapy sessions, both of them concerned over the possibility he could no longer perform at the job he loved, and he'd still let her inside.

Small snowflakes began falling, the dimming afternoon sky set off by the twinkling lights from Main Street. Her eyes widened as she noticed that ugly Christmas sweater wasn't half as glaring as the feelings he'd awakened in her. She'd tried her best at suppressing a chance to love again but failed.

She loved Carlos Ramirez. She loved the way he concentrated on each child while playing Carlos Claus. She loved his focus as he delivered a safety lecture that should have sounded dry and boring but came alive and was fascinating just like him. Most of all, she loved how he accepted her, faults and all, with a failed marriage behind her and a shaky business in her present.

He neared, his knee scooter decorated for the holidays with a giant red puffy nose and antlers. This staid, solid man found such joy in the season, and now that was rubbing off on her despite Pippa spending today and tomorrow with Jack, as she should. Custody wasn't a competition, and she needed to keep reminding herself of that. Pippa would benefit from having both parents in her life.

Carlos wore a worried expression as he asked, "Did I drive off Natalie? She hightailed it out of here in a hurry."

Without another word, Becks closed the distance between them. She kissed him, his warmth mingling with the chill setting in from being outside with Natalie and Danny. With a hint of peppermint and a taste of that Carlos deliberateness she'd come to expect, she savored this moment, the kiss a glimpse of a bright future.

He broke away with a grin. "Where's the mistletoe?" His gaze searched the eaves of the gazebo.

"No mistletoe." She scuffed her boot into the ground. "Maybe I wanted to wish you a merry Christmas Eve."

"That's a pretty incredible way." He rolled back a little, putting some space between them. "I didn't expect that type of greeting considering our last conversation."

Their relationship shouldn't depend on whether the program she chose emphasized life balance or competition.

"I've thought about it. You need to trust I'll do my best whichever way I go with the complex. I want you to respect my decision."

"I can do that." He squeezed her hand. "Come with me."

His words were both a question and a statement, and she followed him.

She stopped in front of the local outfitting store, her lips wanting to curl up at the sight of Santa kayaking while two reindeer were near a cozy bonfire making s'mores. Carlos stood next to her, and she leveled with him. "Is trust always fickle?"

"I don't think so, and that sounds rather harsh after that kiss proved we're beginning to trust each other again." Carlos nudged her, and she couldn't help but be captivated by his joy of the window display. "If Santa can take a break and go kayaking, we can find a way to make it through our issues this time."

"What makes *this time* different?" Her insecurity reared up, and she pushed it down.

"You. Me." He made it sound so simple.

Her phone buzzed, and she ignored it. "Go on." She urged the reserved firefighter, wanting some type of reassurance before she expressed her feelings for him.

"What's between us doesn't come along every day." So far he made perfect sense, and her phone buzzed again. "Believe me, I tried. And what we have? It's too special to cast aside."

"Chemistry can fade away."

"Only when there's nothing substantial behind it." Yet again, her phone vibrated, and she reached in her coat pocket intending to silence it. "Answer it. It must be important."

"We're important." Sometimes the world had to wait, and this was one of those times.

She'd discounted his feelings once, assuming he'd be fine with her decision to go to California, and they'd ended up traveling different roads. She squeezed his hand, and found hope again.

"That's what's different this time, Becks. We're working through our problems together."

The floodgates opened, and out came all of her worries. "With Mountain Vista right now, every instinct I have is telling me to go with Claire's Team4Life program. It won't be as much monetary compensation upfront, but Claire has the potential to expand. Still, my head looks at the numbers Kick, Goal and Score is offering, and I'm back where I started. The amount to come on board is huge."

"There's more to life than money, Becks. Sometimes listening to your gut is what helps you escape those situations where everything around you seems dark."

Well, her instincts had told her to believe in Jack and his ambition, and he'd let her down. That same impulsive spirit told her to buy the property as is and look how that turned out.

"My gut sometimes lets me down, so it's best to think about the logistics and go with what my brain knows is an intelligent business move."

"What about your heart?"

It was telling her there might be another solution. She wasn't the only one with a lot at stake in the complex. Amara and Dante's future also played into the deal. Here, she'd been so focused on herself that she hadn't asked them if they'd be willing to be more than just staff.

Tricia didn't like retirement either.

Maybe she didn't have to be in this alone, personally or professionally.

She sighed and looked around, acknowledging the community that had welcomed her back into its fold when her life had collapsed. Some parents wavered, but many supported her and accepted her word. She needed to look out for those who trusted her with their kids. Even more important than the community's support was the faith of the man standing before her. "My heart says go with Claire and be thankful Pippa likes chicken nuggets."

"Listen to your heart, Becca."

Was it that easy? Did she only have to listen to her heart?

"I'm going to discuss this with Amara and Dante. I hope they agree with Team4Life."

Her phone kept buzzing, and he nodded. "Find out who's calling. It must be important."

"It's probably my mother giving me an update about Dad's rib roast." She retrieved her phone and gasped. "You're right. It's Jack. Hello?"

"Becks? Is that you?"

It took a second for Becks to place Steph's voice. "Is Pippa okay?"

"Yes, but she misses you." At least that's what Becks thought Steph said.

"There's a lot of background noise." *Too much for a small cabin.* "Is Pippa crying?"

"I'm putting you on speaker." Silence greeted Becks for a second until Pippa's sniffles made her heart hurt at the distance between herself and her daughter just then.

Becks gulped and searched Carlos's eyes for some strength. He smiled, those warm brown eyes letting her know she could stay calm and make it better for Pippa. "Hey, darling girl. Is everything okay?"

"Grizzie misses his bed." Pippa came over the line, sounding small and sad.

As hard as this was, Jack and Steph needed her to support them and convey a strong front for Pippa. "And I miss Grizzie, but I love you and we'll see each other soon. Steph and your father love you. You'll have a wonderful Christmas with them."

Admiration came into Carlos's eyes, and a

weight lifted from her. The Becks of two years ago wouldn't have said that. For that matter, neither would the Becks of two months ago, but Jack was trying to have a relationship with Pippa, and that mattered. She couldn't and wouldn't compete with him.

More static came over the line, and Steph's voice sounded nearer again. "I took the phone off speaker. Thank you for that, but Jack and I decided an hour ago Pippa needs her mother for Christmas. There'll be other holidays for us to share with her. We'll be at your house in about fifteen minutes."

She froze just as the line went dead. Carlos rubbed her cheek, his fingers warming her skin. "Becca?"

"She'll be home for Christmas." She met his gaze and beamed. "Pippa's coming home."

# CHAPTER NINETEEN

ON BECKS'S DOORSTEP, Carlos shifted the pillow under his Santa suit and adjusted the whiskers once for good measure. All around him, snow glistened. Not enough for a snowman or hard enough to slide down the hill at Hollydale Park, but enough to wake up to a white Christmas, and that was something in Western North Carolina.

He'd already texted Becks about his plan for Pippa to receive a visit from Carlos Claus on Christmas morning, and he didn't know which of them was more excited to see Pippa's face.

These two had found their way into his heart. With such an uncertain future, he still wasn't sure what he could offer them. But after New Year's? That could be another story, given the doctor was removing the cast soon. Hopefully then, he'd have more answers. He looked down at Tinsel, who'd gotten into the spirit and allowed Carlos to attach a jingle bell to his green elf collar. Tinsel seemed to appreciate not being decked out in full costume.

"A dog has to have some dignity, huh?" Carlos grinned as he rapped lightly at the door.

Becks answered, and he braced himself as Pippa ran toward him, her little legs pumping at full gusto. "Carlos Claus! I missed you."

In a sparkly sequined Santa hat of her own, she navigated around the scooter and wrapped her arms around his right leg. He'd missed this little moppet, and his throat constricted.

"Ho ho ho! Merry Christmas." Carlos scooted inside where Gomez and Morticia bounded toward them and greeted Tinsel, an honorary member of their pack. "From Carlos Claus and Tinsel the Elf."

Pippa giggled. "Doggies are elves?"

"Of course. Elves come in all shapes and sizes, including dogs." He smiled and lifted a red Santa gift pouch out of the front basket. "I have some presents for a good little girl."

Pippa grabbed his hand, and he scooted along to the fireplace where six stockings hung. The last two hanging from the mantel were for him and Tinsel, their names crocheted into bright red-and-white-striped stockings. He faced Becks. "You did this?"

"Do you remember Kris Buhari? Her mom

runs The Busy Bean. We're good friends, and she got me crocheting again."

He went over and ran his hand down the side of his, the stitches perfect and even. "When did you have time to do this?"

"At night." Becks shrugged and grimaced. "It was good to have something to do with my hands while Pippa enjoyed time with her father."

Pippa hopped up and down. "We're going to beach. Carlos come, too?"

"I have a feeling that's special time for you to spend with your dad," Carlos said.

"Jack and Steph visited this morning and then headed out to join Steph's family in Boston. Pippa's going to visit them next May after the European soccer season ends. She's looking forward to being a flower girl." Becks clapped her hands together. "Food or presents first? Hope you haven't eaten yet, Carlos."

"I haven't. How about stockings, then breakfast?"

Carlos thanked Becks for the leather strap to connect his gloves to his belt loop and for the water bottle in the shape of a fire extinguisher. Then he dug down to the toe of the stocking for whatever seemed to be stuck there. He tugged and out popped a rubber ducky dressed as a firefighter. His brow furrowed. "I think I got one of your presents by mistake, Pippa."

She shook her head, and her red curls bounced. "For Carlos Claus." Her grin widened and she hugged him.

"We found it at the festival, and she insisted you needed it." Becks's grin matched her daughter's, and Carlos knew he was a goner. He'd do everything he could to make those smiles appear often.

"You think I'll pass the exam next year." His hesitation threw him.

The tree lights reflected a special glow in the aqua depths of Becks's eyes, and she nodded. "I know no one who'll work harder."

"The cast comes off this week."

"I know."

Her confidence in him left him almost as rattled as the belief lurking in those beautiful eyes. More than ever, his future depended on whether he had ligament damage.

His father had succeeded in finding happiness as a fire chief. He'd never take anything away from that. However, Papa wasn't alone. He thrived with Mami beside him, supporting him every step of the way. It wasn't the position of fire chief that brought him his happiness; it was the love in his life along with his passion for firefighting and for his family.

Just as his parents had assumed things about his life, and wrongly, so too had he assumed too much about his father. Carlos had gotten some of it right, but not all of it.

With Becks at his side during his recuperation period, he could do this. New Year's couldn't come soon enough.

## CHAPTER TWENTY

YESTERDAY MAY HAVE been the best Christmas ever. Becks laughed as the same thought popped into her mind every year, but this time, it was true. She walked onto the pitch, bouncing a soccer ball between her feet.

Christmas morning with Carlos had been perfect, and the afternoon with her family went better than expected. She and Nat had come so far in the past month, and her mother had outdone herself with the turkey and stuffing. Even Becks had dulled her competitive edge during the afternoon Monopoly game and played for mere enjoyment rather than seeking the winner's crown.

Becks dribbled a soccer ball along one of the painted white lines while waiting for the others. Who knew? With hers and Carlos's relationship progressing, next year's Christmas might somehow be even better.

For now, though, her nerves were kicking in. Her idea for a partnership with Tricia, Amara and Dante had come about suddenly, but once she'd had it, she couldn't think of anything else. She'd texted them her offer this morning, refusing to hold off a second longer. No matter how she crunched the numbers, one path ensured this complex would be successful if they were to use Claire's balanced approach with Team4Life, and that was to form a four-way partnership.

Two cars pulled into the parking lot, and Becks picked up the soccer ball. Tricia's sunglasses hid her eyes, and Dante's and Amara's also gave no indication of their decision. She pasted a confident smile on her face and approached the three, all bundled in winter gear.

"Did you all have a merry Christmas? Jack brought Pippa home on Christmas Eve, so I had a wonderful holiday. I'm really thankful for that." Becks stuck her gloved hands into the pockets of her sporty coat. A white puff of breath evaporated in the misty mountain air. "Was it a good day?" Her voice faded like the wind.

Amara stepped forward and rubbed her rounded stomach, a reminder baby Jones would soon be Hollydale's newest resident. "Grandma Louise made a quilt for little Keon. You'll have to visit and see how the nursery is coming along. Dante finished assembling the crib."

Becks swallowed, Amara's avoidance of the text not a good sign. Dante stood behind her and nodded. "Your grandmother's quilt looks amazing in the room."

Becks went to readjust the ball under her arm but instead it fell to the ground, along with her hopes of a future for her complex. She couldn't blame them. Until the past month, Becks hadn't had any business experience, and plunging into something this substantial should have been planned to the tiniest detail. She shouldn't have proceeded with taking registrations until everything was in order.

"I don't need an answer about my offer right away. Please give it consideration. We can discuss this in January. That's all I'm asking." What had she been thinking to text something so important anyway?

"For goodness' sake, let's put Becks out of her misery." Tricia whipped off her sunglasses and perched them on the strap of her oversize purse. "We're all in. Retirement's dull as dishwater for me. I'm committing to this."

Becks faced Dante and Amara. "I understand if you can't because of Keon."

Amara placed her hand on Becks's coat

sleeve. "Our soon-to-be-born son is exactly why we are doing this. We want to have a stake in Mountain Vista."

"Are you all sure? This is a big decision, and I don't want you to rush into anything." *Like I did when I bought the place.* Becks wanted them aware of what they were getting themselves into so they wouldn't suffer from buyer's remorse.

Tricia laughed and shook her head. "You're not getting rid of us that easily. We talked at The Busy Bean before we came here, and we know what we're doing."

Her anxiety dissolved, and Becks gulped in a breath of fresh air. "Glad you're all on board. What's next?"

"Hugs." Amara pulled everyone in for a huddle before they separated, laughter dissipating the last of the tension.

They settled in the office and after scheduling appointments with Penelope and Claire, the four moved on to ways for publicizing the venture with Team4Life in the hopes of increasing registrations in the spring months.

This was coming together, Becks thought. Her dream was becoming a reality with the help of her new partners. Maybe it was time to find out if one particular relationship was also destined for a lasting partnership. She needed the right words to back up yesterday's tender moments with Carlos.

No sooner did she think of him than Carlos texted asking if she had time to talk. Tricia noticed her looking at her phone and said, "We'll still be here if you need to make a call."

Becks excused herself. In the hall, she phoned Carlos, who picked up on the first ring. "I heard from my doctor. Someone canceled, so her office offered me the slot. She's going to take off my cast. Want to come?"

She glanced at the office and then at the phone. It was so tempting to join him, but she had work obligations. "Your cast is really coming off today?"

Amara stepped from the office, mouthing the word *bathroom* and pointing in that vicinity before she stopped. "Is that Carlos?"

"An opening at the orthopedist came up, and he's asking if I could go with him for his cast removal."

Amara nodded. "We'll be fine for a couple of hours without you. It was supposed to be a half day anyway because it's the day after Christmas." Torn between business and Carlos, Becks shook her head, but Amara nudged her and glared. "We're partners now. Go with him to the doctor."

Becks spoke to Carlos. "What time do you want me to meet you there?"

Amara smiled and whistled while heading for the restroom.

"In half an hour?"

"Done." That would give her enough time to wrap up the meeting and check in with her parents about looking after Pippa before heading to the doctor's.

"And Becks? Do you have some time afterward to talk? I mean, about us."

Her heart swelled at the softness in his voice, that same timbre from the time he'd asked her to skip school for a trip to Cape Hatteras. A fresh start with the New Year approaching. A red bow to the year's end.

"That's perfect." It would be the right time to tell him about the changes to the complex before they addressed their future. "See you soon."

CARLOS ENTERED THE doctor's waiting room and headed for the sign-in chart at the desk. He saw Becks rise from a chair, and dread filled his stomach. Thirty minutes ago everything had been fine, but then he overheard a conversation between his father and the battalion chief that left him reeling and had changed his outlook and his plans. He wasn't done reeling yet.

The window slid open after he finished signing his name, and he handed the clipboard and pen back to the assistant. He glanced at Becks, hope shining in her eyes, and his stomach tightened at what he had to tell her.

Becks came over and laid her hand on his arm, facing the assistant. "Hi, Amy, how are you? I heard about your daughter's engagement. Congratulations." She chatted with Amy for a minute while he began composing himself. "Can I go in with Carlos?" Becks asked.

Amy nodded and placed a blue mark next to Carlos's name on the chart. "Dr. Patel is running a few minutes behind since we were closed last week. We're only seeing a few patients this morning, though, and I'm already counting down the minutes until I can go home. You're our last patient today, Carlos."

He nodded his thanks before he and Becks went and sat down. Facing the lovely redhead, he noted Becks's soft apple scent. It stirred so many memories for him. "I talked to my mom. She was so glad I'm coming with you that she and Dad volunteered to take Pippa to the Holly Days Diner this afternoon. We have plenty of time."

"Becks." Before he could say anything else, the door opened, and a nurse led them to an examination room.

After the nurse recorded his vitals, she smiled and left, closing the door behind her. Becks moved from her chair in the corner to his side. He was resting on the table, the thin paper crinkling when she leaned into his arm and squeezed him tight. "Now, I have just got to get this out, so please let me say it. I went ahead and made a big decision about the complex without talking to you first, but it seemed so natural and right. I hope you agree."

A minute of reprieve didn't give him the solace he sought. He rubbed her hand and listened to her as she outlined how she'd asked Tricia, Dante and Amara to become partners in the complex. Then she stopped talking and stared at him.

"What's wrong? Are you upset that I asked them without talking to you first?"

Her pause gave him the opening he needed. "Becks."

The nurse showed up again and removed tools and supplies from the cabinet while Becks scooted back to her chair. "Dr. Patel wants me to take off the cast, and then she'll be in for the examination."

With a soft whir, the small blade of the cast saw cut through the lime-green fiberglass. The nurse removed the bandages and underlayers, and for the first time in a month, Carlos looked at his ankle, the skin pale, the hair plastered against his leg.

"So far, so good. How do you feel?" The nurse checked on him.

He assured her he was okay and she departed. Finally, he was alone with Becks once more. Worry replaced the earlier joy. "Carlos? I'd have thought my accepting business partners would show you I'm ready for other partnerships, most importantly, a relationship with you. When you called me, I thought you wanting me here meant we were on the same wavelength about this. Was I wrong?"

Her gaze pierced his, her tone hesitant and assertive at the same time. That was only one of the reasons he loved her. That was why this was so hard. "Not exactly."

"What do you mean?"

He touched his ankle almost as if he'd forgotten it was there. "When I was at the fire station, I overheard a conversation between Battalion Chief Grayson and my father."

"Since Roberto is his boss, I imagine they talk a lot. What's different about this conversation?" Becks folded her arms across her chest and eyed her coat like she wanted to flee, and fast.

He gave her credit for staying put. "Grayson's finished with his incident investigation. They were talking about his recommendations."

Becks raised her chin. "What did they say?"

Carlos shifted, the sound of the paper crinkling in the awkward silence and the tension growing between them. "Grayson is recommending I be reprimanded for urging the firefighters to continue fighting the fire rather than letting it burn out. Since it had been established no one was inside, we should have pulled out earlier."

Becks all but jumped to his side once more. "I'm so sorry. I'm here for you. I love you, Carlos. You stood by me at the banquet when I worried your family would blame me for your accident. Dr. Patel will hopefully give you good news, and then we'll get you ready for the physical exam and we'll face any reprimand together."

"He's also recommending your company face a substantial fine for failure to comply with county code, especially because of the unresponsive sprinkler system."

She looked stunned. He touched her fingers, which were cold as ice. "Becks?"

Dr. Patel entered, and Becks resumed sitting in the corner, her expressive eyes reflecting all the questions she hadn't had time to ask as well as a wall of hurt.

"Mr. Ramirez, I see you have company. Hello, Becks. Let's get the two of you out of here so you can enjoy the rest of your day." The doctor pulled the stool over and sat probing Carlos's ankle, her smile turning to a frown. "Why don't you tell me what you've been doing since I ordered you to take it easy?"

Carlos shrugged. "Not much." Then he recounted his past couple of weeks under the glare of both women. "It sounds like I was busy, but it didn't seem like I did anything."

Dr. Patel's shiny bob of black razor-edged hair swayed along with her as she shook her head. "That's not minimal activity. That's more than most people do in a month."

Someone knocked, and the nurse stuck her head inside the room. "Dr. Patel, you have an emergency call on line two."

"I'll be right back." Her lips pursed into a straight line as she hurried out to the hallway.

Becks remained in the chair, the distance between them seemingly further apart than when she moved to California. "You were supposed to take it easy and you didn't, is that right?"

"There's been a lot going on over the holidays, and then I couldn't let down the kids at the Christmas festival." No one else had stepped up to play Santa. What else was he supposed to do?

"They had stockings to decorate, gingerbread displays to admire and a fire truck to climb." Becks closed her eyes for a minute and then opened them. Without another word, she donned her coat.

"Becks." She stopped buttoning at his earnest plea.

"This is too much all at once. I'm now officially at fault for the fire, and this news about your ankle?" She gave up and tied the coat belt securely around her waist. "You might never work as a firefighter again."

"I'll find a way."

"Any chance of following in your father's footsteps as fire chief might be gone." She took her gloves out of her pocket and stared at them before shoving them away. Misty tears glistened at the corners of her eyes. "For so long,

I thought I'd never be able to believe in someone else again, but your goodness and sense of duty made me realize there are people who aren't out for themselves. It's ironic, really, though, that the qualities I love about you are what worked against us in the end."

"Becca."

"You're a great firefighter, but I won't stand in your way. You have to find the strength to do whatever it takes to make your dreams come true." She brushed the tears from her face. "I know how much you love your career. I can't take the chance you won't put yourself first and mend your ankle. You have to fight for you."

"I want to fight for us. I should have all those years ago, and I didn't. We're better together." He thought his heart had broken when he ended their engagement, but that was nothing compared to the pain in his chest now.

Her face showed the sadness he felt inside. "You're right. We are better together, but that's not enough. You have to be your best, with or without me."

She moved to leave. "Don't go."

"I have to find out whether my partners want to pull out of the complex or not because of this fine. I also need to consult Penelope about whether there are legal grounds to contest the decision since I literally had just purchased the property." She went back and grabbed her purse off the back of the chair. "Goodbye, Carlos."

With that, his heart left the room with her as Dr. Patel stepped back inside. A vast emptiness took hold of him while she sat on the stool and probed his ankle. "Becks looked upset, and I don't blame her. This isn't good, Carlos. You've suffered ligament damage."

"How bad is it?"

She finished her examination and peeled off her gloves. "Your ankle is more swollen than it should be. Right now, I'd classify this as a grade 1 sprain, but you need to immobilize it for two weeks so you don't tear the ligament and do permanent damage."

Guilt was like a heavy weight resting on his shoulders. "Can I still make a full recovery?"

She met his gaze. "If you keep up what you've been doing, no. You'll tear the ligament by the end of the week. Then you're talking permanent damage and maybe even surgery."

They discussed what he'd have to do if he were to have any hope at resuming his career and his life. An ankle brace, bed rest and a follow-up visit right after New Year's. The odds against him seemed insurmountable, especially without Becks at his side.

Was she right? Had he given up on himself? How could he ask her to trust him if he didn't care about himself enough to do what was best for his future?

There were times in life where a person's future came down to indelible moments. Some of his flashed before him. Meeting Becks. Proposing to her. Breaking up with her. Seeing her from the back of the ambulance. Her and Pippa next to him while he was Carlos Claus. It wasn't a coincidence those all involved the woman he'd never been able to forget, who was now lost to him forever.

"Then it's time for a change."

Even if Becks wasn't meant to be beside him for better or for worse, he owed it to himself to be the best version of himself and fight for what he wanted.

He just wished he could have realized all of this before it was too late for them.

# CHAPTER TWENTY-ONE

CARLOS SAT ON his living room recliner, stunned from his visit to Dr. Patel. Petting Tinsel's silky fur, he was unsure which was the biggest surprise: Ned's report, the extent of the ligament damage or Becks's breaking things off between them. With his heart shattered, he knew Becks's decision was the stunner that had left him numb.

In his heart, he'd always loved her. Had loved her ever since the determined girl beat him to the soccer field intent on becoming the best, her confidence and drive engrained in every part of her.

Now, he'd lost her, and he'd honor her decision.

He wasn't sure how long he'd been stroking Tinsel's fur when a text from Graciela brought him out of his reverie. He blinked and reread the text. This couldn't be right. She wanted him and Tinsel to meet her at the animal shelter? He should tell her he had to stay home and rest, but he had to fight for his dog.

His fingers flew across the screen as she confirmed his fears. Just when he thought his life couldn't get any worse, his sister found the perfect home for Tinsel.

No, all this couldn't be happening at once. Tinsel thrived in his new home, and here Carlos was on the verge of losing him.

This was the second time today he was losing something that wasn't his to begin with. First Becks, now Tinsel.

His throat clenched as he stroked Tinsel's fur, prolonging the inevitable. Tinsel was about to find his forever home where he'd flourish.

No, he couldn't let this happen. How could he convince his sister Tinsel belonged beside him?

What about your policy of no adoptions in December?

Graciela's reply was short and to the point. Owner has impeccable references and is right fit for Tinsel. Been working all afternoon to ensure best for him.

He knew his sister, and there'd be no changing her mind.

Unhappy about Graciela's decision, he gathered Tinsel's toys and placed the dog's favorite terry-cloth chicken on top. Tinsel thought they were playing a game, and Carlos refused to meet his gaze.

"Next month, I was going to talk to Graciela about you, but…" Carlos transferred Tinsel's bag of food to the mobility scooter basket and carried it to his car with Tinsel's other possessions.

But what? He'd waited until everything had to be perfect, just like he'd booked a flight to California all those years ago and then canceled. And now? He'd kept hesitating, thinking the right moment would come, once his cast was off, for him to tell Becks how he felt.

As far as his relationship with Becks, he'd made the same mistake twice, and now he'd blown any chance of having her in his life.

He clipped the leash on Tinsel's harness, assisted him into the vehicle and drove to the shelter where he waited outside, staring at the low brick building. Finally, he turned toward Tinsel. "I'm sure Graciela found you a family who will be able to take you on walks and play with you a lot." Something he wouldn't be able to do for the next while, not with the bed rest he needed to have a real shot at regaining his career.

He was taking Dr. Patel's orders seriously this time. If he was going to get back on track, he'd have to stay at home and rest his ankle, even if it meant complete honesty with his dad about his condition. He wouldn't be able to take that annual exam in February, but he'd work hard on passing the first one after that.

As for Becks and Tinsel?

He'd enjoyed fostering Tinsel, treasuring every minute with this special dog who had a piece of his heart. He loved his time with Becks even more. She'd made this Christmas the best. He'd never look at gingerbread houses the same way. And how she'd stepped in at the last minute at the Firefighter's Christmas Festival? She'd made the perfect Mrs. Claus. Going home with her and kissing her was the highlight of the season.

Tinsel thumped his tail, and Carlos knew he was postponing the inevitable.

"Come on. My sister has a knack for matching dogs with the perfect homes."

He gathered his strength to face the person or family adopting Tinsel and telling them about the dog's breakfast hustle and the way he dropped his toy chicken in front of Carlos at the same time every evening. Only when he felt he wouldn't break down did he take Tinsel into the shelter.

"Took you long enough. I was worried I'd have to send out a search party." Graciela came out from behind the partition and petted Tinsel.

The muffled sounds of dogs barking alerted Carlos to other pets awaiting adoption. "Any chance you'd match this new owner with another dog?"

"You agreed to foster Tinsel until I found him a home." Graciela stared at him. "And I found him the perfect one."

He glanced at Tinsel. The dog was smiling at him as if he were positive Carlos wouldn't leave him here. "Come on, have a heart. Let me foster him a little longer." *Like the rest of Tinsel's life.*

"Do you trust me, Carlos?" She tapped the desk with posters tacked on the front outlining the different fees. "I'm good at my job."

"Speaking of jobs, I have news about mine." With that, he told her about Ned's conversation with their father and his doctor's appointment, including Becks's ending their relationship. "According to Becks, I have no problem trusting others. It's myself I don't trust."

Graciela moved to the front door and changed the sign to Closed. "While I'm upset at her for hurting my brother, I see her point. You make things harder on yourself than they need to be."

Loyal and blunt at the same time. He missed the easygoing sister who'd share her Halloween candy with him.

"Where's this new owner? I'm assuming you found Tinsel a family?" Carlos glanced around the main area, the industrial brown chairs showing wear and tear but no people. "Maybe I should interview them. Make sure they're good enough for Tinsel."

"We have to drive to his permanent home." She grabbed her purse.

"Really? You want me to drive you there? Someone else has to witness my saying goodbye to *my* dog?"

"*Your dog?* Funny you never told me you wanted to make this arrangement permanent. Next time you should speak up sooner. Trust your instincts."

"Will you walk him around the grass out front, please?" He handed her the leash, the reality of his situation wearing on him. "My ankle is beginning to throb."

"You could have asked for help all along. Why didn't you?"

He considered her question. "I did, and everyone did pitch in to walk him, but then with Christmas, I hated to ask since you were all so busy."

"Did you reach out and ask again?"

*All you had to do was ask.* His words to Becks came back at him. How come the most important realizations always dawned too late?

He watched Graciela walk Tinsel around the perimeter of the shelter, and then they proceeded to his car. He hesitated and laid his hand on her arm. "If he's not happy, will they let you know?" Maybe he'd get a second chance if they knew Tinsel's heart already belonged to someone else.

Graciela tucked her purse under her arm. "He's going to be happy. Tinsel has a loving personality, same as you."

"You're right. He does." He bent and rubbed Tinsel's face as the dog licked his nose and cheeks. "But you'll tell me, right?"

"Yes."

He tried to avoid thinking of how hard it would be not to have Tinsel there when he woke up tomorrow.

Or have that unconditional love and support.

He straightened and loaded Tinsel into the back of the truck's cab.

His sister buckled her seat belt. "Take a right out of the parking lot."

He followed her directions. "Tinsel's stuff is in the trunk. After you unload it, I'm heading home and going to bed for two weeks."

"Take a left at the next stop sign." Graciela reached down and pulled out a slip of paper. "Yeah, we're heading the right way. Speaking of Becks, what are you going to do about her?"

"Nothing. I'm doing what I should have done at the beginning. Going on bed rest and giving my ankle a chance to recover."

"Have you told her how you feel?" She huffed out a breath and turned toward Tinsel. "He loves her, right?"

"Yes, I love Becks."

He realized he was in his own neighborhood. It was going to be hard watching someone else walk Tinsel and play with him. The thought of Becks with someone else didn't go over much better. If he did nothing, he'd repeat the same mistake. If he asked for another chance, he'd be going against her wishes. "You had to find him a house near me?"

"Take a right after two streets. Yes, you big lovable dolt of a brother, I did." She folded the piece of paper as he turned where directed. "Then take the next left."

He did so, but then stopped the car abruptly. "Tell the other family no, Graciela. I'm Tinsel's owner. *Please*. Help me take care of him while I recover. I want to be his family."

She laid her smooth hand on his. "Trust me."

Was this what Becks had to do? Learn to trust again after her first marriage ended, only to be disappointed by Carlos when he didn't listen to the doctor?

His heart shattered into more pieces when he pressed on the accelerator and passed Mrs. Smith in her garden. She was the sweet neighbor who lived three doors down from him. *On the same street?* This was ridiculous. "You've got to be kidding me."

"Not at all. Here it is. This is the house. Tinsel's forever home."

He pulled into the driveway, which was full of cars. He recognized their mother's car, and Gisele's parked next to Jordan's truck. "This is my house."

"Of course, it is, and the family that's waiting here is your family. I've known since the festival you two are meant for each other. Tinsel's your dog, Carlos. Embrace the love." She reached over and slugged him on the shoulder. "Someone who loves you very much texted me saying you'd need help the next two weeks while you were on bed rest."

Tinsel started barking and wagging his tail as if sensing something in the air. Jordan waited on the front stoop and ran toward Carlos's car, opening the back door and grabbing Tinsel's leash. "Got him." He waved to Carlos. "I'll take him for a walk and don't hesitate to call when you need me. Your sister's smart, isn't she? That's one of the reasons I love her."

He winked at Graciela and blew her a kiss before Tinsel jumped out and Jordan closed the door.

Carlos turned toward his sister.

"I thought you didn't let people adopt dogs in December."

"You have an in with the manager. I'll make the paperwork official next week. By the way, you need to figure out how to set your relationship right with Becks. She loves you, and I know you love her. It seems to me you need to ask for one more chance." She left him still sitting behind the driver's seat. Her words lingered.

All those years ago, he didn't follow Becks

to California. This time he had to act even if he was on bed rest. How could he use this time to show Becks they belonged together?

He had one idea about how he could show her he'd changed. It was a gamble, but it was a lifeline, and he grasped it tight.

# CHAPTER TWENTY-TWO

BECKS HELD ON to Gomez and Morticia's leash while Pippa glided down the toddler slide at the Hollydale Park playground. A relatively warm winter morning for December 31 brought out energetic kids ready to run off some energy while the adults were happy to tire the children out so they could celebrate the stroke of midnight.

Nat approached with baby Shelby asleep in the sling across her chest, her gaze on Danny, who offered to push Pippa on the swing. "I love it when cousins support each other, don't you?"

Becks listened as Natalie continued talking, her chest an empty shell ever since she ended her relationship with Carlos.

Nat reached out and touched Becks's arm. "You're too quiet."

"I drifted off. Sorry."

"I know, and I love you for admitting that rather than answering my question about time-traveling space aliens from Danny's bedtime story." Nat shrugged. "The things we do for love."

"Love?" She scoffed. "I'm done with love forever."

Nat had the audacity to laugh.

"Oh, Fireball, you love with every ounce of your heart. That's your nature. Mike's the funny one, I'm breezy and you jump into everything."

"You make me sound like a drama queen."

Her twin shook her head. "Not in that way. You plunge in feetfirst and then come up for air, expecting everyone else to be in the pool with you. You only get upset when you're the only one swimming." Danny waved at his mom, and she blew him a kiss.

Nat was right. Becks did tend to jump in feetfirst, from accepting the position on the pro team to the soccer complex to Carlos. All of her roads always led back to him, the solid, dependable, caring man she could see herself spending her life with, except she had walked out on him when he needed her.

"Yeah, well, sometimes it's lonely doing the same thing over and over again. I'd like to have someone in that pool with me."

Nat squeezed her hand. "It's not too late." Nat glanced down as if making sure all this noise wasn't disturbing Shelby. "I'm happy she sleeps through anything."

"You always see everything with rose-colored glasses." Even when winter was in full swing around them with its browns and grays, everything dormant while waiting to wake up and spring to life.

"That sounds like the Becks who returned home from California in a bad place."

This relationship with Carlos had left a hole in her heart, but she wasn't defeated. "No. I'll never be like that again."

"I hear a *but* in there."

Pippa stood at the bottom of the play castle, a determined look on her little face. She'd never been able to climb to the upper level on her own. Danny was beside her. She clasped the side railing of the short ladder and climbed to the second step before falling. She tried again and fell but still, no cries came forth. Becks held on to the leash, ready to hand it over and run to her daughter when Nat reached out for her. "Let her try one more time."

"She's little. She might get hurt." *Same as her mother.* Hurt and scared after a series of disappointments, she'd fallen in love only to leave Carlos in that doctor's office all by himself. Even if she wanted another chance with him, why would he want her back when she could abandon him again?

Danny helped Pippa brush herself off, and she climbed the three rungs of the ladder this time. She scrambled inside the top of the castle, her grin stretching from ear to ear. Danny followed and cheered.

"They make a good team." Pride laced her sister's voice. "Just like me and my older sister."

"Only by twenty minutes, and don't you forget it."

"In case I've never said the words, I'm proud of what you've accomplished with your soccer complex."

Becks leaned against the swing post. "I signed those partnership papers at Penelope's office yesterday, and Team4Life and Claire are also now on board with Mountain Vista."

"Oh, Becks. That's wonderful." Nat frowned. "I thought there was some holdup."

"Penelope talked to Roberto Ramirez. Since I showed good faith having made substantial modifications for the safety of the property and brought the buildings up to code, everyone agreed to move on without legal action."

Nat's frown turned into her sunny smile. "I'm proud of your tenaciousness. Others who've been through your situation might have given up." She nudged Becks's side. "Are you really giving up on you and Carlos?"

"I left him in that doctor's office. I ran because I was scared of getting hurt again and trusting him with my heart."

"You need to admit that to Carlos, not me." Her twin checked on her daughter, stirring from her nap. "You know the best part of life? You get to have second and even third chances to get things right."

Her niece started burbling, waving her tiny fists, and Nat rose. "Tomorrow's a fresh start, a new year. Why don't you take Gomez and Morticia for a long walk, sooner rather than later since I think the weather's about to change? It's going to be cold, and I bet it rains later. I'll take Pippa back to my house, and she can play with Danny and Shelby."

Becks protested. "You've already done so much for Pippa."

Nat shook her head. "She's more resilient than you think. Maybe you should walk the dogs in the direction of a house belonging to a certain firefighter? Being honest with him and telling him how you feel might be the best way to ring in the New Year."

Nat was right, and the answer was obvious now. She and Carlos had the potential to be a strong team. Love wasn't some ideal. It was messy and beautiful and exciting, and every muscle in her body ached for the man who made her laugh, made her pulse race and helped the world be a better place just by being in it. Part of love was standing by someone, and if she trusted him to rush into burning buildings and save others, wasn't that enough? Wasn't that everything?

The truth was, she'd ended any start of a relationship before Carlos could so she wouldn't be hurt again.

She owed it to the both of them to ask for one more chance, but first she needed something special to bring with her.

"I'll only take an hour."

Nat grinned. "Take two. One for each of us."

# CHAPTER TWENTY-THREE

THE STIFF BREEZE picked up, and the sudden gust of cold, a marked difference from the almost sultry weather on the playground, pierced her blue Anorak coat. Gray clouds billowed in, promising a night of rain or sleet that would maybe even provide a few sprinkles of snow to greet the New Year. Becks hurried onto Carlos's front porch with Morticia and Gomez.

She loved Carlos, and her brain, instinct and heart all agreed. This relationship was right. He'd make her laugh and keep her grounded, and she would make sure he always reached for his dreams, and looked out for himself, so he could continue taking care of the community he adored.

Would he be willing to go for a third try with her?

She felt the Christmas ornament necklace in her pocket, thinking of it as a good luck charm. Finally, she pressed the doorbell. Holding her breath, she waited a moment as the door opened, expecting her first glimpse of Carlos. But the person walking Tinsel was shorter and stockier than Carlos. What was his name? Ah, yes. This was one of Carlos's fellow firefighters, Jeff Bukowski.

Hope overtook her as Gomez and Morticia propelled themselves toward Tinsel. For the first time, she took note of two cars other than Carlos's in his driveway. If Bukowski was walking Tinsel, Carlos had asked for help and really was resting his ankle.

"Happy New Year's Eve!" Becks said. She bent down and patted Tinsel. "Hey there, boy. Everything okay with Carlos? You're taking good care of him?"

Tinsel thumped his tail once as if responding in the affirmative.

"Same to you, Becks. You know dogs don't talk, right?" Bukowski reeled in the leash.

She smiled. "Ha ha. Would you mind if I took over and then returned Tinsel to Carlos?"

Bukowski glanced at the house and then Becks again. "I told Carlos I'd do this, but I have a feeling he'd like to see you."

He handed her the leash and waved while making a beeline for his car. The dogs played for a minute and then she led them to the house. She knocked on the door and stepped inside where she discovered the owner of the other car. Fabiana hadn't caught sight of Becks yet; she was in the kitchen stirring something and whistling to the salsa music that filled the air. Becks closed the door behind her, and Fabiana turned.

"Was Tinsel a good dog, Jeff? You weren't gone for long." Her voice faded as she met Becks's gaze. "Oh."

Becks gulped and considered how much colder it was inside, compared to outside. She should take Gomez and Morticia home and burrow under a blanket with Pippa until they greeted the New Year together.

But she'd never been one to shy away from a challenge.

"Hi, Fabiana. Do you need help in the kitchen?" Becks released the three dogs and made her way to the woman's side.

Fabiana crossed her arms. "Why are you here?"

Becks took a deep breath, resolved to set things to right with Carlos's mother. "I know I'm responsible for Carlos's injury, and I know you have every reason to be upset with me about that. If someone hurt Pippa, I'd be angry and beside myself, but I love your son, and if we start something that will hopefully last, I can't have your disapproval hanging over me."

"Disapproval? Where'd you get that idea?"

At least she hadn't laughed or stomped out at the prospect of Becks and Carlos together. "The cupcakes. The seating at the celebration dinner. The fact I'm responsible for his injury."

Fabiana loaded a coffee pod into the machine. "I'm old-fashioned and prefer home-made desserts to store-bought confections." She ticked off a finger. "I was upset at Carlos, who switched the cards without telling me." She tapped a second finger. "I love my husband enough to know this career is in his blood, same as it's in my son's. I've been a firefighter's wife long enough to know if it wasn't arson, you aren't responsible. This was an accident, and firefighters learn to be prepared for anything." She raised her ring finger and reached for her cup of coffee before facing Becks. "Your lips are blue. Do you want me to make you a cup of coffee?"

Becks nodded, unsure of what was happening, but Fabiana talked the whole time, their camaraderie from the days she dated Carlos back in full force. It was as if she was preparing Becks for the rigor of being a firefighter's significant other. She thanked the older woman for the coffee, the warmth of the mug heating her cold hands.

Roberto entered the kitchen, shaking his head. "Why our son didn't just talk to me first is beyond me. He would have found out Ned had started our conversation with thoughts about what he originally might recommend before he gathered all the facts and came to a different conclusion. Carlos will need to complete a refresher course on procedures and communication before he's back on the team." Then he realized Becks was there. "Oh, Becks. Happy New Year's Eve."

Becks nodded. "Hello, Fire Chief Ramirez."

Fabiana slipped an arm around Becks. "He's Roberto, darling. For now. We'll talk again in a few months about calling us something else, and I can't wait to spoil Pippa."

Becks opened her mouth but not before she saw Roberto catch on to what his wife was saying. "Come on, Fabiana. Let's go home."

"But Carlos and Becks need—"

"Some alone time." Roberto interrupted his wife. "They don't need our help. See you soon, Becks."

They bundled into their coats and left.

"Bukowski, is that you?" Carlos's voice came from the rear of the house. "Is Tinsel okay?"

The dog thumped his tail at hearing his name, and Becks went to Carlos, the three dogs following behind her. She reached into her coat pocket for her Christmas ornament necklace and placed it around her neck before inhaling a deep breath and walking into the bedroom. "Nope, not Bukowski."

Carlos dropped his knitting needles and one of the pillows behind him fell to the floor. "Becks?"

Not Becks, she wanted to be Becca to him and him alone. Exhaling a shaky breath, she made her way to Carlos. Around his neck was that awful scarf she'd knitted for him. Suddenly, she couldn't find the right words, or any words.

The dogs jumped onto the bed, and Carlos began laughing. She joined in and everything clicked into place. This felt right.

This felt like home and love.

"I shouldn't have walked out of Dr. Patel's office."

He laid his hand gently on hers, the electric spark waking her to the attraction between them that had never gone away. "You were right. I didn't want to face something scary and unknown. I didn't trust myself, but when you said what you did and left, I realized something."

Silence stretched between them, and curiosity nipped her, the same way Gomez was biting Carlos's blanket. "What?"

"That losing you is scarier than any future I can imagine. I don't want a future without you in it."

Her heart, which already belonged to him, melted, and she knew she wanted to always be by his side. "So, you're taking care of your ankle?"

He held up the knitting needles and showed her a scarf in burgundy and deep yellow. "This one's for you." Then he reached over and brought up two balls of yarn, pink and aqua. "These are the colors for Pippa's scarf. Then I've promised Graciela some blankets for the dogs at the shelter."

A man who knit? That might be the sweetest and most endearing trait of all. There were a few dropped stitches, but the six-foot scarf showed how seriously he was taking the doctor's orders to rest his ankle. "It's beautiful."

"Not as beautiful as you. I know it's a lot

to ask to stay by me when I don't know what the future holds."

She silenced him with an index finger to his lips and then touched her necklace. "As long as we're together, we can face anything."

He smiled and she smiled back. Then she lowered her finger and he spoke. "For so long, I thought my father was happy because he found the profession that suited him," Carlos said. "I thought I had to follow in his footsteps or I wouldn't find that same happiness."

She understood that since she'd fought the exact opposite force. For so long, she thought she had to walk alone and carve a separate niche from her twin who found happiness just in being alive. "When I couldn't follow in Nat's footsteps, I thought I had to be the best in athletics to be happy."

"Just like soccer is a part of you, firefighting has taken ahold of the deepest part of my core, or at least I hope it will again."

"If not, we'll navigate that together. Whether you work with safety codes or go into teaching, you'll tackle it with that same thoughtfulness and courage that's a part of you." She snuggled beside him.

"As long as you're with me, my future isn't as scary. I'm sorry I didn't support your dreams in the past, but I'll be there for you every step of the way with your complex from here on. I'm a fast learner, Becks. See, I'm almost done with your scarf. It was the best way I could think of to show you I'm taking me seriously, and that I'm trusting my intuition. I'll give us that same consideration, too."

"I only insist on one thing."

"What's that?"

"That I'm your Becca."

That slow grin curled his lips upward, and he moved closer. "I love you, Becca."

"I love you, too." The dogs stuck their snouts between them while she and Carlos gazed deeply into each other's eyes. Their kiss started with laughter, the way the best things in life always did.

# *EPILOGUE*

THE POLAR PLUNGE wasn't the way most people would choose to start Valentine's Day, but then again, his girlfriend wasn't the conventional type, and Carlos wouldn't have Becca any other way. Her penchant for everything new balanced his more traditional, cautious approach to life. He loved Becks, and that's why he found himself outside at five in the morning, supporting her and the other Hollydale residents on the shores of Lake Pine.

He waved to his father at the starting line alongside his sisters and their significant others. Mami approached him and they stood next to her friends, the Matchmaking Mimosas. They'd adopted him as one of their own, giving him credit for matching Hyacinth with Max, who were both also waiting in the group of people about to dive into the freezing cold depths.

Carlos would have considered it, but his physical therapy was going well. Two weeks of constant bed rest had helped heal his ankle, and he was set to take the physical next month with all signs pointing toward returning to firefighting. In the meantime, Pippa squirmed in his arms.

"Pippa go swimming."

"No, young lady. I have my orders from your mother that you are to stay dry."

He'd miss Pippa this summer when she flew out to California for her father's wedding. If he had his wish, Pippa would be a flower girl twice this year. His grandmother's ring was already out of the safety deposit box waiting for tonight when he'd propose to Becca.

One of Becca's business partners, Tricia, held up the starter's pistol and counted down from three before firing it. Then the fifty participants ran and jumped into the lake, raising money for a good cause. Within minutes, Becks arrived at his side, dripping and shivering in her wet bathing suit, a warm blanket around her. He handed Pippa to Becks's mother, Diane, and wrapped an extra blanket around the love of his life.

"Thank you. That water was colder than I expected." Her short red hair was plastered to her scalp, and those blue eyes shone with vitality.

"I'm always here for you, Becca." He smiled and loved the smile she gave him in return.

"Will you marry me?" Her expression was full of hope.

He tugged on his ear, teasing her. "Did you just ask me to marry you?"

Her grin widened, and she cleared the wet hair from around her ears. "Yeah, I did."

Taking the plunge with her every day of their lives was one decision he didn't have to mull over. "I love you, Rebecca Harrison, and yes, I'll marry you. Your ring is waiting at my house. Mami brought it over since she knew I was proposing tonight."

Pippa and Becks whooped with joy before he leaned over and kissed his Becca, the moment bursting with the promise of a lifetime of love.

\* \* \* \* \*

*For more charming, small-town romances from author Tanya Agler and Harlequin Heartwarming, visit www.Harlequin.com today!*

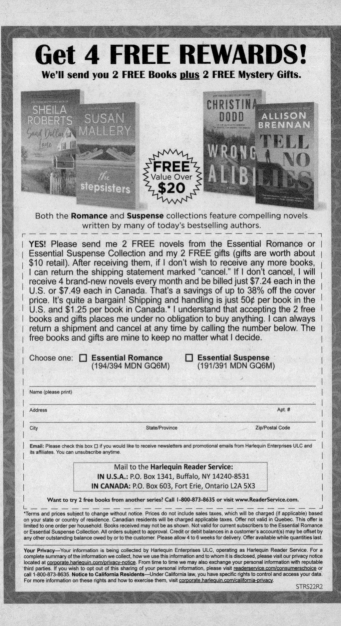

### #443 HER FAVORITE WYOMING SHERIFF
*The Blackwells of Eagle Springs*
by Cari Lynn Webb

Widower and single mom Adele Blackwell Kane must reopen the once-renowned Blackwell Auction Barn—if she can get Sheriff Grady McMillan to stop arresting her on town ordinances long enough to save her ranch. Can love prevail in county jail?

### #444 THE SERGEANT'S CHRISTMAS GIFT
by Shelley Shepard Gray

While manning the NORAD Santa hotline, Sergeant Graham Hopkins gets a call from a boy who steals his heart. When he meets the boy's mother, Vivian Parnell, will he make room in his heart for both of them?

### #445 THE SEAL'S CHRISTMAS DILEMMA
*Big Sky Navy Heroes* • by Julianna Morris

Navy SEAL Dakota Maxwell is skipping Christmas—and not just because his career-ending injuries have left him bitter. But Dr. Noelle Bannerman lives to heal. And she'll do that with physical therapy...and a dose of holiday magic.

### #446 AN ALASKAN FAMILY THANKSGIVING
*A Northern Lights Novel* • by Beth Carpenter

Single mom Sunny Galloway loves her job as activities director of a seniors' home—then Adam Lloyd shows up, tasked with resolving financial woes. They have until Thanksgiving to save the home. Can working together mean saving each other, too?

# HARLEQUIN
## PLUS

Announcing a **BRAND-NEW** multimedia subscription service for romance fans like you!

---

## Read, Watch and Play.

Experience the easiest way to get the romance content you crave.

Start your **FREE 7 DAY TRIAL** at
<u>www.harlequinplus.com/freetrial</u>.